LILY WHITE LIKE ME

CHRISTIAN MARK

Copyright © 2022 by Christian Mark

All rights reserved.

No portion of this book may be reproduced in any form without written permission from the publisher or author, except as permitted by U.S. copyright law.

All the author's royalties from this book will be donated to:

The Salvation Army
National Headquarters
615 Slaters Lane
Alexandria VA. 22314
PH: 800-728-7825

This book is dedicated to John Howard Griffin and Dr. Martin Luther King, Jr.
Two men who saw a wrong and tried to right it.

Chapter 1

1974

I rushed out of White Hall dormitory, took a quick right, and walked up to Huntington Avenue. The midafternoon traffic was light at this time of day. I waited for the light to change before I crossed and then made my move. I was late for the play today and I needed to do some prep work in my dressing room and work area before the actors and actresses arrived. It was a beautiful March day, and Spring was in the air. The Northeastern students were all going without winter coats to coax the Spring season to come early to Boston. The dirty snow on the side of the road was melting and going down the storm drains.

I quickened my pace. Down the street up ahead I saw one of my friends, Willie Shaw. He was coming right at me, balancing several textbooks under his arm. He was very tall, with a very white complexion, and dressed up in faded dungarees and a Northeastern sweatshirt. The many freckles on his face jumped out at me. He was a fun-loving kid I had met freshman year, and we had been friends ever since. I grew up in Winchester, and he lived in the neighboring town of Lexington. We had a lot in common and just hit it off from the beginning. He also was very smart and helped drag me through several freshman seminar courses before I got serious about studying.

I kept thinking freshman year was really thirteenth grade in high school. He also had my back when we would go out in a group to several dive bars for cheap beer, and get into a jam with the locals. Being from the suburbs, I forgot that the college campus bordered Mission Hill, which was part of Roxbury, and had a lot of poor city kids, housing projects, and crime.

"Hey Jimmy, how are you doing today?" Willie said with his usual jovial voice. "I missed you at the EL Center this morning for coffee."

"I'm sorry man," I said back with as much empathy as I could muster. "I had to cram for a sociology exam tomorrow, and I still haven't got a grasp of the material." I was really lying, and slept in since my dorm neighbor was having a party next door, and the music they were playing reverberated through my wall all night, and I could not sleep.

"I understand, Jimmy. No problem. Come on up to my room tonight if you finish studying and we can catch the Bruins and Flyers game on TV. Hopefully there will be a few good fights." He finished with a laugh.

I gave him the thumbs up and said I had to get to an afternoon performance of *Othello* at the Blackman Auditorium, and he understood, and sent me on my way. I picked up my pace and turned the corner just as a Green Line train went by me down the street with the clickity clack sound I had become so used to, since the trolley tracks were right outside my dorm window. The sounds of the city always reverberated into my room until the wee hours of the morning.

I crisscrossed my way through the quadrangle and headed up the steps of the EL Center building. It was several stories high, with distinctive gray brick and blue-smoked windows. I held the door for a group of good-looking girls to come out. I could swear the last girl gave me a wink, and I smiled back. I walked through and opened the main door of the Blackman Auditorium, then entered the big hall. I walked down the graded slope towards the stage, past all the maroon felt seats.

Today's performance of *Othello* would go off without a hitch. We had already had two shows over the past week, and they came off without a problem. My job as a makeup artist was a behind-the-scenes gig and was well within my training. My mother was a hairdresser by trade, and knew I had an interest in it from an early age. She would take me to her shop when I was a teenager and show me the finer points of makeup and skin preparation. I took to her trade naturally and she would have loved me to come into the business and take over, but my father and her wanted me to get a college education, and chase my dreams instead of theirs. In high school I practiced my trade with makeup and hair for several drama productions, and had met so many nice people and their parents over time. I dated several pretty girls in high school because they knew I was comfortable in my own skin with a job that would normally go to a female.

As I went up the side stairs onto the stage Mr. Steeger, the director, came out from behind the curtain and welcomed me.

"Mr. McPherson, I'm glad you could join us today," he said with just a touch of good natured sarcasm in his voice. "Several of the actors and actresses are waiting outside your makeup room to be prepared for the production." He looked at me for recognition and I nodded.

I breezed past him with a wave, smiled, and said I would handle it since I had little time to waste. He looked down at his clipboard, turned, and disappeared through the curtain, off to talk to someone else.

I walked down a dimly lit hallway which led to my dressing room, and past several stagehands, getting scenery ready, painting last minute backgrounds, and swinging walls with a big boom to prepare for Act One, Scene One. Looking ahead I could see a line of people outside my room. It was Desdemona, daughter of the Venetian senator; Emilia, who was playing a prostitute in Cyprus, and Cassio's favorite girl; and Emilia, Iago's wife. They were all standing there with nervous anticipation, wanting to get ready so they could do a last minute rehearsal of their lines before the play started.

I waved Desdemona into my room and shut the door, just as the other two girls were peppering me with reasons why they should be first. The young girl peeled off her coat and took her shirt off, which left her with just a red bra, showing off her ample breasts. I did not give it a second thought since she did not want to get make up on her clothes, and during any play production actresses and actors were always on the run to change clothes. They might also be playing other parts in the production. Nudity was part of the world I played in, and it became very second nature over time.

She sat there in her chair staring at herself in the makeup mirror. I looked at a list of things to do, which was taped to the upper left hand corner of the mirror. It was numbered and stated: Replicate characters; Enhance appearance; Alter makeup during production for lighting; Access skin type; Examine sketches, photos, and plaster models to get image; Create character models; Get shade from stock and/or mix oil & grease to get correct effect; Cleanse and tone skin before make up application; Requisition wigs and beards before production. I quickly looked at the list and knew I had everything I needed to get ready for today's event.

I started chatting it up with the young woman while I prepared her for her performance today. As I went about my duties to transform her, she seemed to relax more and more. She was a beautiful young woman, and I changed her into character within twenty minutes. Her own mother would not recognize her now. I took off the white sheet I had covered her with and said she was ready, and she thanked me, and I sent her off to wardrobe to get dressed. The next girl entered immediately, and I started with round two.

After several hours of preparing the cast, I finished and made my way to the front of the stage, right behind the curtain. The stagehands were darting here and there, so I made my way over to the far right and peeled back the curtain. Today's performance of *Othello* by William Shakespeare would be sold out. It also was free to the public and reserved for several inner-city grammar and middle school children. Most of the kids were Black, and poor, and Northeastern University provided opportunities for the poorest children in Boston with these types of outreach programs, and scholarships.

As I looked out, I could see so many young children streaming in with their teachers and school administrators. They were so excited, and talking back and forth with their classmates. They all looked so happy, and you knew that so many of them came from poor homes, and poor circumstances. Looking at their happy faces you would think they had not a care in the world. It was amazing how resilient children were no matter what they were exposed to in life.

We would make today's production the best, and they could go home to their schools and family, and tell them how fun it was, how interesting it was, and how much they learned about history. Maybe we would interest a few of the pupils in a life in the theatre. I daydreamed for a quick minute about what my future held, since I was a senior and would be making my way out into the world soon. I had always dreamed of a life on Broadway, or in Hollywood, but still had not made the move to get serious and switch gears from college student to working professional. I was having too much fun and did not want it to end. I would cross that bridge when I came to it.

Chapter 2

I WAS HEADING DOWN Forsyth Street at Northeastern University, looking to park my car in the back lot, behind the EL Center. There was no parking in the lot across from White Hall, and I did not want to get towed. The midday traffic was not too bad as I meandered down the road, but most Boston drivers had little patience for any cars slowing them down to their destination. My yellow Chevy Vega was sputtering as I tried to shift gears, and fine tune the radio to WBCN rock radio. Charles Laquadera's voice came on introducing the latest song, and I was hoping it was one of my favorite groups. Most of the music that was presented on this station was from new rock and roll bands on their way up the ladder of success.

As I peered in the universities back parking lot my heart sank seeing the "All Full" sign posted beside the security booth. I thought for a moment I might pull in and beg the guard to let me drive around and see if there were any spaces available. My blood pressure began to rise as I knew I had to be at a sociology class over on the other side of campus in a short time, and I did not want to be late. I looked at the guard's face and his expression said it all. He frowned at me, knowing what I was up to, and waved me on down the street.

My pulse increased as I took a quick right and went by the housing project across the street from the campus. It contained several six-story red brick buildings designed in an L shape with white steel framed windows that had paint chipping off. If you looked in close, you could see several people looking out the windows over the skyline, and many Black men congregated outside talking, laughing, and passing the time of day. There was trash strewn over the property with many old model cars, and a few junk cars that people just gave up on. The city had not had time to come and tow them away.

I closed my windows and proceeded down the street, up into Mission Hill into an area I had never been before. Around the turn of the century, it had been a wealthy Jewish section of Boston, with beautiful Victorian homes. Then, as time went on, the Jewish citizens moved over into Brookline, which was more affluent, and the Irish crowd started immigrating there and building more multifamily dwellings. It was a thriving community, spilling over into Dorchester and Mattapan. In recent years, more and more people moved out due to a bad economy, the influx of Black residents, a rising crime rate, and depressed real estate prices.

To add to the downturn, a federal judge, Arthur Garrity, had made a ruling which would impact the racial complexion of Boston for years to come. His federal mandate said that Boston schools had to be racially integrated in order to make sure all children were going to good schools and receiving a decent education. The ruling mandated that many children of color were sent into all-white areas of Boston to attend school, and the reverse was done with white children being sent to all-Black schools on the other side of the city. The unintended consequence was that no one was happy. Parents were outraged sending their children where they were not wanted, and people started selling their homes in Boston and moving to the suburbs to make sure their kids were not affected by this travesty.

The Boston police had to be activated to keep everyone in line and make sure it was a smooth transition. Of course, it wasn't, with eggs, rocks, and insults being hurled at innocent children who were just trying to go to school and get an education. Local politicians voiced their displeasure, and promised things would get better, but they never did. Things only got worse in all sections of Boston, and it turned into white flight. To escape the declining school systems, white families who could afford it sold their homes and moved out of the city into the suburbs, with predominantly middle-class white school systems offering a good education. The outcome was a dwindling tax base and city services not being attended too. Poor families who could not get out were left behind, and animosity between the Blacks and Whites increased. The beautiful city of Boston was labelled as a racist place for people of color to live, and the atmosphere was tense, especially for an unsuspecting white college student from the suburbs.

As I proceeded in my car down the street, I was looking here and there for street signs and any landmarks that looked familiar, hoping to weave my way back to Huntington Avenue and into familiar territory. I kept driving and shifting, and my hands were starting to perspire as I was going. After a while, the only people I saw were Black people walking down the sidewalks, pushing baby carriages, riding bikes, and going about their normal day. I wasn't sure if I was getting nervous because I was lost, or if I was not used to being the only white person in a Black environment. Growing up in an affluent suburb right outside Boston, I was not exposed to an interracial background. My hometown only had one Black family, and the only other people of color were Metco students. This was a state program that took Black high school children from Boston or other city school systems and sent them to suburban school systems that had mostly white pupils. The reasoning was the same as busing. It was to expose the city kids to a better school system, and in return they would get a better education. The kids they sent to our school were very nice, and mixed in easily with the teachers, and their new friends. I did not have any of them as good friends, but I was always polite and friendly to them and tried to help if they had any questions about the school or directions to a classroom.

I looked around to see if I could pull over and ask a resident how to get back to the main street. I peered from side to side of the street looking for someone who was non-threatening, and close by. My eyes were straining as the afternoon sun was going down in the west, setting off a glare that reflected off my windshield into my eyes. I reached for the radio dial to turn it down in order to concentrate, when all of a sudden I heard this loud bang, and then I saw a red brick bounce off the hood of my car and go off the other side. I immediately looked to my left and the sun glare hit me straight in the face and obstructed my view of where the object came from. With the music down, I could hear several young men yelling "Honkey go home!" They were laughing and getting a big kick out of it. I strained to look out my window and over the hood of my car for any damage.

The voices outside my window went from laughing to an angrier tone, and I pushed down on the accelerator to get down the street and into friendlier territory. I was muttering and swearing as I was driving, and wondering why someone had done this. I had not provoked these guys to do such a thing. I kept replaying the episode over in my mind. My parents always said stay out of places where you don't belong, but I thought they meant strip clubs and dive bars. As a college student on a campus, I thought I was insulated from the bad things that go on in a major city, but I guess I was wrong.

I made my way back to the White Hall parking lot and inspected the damage to my car. It was a small dent and paint chip, but I would wait until the summer to fix it when I had more time, and more money.

I raced into the building past security, which was really just two upper classman checking student passes to make sure you belonged in the building. I shot up the stairs to the second floor, not stopping to talk to anyone. I plunged my key into my dormitory door and opened it up. There, sitting at his desk, was Jeffrey Estridge. He was a rich junior from Connecticut and his father owned a big electronics company in the state. He told poor Jeffrey that if he ever wanted to be president of the company he would need to go to Northeastern University and get a degree in electrical engineering. This was the hardest curriculum in the school. His father was a Northeastern alumni and graduated with the same degree in the forties.

This poor kid studied every hour of the day unless he was in class or with his girlfriend. He was deathly afraid of his father, but he grew up with all the nice things in life and knew it would stop unless he followed in his father's footsteps.

As I entered, he looked up from his textbook and calculator, and gave me the head bob. I smiled, and gave it back, grabbed my sociology text and notebook off my desk, and said, "Later." I slammed the door behind me by mistake and raced back on to Huntington Avenue, and to my afternoon class. I was still upset about my reception in the Roxbury neighborhood. I kept replaying it over and over in my mind. The college courses I was taking were starting to expand my mind about the world, and have me better understand people, groups, and places. I was very naive and still trying to get my feet on the ground. Hopefully today I would learn something new that would inspire me.

Chapter 3

I scooted down Huntington Avenue, crossing over Hemingway Street, tired from studying for a history final. It was about nine o'clock and the school library had just closed. I could not believe the school year had gone by so fast, and my college career was coming to an end. I had four finals to take before graduation. This course on Civil War history was hard since the professor was Middle Eastern, and had a heavy accent. I sat in the front of the classroom to listen, but my notes were very fragmented. Most of the good notes I used to study for this final exam came from outlining my textbooks, which took a lot more time. I felt good about my prospects to do well on the exam, since it would be essay format, and I had a wealth of knowledge on the subject.

As I walked up to White Hall, my residence dorm, I saw a lot of classmates coming and going. I gave a few waves and head bobs as I walked by but did not want to stop and get into a long drawn out conversation. I breezed past the two security people sitting at the front desk and flashed my school ID, and they waved me through. As I climbed the only stairs to the second floor, I thought twice about going up to my friend's room and watching the third period of the Boston Bruins hockey game. They were in the Stanley Cup playoffs against the Philadelphia Flyers, and the series so far had been exciting and a slugfest. I was bouncing the thought in my mind for a few seconds, and then thought better of it. I knew I had that final early the next morning and wanted to be fresh for the test. My time in college was coming to an end, and I wanted to finish up strong.

As I stepped out into the second-floor hallway, I noticed the red carpet and gray painted walls. I could hear the low bass beat of a song as I walked further down the hall to my room. I looked ahead and in front of me were several Black students who were standing about the hall, with red cups in their hands, and smoking cigarettes. As I approached them, the smell of marijuana was wafting out of the open door to the room. I thought to myself, this was an odd night to have a party, and then it dawned on me that the Black Fraternity at Northeastern had meetings once a month. My neighbor, Usae, was a Black student from Uganda and was the head of the Black fraternity. Their fraternity house was up the street in Jamaica Plain, but it made more sense to have meetings here if it was something simple and saved the members time, since everyone did not live at the house.

Usae was the head of the fraternity and very popular. His father was a higher-up in the Ugandan government, and sent his son to Northeastern University to get a degree in electrical engineering. He told me his father was in charge of the energy sector of the country. In charge of building dams, power plants and making sure the country's electrical needs were met, even though it was a third world country with minimal basic services. He wanted his son to be his man on the job surveying new ideas to improve the country's electrical grid and bring the country's energy needs into the twenty-first century.

Usae spoke perfect English and had a mild British accent. We had known each other for three years and were very friendly and got along well. We did not socialize much, since I hung with my liberal arts friends and he hung with his Black friends and the electrical engineering students. He knew my roommate very well, and liked him, since he was a laid-back dude and loved to smoke pot. That automatically put me on the good list with Usae.

I put my key into my door and twisted the lock. The door opened to blackness. I could barely see in front of me. As I looked into the distance through the window, I could see the lights and cars on Huntington Avenue. My eyes adjusted and I reached for the study light on my desk. As I switched the light on, my eyes went black for a second and then adjusted to the light. I heard some movement in the upper bunk bed to my right, and I saw my roommate and his girlfriend nude laying there sleeping. They had had their normal daily romp whenever I went out to do whatever. Both of them were young at heart, and had not experienced any freedom over their high school years, and were taking full advantage of the freedom of being away from home.

I twisted the desk lamp down as low as I could to dim the light in the room, and they pulled the blankets over themselves and went back to sleep. I went over to my dresser, grabbed my bathroom toiletries, and made my way down the hall to the men's room to get washed up for bed. The hallway was vacant except for a few party-goers relieving themselves. I looked into the mirror and noticed dark circles under my eyes since I had been burning the midnight oil with final exams, Bruins playoffs, and my normal senior partying with my friends. I thought for a second about leaving college and getting a job and starting a new life. My father wanted me to follow in his footsteps as a business desk jockey, but I was not sure what I wanted to do. He was a traditionalist, and I was a wet behind the ears college student, still believing you could be anything you wanted, and do anything with your life. I had learned so much at Northeastern, and my mind had expanded to all the possibilities that the world had to offer.

I went back to my room and snapped off the light and crawled into bed. I lay there with my hands over my eyes, blocking out the glare from the streetlights. I could hear the clickity-clack of the Green Line trains going by, and voices of students and passersby. I loved the sounds of the city and wished I could extend my stay here in Boston for a long time. I knew, based on my lack of income, I would have to move home, get a job, and save my money.

As I lay there, I started drifting off to sleep, and dreaming about all the good things in my life. As I maxed out in my REM stage of sleep, I dreamed of girls, sports, college, and all the things that made a college student excited about life. I floated and floated through my dreams, and it was so tranquil.

After some time, I was abruptly awoken from my dream by a loud sound. I could hear voices laughing, and a loud bass sound from music coming through the wall. I was groggy and reached and placed my hand on the wall to my right. The bass sound from the music was vibrating through my hand. I lay back on my pillow and tried to relax my mind back to sleep. As I looked over towards my desk, I saw the desk clock with its red digits reading one thirty AM. My pulse started to beat faster and faster as my mind focused on the noise and music, and not drifting back to sleep. I rolled over and faced the opposite wall, and tried to concentrate on counting sheep, but after several minutes it was no use.

The noise was taking over my subconscious. I needed to get some rest so my mind was sharp and I would be at my best for the big final exam. As my mind raced, and my anxiety overtook my body, I started to get mad. I could hear the voices in the next room, and the music was way too loud for this time of night. Usae should have known better since this was finals week, and as I pondered that thought, I sat up, got out of bed, and pulled on my pants. My body was half asleep as I stood in the dark room, and looked up to the top bunk, where no movement was forthcoming.

I opened my dormitory door and the hall light seeped into the room. I quickly stepped out and closed the door behind me. As I looked down the hallway it was vacant. The next door party had been brought into my neighbor's room. I could still hear the loud music and jovial voices emanating from inside. As I stood outside I rehearsed what I was going to say, since I had a good relationship with Usae, and my college experience was coming to an end.

I stood there for a few minutes, and then rapped on the door. I waited for a few seconds and then knocked again, even louder. I heard some rather loud guys with a city slang, and then the door flew open, and a tall thin Black man was standing in front of me dressed like Superfly, with a large afro hair style, and a matching hat. The yellow and white colors were so bright I could have used sunglasses. The guy's facial expression turned from one of glee to very serious. I stepped back one step to not be looking straight up into his eyes.

I said "Is Usae here? I want to talk to him for a minute," in my firmest voice.

His expression turned even darker as he looked down and said, "Listen man, whatever you have to say to my friend, you can say to me," he spouted indignantly. "Usae is busy."

I stood there, pondering. Should I just forget about it, and go back to bed, or should I tell this guy to keep the noise down? I continued to look straight into his eyes, and he never broke eye contact.

"I just wanted to let you know that I live next door, and the music and noise is keeping me awake. I was wondering if you guys could just turn down the volume a little bit?"

The guy's expression turned from one of seriousness to one of anger. He started stepping towards me, and said, "Man, who do you think you are telling us what to do? We have every right to have a meeting with our fraternity brothers, and you don't own this building." As he finished, several brothers from the room turned and noticed what was going on and walked out behind their friend and stared me down. "Hey guys, this motherfucker doesn't like our party or music."

I kept backing up, and the men jeered at me, and supported their friend. I noticed a few friendly faces from the past, but they were not friendly now. I started trying to think of a quick way to talk my way out of this and get back to my room in one piece. The big man in front of me was obviously drunk, and I was not going to be able to reason with him. He was clearly a city kid from Boston and not a foreign student, and he had a chip on his shoulder. He kept backing me across the hallway toward the opposite wall, when out of nowhere Usae came out of his room and stepped between me and the tall man.

"Hey Jimmy man, how are you doing? What's this all about?" he said with his native British voice.

I was just about to respond when the big man spouted, "This mother doesn't like our music and I told him he is not being very neighborly."

I responded quickly, "Usae, I have a final exam in the morning, and I can't sleep with the noise. I was just asking your friend here to turn it down a bit." I looked back at his friend, and he looked like he was going to blow a gasket. He made a move towards me.

Usae stepped right in between us and said, "Malcom, chill out man. We are having a good time, and Jimmy is good people. He is family." As he talked, he was pushing his friend back towards the room from which he came. The entourage started backing up and disappearing into the room. The big guy was moving backward very slowly and giving me a curt smile. As he receded, Usae said in his usual jovial voice, "Jimmy man, so sorry about the noise. My brothers and I will keep it down so you can get your beauty sleep." He started chuckling in his usual laid-back manner.

I thanked him and turned toward my door. As I stepped in and closed it, I was in a state of blackness. My heart raced from the confrontation, and I was so mad at that guy. I had never experienced that type of behavior in my four years of college. As I rested in my bed, I had a million thoughts going through my mind. I tried to do some meditation in the dark until my body relaxed and melted into the mattress. I drifted off into my happy place.

Chapter 4

I scooted across the quadrangle headed towards the Daniels Building on a beautiful spring day. The sky was a light blue with no clouds, the flowers were blooming, and everyone had a spring in their step. They were looking forward to the end of the school year. My final exams were over, and I was excited and apprehensive about my college career being over and heading out into the world to make my mark. It had been a great time, and I had learned a lot, and met so many nice people. I had no idea what I wanted to do with my life, and I needed to ponder the thought since my parents would be peppering me with questions about my future once the graduation high had worn off.

For some reason Dean Smith, who was the head of the history department and my guidance person, wanted to see me. I was surprised because I knew I aced the history final and could not think of why he would want to talk to me. We always had a good relationship, so maybe he just wanted to say goodbye, since we might miss each other at graduation.

As I climbed the gray granite steps of the administration building, I made my way through a congregation of Black students who frequented this area to hang out and talk to their friends. They had an air of excitement and were talking about the same things I was thinking. What they were going to do for the summer, and what the future held. Also, the spring Boston sports season was kicking in, and so many of the people were discussing the Celtics, Bruins, and Red Sox.

I began to sidestep the crowd and make my way towards the front doors. I said hi to a few of the students I knew from my classes or drama classes, and then a man stepped into my path.

"Jimmy man, how is it going?' the young man asked.

I turned my head and saw Usae standing there with his usual big smile. He was always in a good mood and was the life of the party. People naturally migrated to him because he made everyone feel good, even if you were having a bad day. I turned to him and gave him my usual head bob, and said hi, but I was in a hurry. I tried to sidestep him, but he grabbed me around my shoulder.

"Jimmy, Jimmy, where are you going in such a hurry? School is over, and it's time to celebrate with the brothers," he laughed as soon as the words came out of his mouth. "I'm so sorry about the other night. Our fraternity meeting got over sooner than we thought, and the drinks started flowing. I hope you did okay in your final exam?" he stated with as much empathy as he could muster.

"No problem, Usae. Everything worked out okay. Are you going back to Uganda after graduation?"

"No way man," he said, raising his voice. "I'm enrolling in graduate school and getting my master's degree in Electrical Engineering. I don't want this party to end," he bellowed.

I chuckled at his good nature and understood why he would not want to go back home since he was having so much fun in Boston.

I told him I was late to a meeting and guaranteed we would catch up before I moved out of my dorm after graduation. As I made my way towards the doors, I spotted Superfly out of the corner of my eye. He was talking to a few of his classmates and had a big smile on his face. It was quite a contrast from the other night when he was spitting four letter words at me and ready to do battle. I picked up my pace before he saw me and made my way into the building.

The inside of the Daniels Building was very similar to most college campuses and buildings. The walls were made of white plaster, oak trim, and had high ceilings. The brown and white tile floors were highly polished and reflected the sun light beaming in the windows and front doors. As I entered, I saw a trophy case with many academic and sports trophies and commendations that the students of Northeastern had won over the years for a high level of achievement. As I stole a quick look, a proud feeling of accomplishment came over me that now I was a graduate of such a fine school.

I stepped out of the elevator on the second floor of the building and made my way down the long hallway until I stood in front of the door that said "Dean Smith" in black letters across a smoked glass mahogany door. I pushed the heavy door open and made my way into a small anteroom and noticed Dean Smith's secretary with her back to me pulling a file out of a steel gray cabinet. She looked to be about seventy years old with white short gray hair. Her dark blue wool outfit struck me as odd since the weather outside was beautiful.

I cleared my throat to let her know I was behind her, and she twirled around and looked a little taken aback.

"Excuse me miss," I said, "I have a ten o'clock meeting with Dean Smith. My name is Jimmy McPherson." I waited a few seconds for her to collect herself.

She looked me up and down and then at the file in her hand and responded," Yes, yes, Mr. McPherson. I saw your appointment with the Dean on my calendar. He is just tying up a few things and will be with you in a minute. Why don't you sit and make yourself comfortable?" she said with an air of snobbery in her voice.

I turned and seated myself in a nice red leather chair, grabbed a copy of the Northeastern University magazine, and started flipping the pages. The Dean's assistant went back to her work, and I looked at the large old clock on the wall. When it was quiet, I could hear the tick tock of the clock, and I wondered if this droning noise bothered the woman as she concentrated on her daily activities. As I turned the pages, not really paying any attention to what I was reading, the door of Dean Smith's office flew open, and the Dean came out to meet me. As he walked, the woman from behind the desk handed off a file to him, and he did not break stride.

I stood up from my chair, and approached the Dean halfway across the room, and stretched out my hand.

"Nice to see you again, Dean," I belted out with as much enthusiasm in my voice as I could muster. He grabbed my hand and shook it firmly with an air of superiority.

"So nice to see you Mr. McPherson," he responded with a serious look on his face and in his voice. "I'm sorry to bother you today since I'm sure you are getting ready to wrap things up around here, but some concerning news has come to my attention, and we will need to discuss it."

My heart dropped as he said the words. What could be so important as to drag me in here the day after finals wrapped up? I was looking forward to all the on-campus celebrations before graduation day. The Dean turned on his heels and walked into his office; I hurried behind him with a pit in my stomach.

As I entered the Dean's office, I looked around in awe at all the beautiful painted pictures of landscapes, Boston buildings, Boston Common, and all kinds of degrees and commendations mounted on the walls. The room had white plaster walls, with mahogany trim and chair rails, and with a plush light tan rug.

I closed the door and sat in a one of two chairs facing the Dean as he slid behind his big, beautiful desk with a nice leather blotter in walnut shade. As I settled into my chair, I could see the man flip open a folder holding all my academic information. He was studying it attentively and then slid his horn rimmed glasses down his nose. I looked over his face to see his body language and see if I could get a clue as to what this was all about.

"Well, well, well, Mr. McPherson," the Dean said with an exasperated voice. "I'm sorry we had to meet under these circumstances, but I just got your marks back from your final exams, and there seems to be a problem."

I was looking straight at him and tried to go over in my mind how finals week had gone, and why he would be saying this to me. I knew I did not ace all my studies, but I had a good feeling walking out of each final that I would have a passing grade. As I scanned my mind for the weak link the Dean let it all hang out. He flipped the folder open, then shut, then open, and then let out a big exhale.

"Well son, I hate to break this bad news to you, but you failed your computer analysis course with Professor Eisenblate. It looks like you did not go into the final with a strong grade, and then you flubbed the exam. He looked up with a look of pity written across his face.

The news hit me like a freight train. Then reaching back in my mind the truth came through. I was not a computer person and had no good friends to drag me through the course. I had known I would have to take this course since my sophomore year, in order to get my Bachelor of Science degree, and I always avoided the course and kept putting it off thinking I would get more computer literate over time. This only made the situation more anxiety filled. I remembered listening to my good friend in the dorm complain about Standard Fortran programing and running programs with all those IBM computer cards with punch holes., then figuring out where the errors were in order to fix the punch holes and get the program to run correctly. The more I thought about it, the truth bubbled to the surface. I struggled the whole semester with the class and went into the final with a D average. The final was all multiple choice and short answer, and I figured I could BS my way through. I obviously blew it and now I was going to pay the price.

Dean Smith kept looking down his nose at me for a response. I could see from his body language he had given this message before, but did not like bursting a student's bubble, especially when it had to do with graduation.

I tried to muster as much confidence as I could to ask my next question. "Well, Dean Smith, could I talk to Professor Eisenblate to see if he will change my grade to pass/fail?"

He looked at me with another pathetic look, and responded, "Mr. McPherson, you cannot change an F for a grade into a pass/fail. The lowest mark you can get is a D, and this is clearly an F. Besides, the esteemed professor has left for Israel for a sabbatical this summer and will not be back until the fall." His voice seemed very forthright and forceful.

I melted in my chair with a thousand thoughts cascading through my mind. My parents were going to be furious. They were so happy when I got into college, and I would be the first one to graduate in my family. The graduation was scheduled for three weeks from now at the Boston Garden, and Senator Kennedy was going to be the commencement speaker. My parents were lifelong Democrats and held the Kennedys up as royalty. After the graduation, my mother and father had planned a big family party with all my relatives attending. A wave of panic set into my chest and stomach. What was I going to do? How could I let them down like this?

Dean Smith let me stew for a few moments and then tried to throw me a lifeline. "Well son, this is not the first time this has happened to one of my students. Looking over your file, you have a reasonably good academic record with steady improvement since freshman year. Your coop advisor said you were hard working at your jobs along the way, and coworkers liked and respected you. Overall, you had a good solid college career, and because of that I am going to give you a lifeline to help yourself." The Dean sat back and looked straight at me.

I sat there dumb founded, saying *what is a "lifeline?"* over and over in my head. My heart skipped a beat and my confidence soared.

"I am going to give you a one-time chance to do a thesis paper over the summer on any concept, as long as it has to do with history, political science, or sociology. It will have to be significant, moving, no less than fifty type-written pages, and due the Tuesday after Labor Day. If I am satisfied with the paper, you will get a passing grade and your diploma will be mailed to your resident address."

I grabbed on to the lifeline, and a smile came across my face. This was my ticket out of the doghouse. Being a history major I could pull off a fifty-page paper in my sleep. Dean Smith had saved my bacon with my parents and my college career. I was not going to let him down, and in fact I was going do a thesis paper that would blow his socks off. I quickly thought of all the possibilities in my mind.

He looked back at me, closed his folder and said "Mr. McPherson, I hope you won't let me down? In fact, you can walk with your class at graduation and participate in all senior activities next week."

I was so happy to hear the news I leaped from my chair and reached out my hand to shake his. As he grasped my palm, I started shaking his hand so hard he regripped his hand as to counter my grip. A smile came to his face, and he said, "Son, don't let me down. I am counting on you. Now go have some fun."

I ran from the office almost skipping down the stairs to the first floor, out on to the front steps. All the students were gone, and only the underclassmen and women were meandering around the quadrangle and education buildings. I ran down the stairs two at a time trying to think of what to do next. As I waited to cross Huntington Avenue, I looked down at a newspaper stand and saw the local Boston newspaper with a headline which read "Busing Problems" in big bold print. Under it was a picture of a Black lawyer who was coming out of City Hall, and a White resident of South Boston trying to spear him in the stomach with an American flag. I stared at the picture for a few moments, pondering all the racial problems busing had caused the city of Boston and turned good people against each other for no good reason. I understood that every parent wanted to give his or her child a decent education, but was this the best way to accomplish it? The division was strong, and this message was resonating across America that Boston was not welcoming to the Black community.

I stood daydreaming for a few seconds, pondering what Black people had to endure on a day-to-day basis. Why were people still struggling so much since the Civil Rights act was passed in 1964, and why hadn't so many of the Black citizens climbed the ladder to achieve the American Dream?

I stood for several minutes thinking about the past week with my car trip through Roxbury and my run in with the brothers from the Black fraternity, and then it hit me like a freight train. I knew what I was going to write my thesis paper about. I would explore Black America and get right down to ground zero, and put myself in their shoes. I would travel America this summer and tour several major cities. I would use my makeup talent to change my complexion from white to black. That way I could blend into the background and see how minorities lived, and how they felt about things. Once I accumulated all the information, I would come back and write a thesis paper that would blow Dean Smith away.

I ran across the street and went into the Cask and Flagon Pub to fine tune my game plan over a few draft beers and a roast beef sandwich. I was very proud of myself, not knowing what the future travels would bring.

Chapter 5

I TRIED TO PEEK out over all my college friends and classmates to see how many people were sitting in the seats at the Boston Garden. I could not believe this day had come so fast. I remembered back to my freshman year being a wet behind the ear nobody, and trying to survive my first year seminar classes. The jump from high school to college was a huge divide, but I learned the ropes, with the professors' help. What I really learned, which was most important, was I would have to study really hard to get good marks in school. I tried many ways to avoid hard work, and be sociable, but the hard truth was there was no substitution.

As I peered out over all the heads and graduation gowns, I could see the crowd growing, and the excitement building. My parents would be in attendance, and they were never so proud of me. They were an older couple, and I was the first person in my family to graduate from college. Over the five years of school, and my coop jobs, they were always supportive and were available to bounce a question off or get some worldly advice. They had grown up during the Depression and World War II and knew what real hardship and sacrifice were. They had dropped me off in front of the Garden, and told me what section they would be sitting in. I could not tell them where I was sitting since there was no dress rehearsal, but I wore a florescent tassel on my graduation hat which stood out like a sore thumb. I told them once I got seated, I would stand and wave to them to get their attention.

I was getting my bearings and chit chatting with some friends when someone came up behind me and knocked my hat off. I thought someone had bumped into me by mistake, but then I turned and saw Willie Shaw standing there all dressed up in black with a big smile across his face. The smile grew even bigger as he thought of something funny to say.

"Hey Jimmy, can you believe a couple of lunkheads like us are going to be college graduates?" he bellowed. "I have to keep pinching myself. My parents still can't believe it."

Everyone around us snickered and that only made Willie more comical than ever. I gave him a shoulder to the chest and knocked him back a few feet and then picked up my cap off the floor. I patted Willie on the back. "You are right man," I agreed. "My parents feel the same. They did not feel I could pull this off." I was fibbing of course because I had no idea how they felt about my scholastic ability. My father worked three jobs to pay the bills, and my mother ran the hairdressing salon, and was happy with my drama career, and hoped I would come into the family business, once I settled down.

I looked up from my conversation with Willie and saw Mrs. Atkins, our assistant Dean, waiving her arms and telling us to get in line as we had been instructed, and get ready to march into the Garden and the seating area. Willie high fived me and ran farther back in the procession line to find his spot. I waved to him walking away and turned to insert myself between two school classmates to be in the right order. The excitement was building and there was so much jubilation in the air. I could barely keep it together.

All of a sudden, the Northeastern band began to play, and Mrs. Atkins gave us the cue to start marching. My feet started moving and then I was swallowed up in a big pile of humanity. I was being swept along like a fish in a fast-moving stream. As we came into the big hall, I thought about all the championships that the Celtics and Bruins had won in this building. I had never been down on the floor of the Garden, and it gave me chills to think about the history of it all. The place was packed, and up front was a beautiful stage with the Northeastern logo on the front and several chairs lined up with all the Deans of the various departments and all the speakers standing in front of their chairs. The podium was made of dark oak and had the NU emblem hung on the front. As I marched, I saw Mrs. Atkins stopped in front, guiding us into our correct rows. I turned and walked in and sat next to a nice young girl who I did not know. She looked somewhat familiar, but I'm sure she was probably in some of my bigger seminar courses and not the small classroom size courses. She smiled at me, and then I stood and looked to where I thought my parents would be sitting. I began to scan the sections, and looking up and down, and then I spotted my mother waving to me. She was so happy, which made me feel proud of myself. My father gave a quick wave and then looked down to scan the program.

I looked back at the girl seated next to me and she said, "You are lucky your parents were able to come to your graduation." She had an air of apprehension in her voice.

I was taken aback for just a second and said, "Where are your parents?"

"I'm from California and they couldn't afford to pay for the airfare to Boston and stay in a hotel for a few days. I wish they could have been here," she stated with a despondent tone. "They are so proud and happy for me. I am the first in my family to graduate from college."

I felt bad once I heard her story and told her how I lived only seven miles from Boston, and I was also the first to graduate from college in my family. I kept the conversation going to put her mind at ease and enjoy her big day. She was very good looking with long blonde hair, blue eyes, and a great tan. I can't believe I missed this girl in five years at school. I told her about my road trip for the summer, and she said to stop in and see her if I made it to California. I was elated that she would make the offer, but I knew right now there were more questions than answers as to how I was going to pull this off, and write my thesis paper.

After a few minutes, the proceedings started, and the garden heated up on this warm Sunday afternoon. There seemed to be many speakers and lots of cheers rising from the various factions in the hall. I was listening attentively, but after a while my interest started to wane. I kept looking over to my left to see what my parents were doing. They were looking at the stage, and I started daydreaming until the final speaker, who was going to be Senator Edward Kennedy from Massachusetts. I was so excited to hear his speech. Since I was little, the Kennedy family was so influential in Massachusetts, and national politics. In my parents' eyes they were like royalty. I flashed back to when I was in fourth grade and the teacher came in with tears in her eyes and told us to go home. When I got home my mother was sitting at the kitchen table with a despondent look on her face and told us that President John Kennedy, Ted's brother, had died. It was an awful three days after in our country and it was like a household member had died.

I snapped out of my funk, and then focused on the stage just in time for the Chancellor to introduce Mr. Kennedy. There was a resounding roar as all the people in the hall stood up and cheered. This man was bigger than life. He carried his speech in his hand and made his way up to the podium and smiled. He looked up and waved to the crowd, and waited for the cheers to tone down. It went on for a few minutes and then the hall was quiet. His speech was part political, part about Vietnam, and part motivational. He had that Kennedy accent, and had a way of making any speech one that you would never forget. I looked over at my parents and they hung on every word he was saying. The speech took about forty-five minutes, and it went by so fast I couldn't believe it. The crowd gave him another standing ovation, and then it was time for the diplomas.

Edward Kennedy's speech sent me back to what John F. Kennedy and Robert Kennedy endured enforcing civil rights, equal education, and trying to solve poverty in the Black community. They had met with so much resistance and hate, and in some cases had to bring in the National Guard to enforce federal law. I tried to think about how I would feel if I were in their shoes.

    I looked over to my right and I spotted Mrs. Atkins walking down the center corridor and getting people ready to march up to get their diplomas. The symphony part of the band started playing graduation music, which fit the mood, and the liberal arts department would be the first to go to the stage. After a few minutes I got my cue and started moving. I walked up to the stage, turned to my left and headed for the stairs. As I peered across to the center podium, I spotted Dean Smith. He was all dressed up in black with a blue colored ribbon across his chest, and a matching tassel on his cap. His glasses looked new and were reflecting a glare from the lights on stage. I walked in line towards him as he was handing out the pieces of paper. I kept thinking about what hand I would receive the diploma with, and what hand I would shake his with. Before I knew it, I was standing in front of him. He read out my name and handed me a folder with the NU logo on it. He shook my hand and gave me a smile, which I interpreted as you better come up big with this thesis paper and have it to me right after Labor Day. As I walked off the other side, I quickly opened it and looked down. The diploma was blank, and a little yellow sticky note said my name on it. I quickly took the sticky note and stuck it in my pocket.

    The reality of the situation started sinking in, that I had a long road ahead of me, and not just in a literal sense. I had told Dean Smith about my road trip to tour major cities in America and see what Black citizens in this country's lives were like, and their trials and tribulations. I had never even thought about other people growing up that lived in lesser circumstances. I always just assumed that every child in America grew up just like me. Once I went to college, and started opening my mind to the world, I knew this was not the case, and that with the Vietnam war, the draft had been stacked against people of color. The war had ended in January 1973, but the damage was done. There was so much death, and destruction, and so many of our young people were coming home broken. They were not received back as heroes but as goats, which only made their assimilation back into society that much harder.

I snapped out of my dreary thoughts and flipped open my diploma and kept thinking in my mind of an excuse to tell my parents as to why my name was not on it. I pondered the thought, and then I sat down next to my pretty classmate and dreamed about my after party and seeing all my family and friends. Today was going to be my day and nothing was going to spoil it.

Chapter 6

My sweaty shoulders were starting to ache as I turned the socket wrench on the oil plug to my 1973 Chevrolet Vega sedan. It was tight quarters under my car, and the bolt I was trying to loosen was on extra tight. Before I used all my might, I tried to remember clockwise or counterclockwise to undo a screw or a bolt to the car. I recollected in my mind for a few seconds, and then gave it all my might, and felt some relief as the bolt broke free, and I threaded it off until the oil started flowing out of the engine into the bucket I slid into place. As it started to drain, I wiggled out from under the car and stood up, feeling creaky as an older senior citizen. I adjusted my body in several different directions to work out the kinks until I would have to go back under to twist on the oil engine filter.

As I stood there looking from the driveway back to my house, I started to ponder all my childhood memories of playing baseball and football in the back yard, having street hockey games on the street in front. Also, the fun we had riding our bikes and skateboards up and down the road. I had so many good times with my friends, and block parties. A thousand thoughts were shooting through my mind, and I just couldn't believe that twenty three years of my life had gone by. It was all too quick, and I knew life was about to get serious, and would never be the same as it had been.

As I daydreamed, I looked up at the basketball hoop mounted over the garage door in front of my car and had a flashback of playing Horse with my friends. We were all about the same level of shooting and the game usually ended with an argument about a foul or something that the other contestant had forgotten to say or do which should disqualify them from winning. It always got heated, but in the end, we had fun, and we ended all friends. The prize was heading into the house and rifling through the refrigerator to see if my mother had any ice cream or cookies stashed somewhere.

I heard a bird chirp, and my concentration was broken. I grabbed the oil filter, removed it from the box, and bent down to slide the bucket of oil out to the other side of the car without spilling it. I was very careful to move it an inch at a time until I could go around the car and pick it up. Once that was accomplished, I positioned my body near the oil plug, and began screwing on the filter. After the first few turns, I knew I had cross-threaded the filter and plug. I turned it counterclockwise to start over again. Once I completed the task, and I was sure both were on tight, I shimmied my way from under the car. I picked up the used oil and moved the bucket to the corner of the garage door so no one would trip over it by mistake. I would dispose of it later. After that I grabbed five quarts of Quaker State oil from a case in the garage and then popped the hood to my car. I looked over the very clean aluminum block engine and scanned for the oil cap. Once I screwed it off, I began adding the oil until the five quarts were gone. Then I put on the cap and closed the hood. Now it was test time. I jumped in the driver's seat, put the keys into the ignition, and turned the key. The engine fired up and came to life and purred. I was so proud of myself for a brief second. I jumped out of the car and climbed under to make sure no oil was leaking from the oil filter. As I laid on my back looking up at the filter a sense of accomplishment washed over me. I was ready for my cross-country trip.

I felt the warmth of the engine radiate down on to my face when all of a sudden I felt someone kick my foot, which was sticking out from my car. I could hear some muffled voice, but I could not make it out because of the car engine noise. I shimmied my way out, figuring it was a friend coming to say goodbye.

As my head started to clear the under carriage, I was ready to let loose with a wise ass remark, when I saw my father looking down at me with a frown pasted all over his face. The last few days had been hell once I told my parents of my plan to take a cross country trip after graduation. They were not pleased, since my mother and father had grown up in hard times, and had spent quite a bit supplementing my education. They felt I should go out immediately and look for a professional job that I could make a career of. After my graduation party, I broke the news to them about Willie Shaw and myself going to drive across the country in my car, and back, to see America and all it had to offer. I told them that I still had several hundred dollars in my bank account, that I had earned through my coop job at Northeastern University, and would not be a burden to them. I promised them I would be back before Labor Day, and then I would seek permanent work in my chosen profession. Little did they know I would be travelling by myself, and only used Willie as cover, so not to worry them. They also did not know Willie's parents and would never call them to check up on me. I also had not discussed that I was not planning on getting a traditional job when I returned, but instead I planned to go to New York and try to break into a Broadway theatre company that could use my skills as a makeup artist. I wouldn't even think about discussing that with them until well after Labor Day.

As I wiggled my way from under the car and focused on my father, I finally made out what he said.

"Supper is ready, and on the table if you care to come and share a last meal with us."

There was an air of sarcasm in his voice which tore through me and really hurt. I was always very close to my parents, and had been a good student, and never caused them any problems. My father had been active in my school sports, and never missed a hockey game or a baseball series. He taught me everything I knew about the sports, and I was an average player that always had fun participating. We never

ever had any cross words with each other, but I rationalized that he was having trouble letting go, and had never thought that someday soon I would be leaving the nest. He turned his back and headed into the house and disappeared.

I made sure nothing was left in the driveway and then scurried into the house and headed upstairs to change my clothes and wash my hands. It took me about ten minutes to get myself together, and then I came downstairs and walked into the dining room and sat down at my place setting. My mother and father were in the middle of eating when I arrived, and my plate had been filled with meatloaf, mash potatoes, and green beans. It was piping hot and it looked so good. My mother was an excellent cook, and she never disappointed us with her meals.

After I sat down, I immediately grabbed my fork and took a bite of meatloaf, and then washed it down with milk. The food tasted great sliding down my throat. My taste buds came to life, and I wondered to myself when I would have a meal as good as this in the next few months.

I thought for a moment until I heard my mother say, "Jimmy, your father and I are going to miss you when you leave, but we understand you want to take an adventure and find yourself." She finished with a quiet solitude to her voice. I looked over at my father, and he gave a quick grunt and then lost himself in the mashed potatoes.

My father was a straight shooter and worked very hard to get to this point in life. He seemed unbiased about the subject of race, and I had never heard a bad word come out of his mouth. I knew he volunteered through work in an organization called Junior Achievement, which worked with inner city youth to show them what business was all about, and the road map to take in order to accomplish your goals in life. He never really discussed the program or the poor children he had mentored, and what their track record of success was.

A wave of relief poured over me. "Thanks Mom and Dad, I really appreciate you supporting my cross-country trip, and when I get back, I will buckle down, and get out into the working world. I am so excited to come back and tell you about all the great things I have seen along the way," I spouted with an air of satisfaction.

My father looked up, took a sip of his coffee, and then looked at me with those deep piercing brown eyes. He was tapping his index finger on the tablecloth, and I could see he was really thinking and choosing his words carefully. Out of my peripheral vision I could see my mother staring straight at him with that look.

"Well son," he said in a low tone voice, "your mother and I are very proud of your accomplishments, and how well you did in school, and we just want you to get settled, so we can have a little time to ourselves."

As I heard his words, I felt some self-satisfaction and guilt washing over me at the same time. I was so elated from what my father had just said, but at the same time felt guilty that I had not told them that the reason I was going cross country was because I flunked one of my last courses and needed to make up a class before I really graduated. I sat there for a few seconds knowing how hard it must have been to say those words to me. He was never a touchy feely type of Father and could never hug me or say any words that came from his heart. This is the best I could ever hope for.

"Thanks Dad," I responded with an upbeat tone. "I appreciate everything you and Mom have done for me, and I will not let you down." I looked over at my mother, and she had a big smile on her face, and gave a loving look across to my father. I buried myself in my meal, not wanting to spoil the moment saying something stupid. I also made sure I did not fill up my stomach all the way. I needed to save room for my mother's lemon meringue pie. It was the best I ever had anywhere.

I retired to my room after dinner with a thousand thoughts going through my mind. I had never been away from home by myself, except for college. I was always under my parents' care, and now I was making all the decisions, and good or bad I would have to live with the outcome. This time tomorrow night I would be living in another city, and trying to make my way in the world, and accumulate information on the Black experience in order to write a well thought out thesis paper, and graduate from college. I would stay in homeless shelters at all the cities I visited to have some level of safety since I was not a street-smart kid. It was an exciting thought and also a scary one.

I pored over my Triple AAA United States map to lay out my journey and pinpoint all the cities I would visit along the way. I decided on a northern route across the country, and I would hit a lot of the rust belt cities. I drew with my magic marker across the map hitting several cities along the way until I got to Chicago. Then I turned south and made a turn in the middle of the country and turned back to the east coast. It would be a long journey, and I would spend a week in every city to get a perspective on different people, and their circumstances.

I thought in the back of my mind about my car, and if it would make the trip and get me home safely. My anxiety level started to climb as I thought about all the things that could go wrong with my car, and then I started thinking about money, if I ever needed to fix the car along the way. I had taken all my savings out of the bank in cash and had a special money pouch I had bought that I wore on my body. Even if I got robbed along the way I would only lose my driver's license, emergency contacts, and a few dollars.

As I looked over the map, I was amazed at what a big, beautiful country this was, and all the opportunities it presented. I knew based on my studies in college that it was not always the same for everyone, and I was lucky to be born into a nice middle-class family that gave me the opportunity to have a good life. I gazed across all the cities I would be visiting, and wondered what they would be like, and the people I would meet along the way. I tried to focus my thought process to just accumulate information for the term paper, and not get caught up in people's emotions or circumstances. I was always an empathetic person, and cared about my fellow citizens, but I wanted to capture the details of what I was writing about, and not get sidetracked.

After what seemed like a long time, I stood up and looked around my room and noticed all the posters of my favorite sports athletes and rock stars. I scanned my high school letters for hockey and lacrosse and then looked at my team pictures in detail to spot some of my old friends who I had been close to since childhood. I continued to turn my head and look around in a three-hundred-and-sixty-degree circle, and a rush of memories came over me. I thought about my first twenty three years of life, and how much I had accomplished, never thinking that the next part of my journey would be the most interesting.

I looked down at my suitcase and double checked my clothes, my makeup, and some street clothes I had picked up in Boston to make me look like a Black city kid. I checked my wigs and tried a few on to make sure they fit. Then I neatly packed everything away and closed the lid of the suitcase. I wished I could apply my first round of blackface tonight, but that would be impossible, in case I ran into one of my parents in the morning before I left to hit the road.

I laid down on my bed and looked up at the ceiling, thinking about all the possibilities, and had a secure feeling that I was up to the task. I would use my college degree and knowledge to open my mind, and experience life. I had no idea what that meant, and that the next two months of my life would change me forever.

Chapter 7

I was cruising down Route 90 in northern New York state on a beautiful June day. The flowers were in full bloom, the sky was a light blue, and the grass was green. I was feeling great and was optimistic about my little adventure. As I looked down at the speedometer, I felt a big truck speed by me, which caused a suction for a moment into its path. I jerked the wheel back to steady the car. Just then I heard my eight track player put on a great Rolling Stones song from summers before. I began to sing along in a loud fashion since my windows were down, and the wind was blowing through the car. The road was straight, and I saw a sign on the side of the road which said Syracuse, New York, five miles.

A pitter patter went off in my stomach as I knew I was fast approaching my first stop to start my case study in sociology, and the civil rights moment. I had already made a reservation at the Holiday Inn near Syracuse University. I felt I could spend one last night there and prepare myself to move into the ghetto and start my masquerade. My bag was packed with all my supplies, including school supplies in order to document my journey. I had many tattered clothes, and drama school clothes in order to dress the part. My training as a costume and makeup artist would come in very handy as I started to live my double life. I felt the only way I would get an honest interaction to document what it was like to be Black was to become a Black man living in the city, and be exposed to everyday life as my subjects lived it. I knew a little of the Black experience from living on the edge of the poorer section of Boston while attending Northeastern University, but it was only from a superficial view, and I needed more detailed exposure in order to capture the true state of things.

As I was daydreaming my way down the highway, I saw the exit for Syracuse, and pulled off the ramp which brought me down into the city. After pulling into a gas station for directions to the school, I bought a soda and was on my way. I was on an artificial high and was thinking about all the possibilities. As I got closer to the school I could see a clear distinction of boundaries with a beautiful campus on one side of the street with a nice fence, beautiful buildings, perfectly manicured flowers, and grass that looked even better than their publicity guide showed. On the other side of the street, it looked like a working-class section, with modest wooden and brick multistory buildings with small yards, and with a lot of junk accumulated in the area. I saw mostly old-model cars in the driveways lining the street, and also on the street. As I peered over to the campus I saw a few professors and students walking from here to there. The school population was at a minimum due to the summer season. Most students had gone home and would not be back until the fall.

I looked up all of a sudden and saw a homeless person with a shopping carriage right in front of my car. My heart leaped out of my chest, and I slammed on the breaks. The car came to screeching halt as my eight track tapes flew around the interior, and the suitcase in the back seat bounced off my head rest and gave my neck a quick jolt. The car stopped before I hit the man, and our eyes locked with each other. He was maybe forty years old, with tarnished style clothes that had many holes in them, worn shoes, and he wore a black knit cap, which was out of season based on the warmer temperatures. His shopping cart was filled with various possessions that I'm sure had more value to him than the open market. His skin was dark, which made his eyes seem whiter than they were. He had a look of depression and desperation in his eyes and waved to me in a simple manner to let me know he was sorry. He tried to cross the street as quickly as possible. He had a significant limp which impeded his progress. Once all was clear I pulled up the street into the hotel I was looking for, and checked in.

I LOOKED ACROSS THE dining room in the hotel, having what I thought would be my last great meal for a while. After my dessert, my waiter seemed to disappear. The steak dinner had been great, and cooked to perfection. The dining room was moderately filled with mostly college age kids and their parents. I'm sure the students were taking summer classes to make up courses they had flunked, or added courses at a more rapid pace to graduate early. Maybe a few of the kids were taking a course that was not offered during the regular school year. Either way, it was a good deal since the classes were shortened, and you could make up ground faster.

As I scanned the room, I could see a three-piece band setting up in the corner. The men were all Black, had matching white and black outfits with shiny black shoes. One was a drummer, one had a guitar, and the other pulled a saxophone from a beautiful carrying case. They reminded me of the Temptations. I was tempted to stay, and get a drink at the bar, but I knew I had serious business to attend to and this would be a distraction I would regret in the morning. I took the safe route, and flagged down my waiter, and made my way up to the room for the night.

As I CAME OUT of the hotel bathroom, I peered out the window at the Syracuse University campus across the street. It had a magnificent look at night with the lights reflecting all over the area. You could see a few people going from here to there. I saw a few guys that looked like basketball players going into a gym which I could see in the distance.

Most of the guys were dressed in different uniforms, so I assumed it must be a public night league that the school let use the gym. From closer observation, the men looked to be a little older than college, and were walking briskly to the gym entrance.

I glanced down at the television news that was on some local station, and a reporter was talking in front of a police car with crime scene tape shown in the background, describing a murder that had taken place several hours before. It seemed a young man was walking down the street minding his own business when a stray bullet from out of nowhere struck him in the head and killed him instantly. Many police were scanning the sidewalk for bullet fragments, and then it cut to a Black family being interviewed. It looked like the mother and sister of the victim, and they had tears rolling down their faces, and anguish pouring out of their bodies. I focused more on them as the interview progressed, and could not imagine what they were going through. From what they made it sound like the boy was a model student, and musician, and would have been on his way to college on a state scholarship, and now all that was left were shattered dreams.

I tried to block it out and picked up a chair from the room and brought it into the bathroom. I sat down and opened my makeup kit and began applying my blackface. I had done this a million times for various school drama productions and could make a white person look Black in my sleep. I was very careful around my eyes to avoid hitting my eyeball with the black substance. I used a mirror behind me to make sure my neck area was completely covered, and then started applying the paste to my hands and up my wrists. It would take a half an hour for the makeup to dry, and then it would not come off unless I wanted it to.

I began singing in the mirror pretending to be a sixties front man from a group like the Temptations or Stevie Wonder. I began to sing all of the two groups' songs, and bob my head back and forth. I even threw in a little Diana Ross and the Supremes for good measure. After some time had passed, I walked out of the bathroom and over to my suitcase, pulled out a black wig, and firmly fit it on my head.

I turned to the mirror and adjusted it to fit just right. As I gazed into the mirror, I was amazed that I had transformed myself into a character I would play for the next two months. I had been around the theatre my whole life, and had participated in several school plays and acted many parts over a period of years before I decided to have costumes and makeup be my specialty. I tried to justify in my own conscience that I was playing a part in a play to accumulate knowledge, and to understand how other people lived. I felt it was very altruistic of me to do this, and for a split second I was very proud of myself, and then I realized I had not done anything yet, and my mood changed to one of anticipation to one of self-doubt.

I took off my wig, placed it on the holder, put a towel over my pillowcase, and decided to get some sleep. Tomorrow would be an eventful day, and the start of my summer adventure.

I HAD SLIPPED INTO a vast dream world. As I drifted into a deeper REM, I could only think of Minstrel shows, and I was part of a Virginia company that was playing at a theater in Boston. I was playing a Banjo, and singing about "My Old Massa," and how much we loved him. There were several men standing up on stage with me singing back and forth. The second part of the show was political, and making fun of ourselves, whether it be our voice or our situation.

Minstrel shows had been born on the plantation and then became popular as a form of entertainment for the masses through vaudeville, and other travelling shows. After the Civil War, and during Reconstruction, many national theater producers brought the shows up to the northern cities where they were in big demand, and the citizenry could get a cross section of how the Black experience had been in the South.

I looked out into the audience as I strummed my banjo, and they were all white people, well dressed, and were upper class. The women and men were star struck by us, and seemed to love our performance. We jibber-jabbered back and forth, and the crowd was laughing loudly.

As we accentuated our negro southern slang dialect, I looked into a man's face in the front row, and something finally rang in my mind and heart. These people were not laughing with us but laughing at us. As I scanned the crowd in more detail, the jeers and laughing became louder and louder, and more repulsive. Why did I put myself in this situation? The harder I looked at people the noise level rose. I realized the patrons could just as well be looking at animals in the zoo and get the same level of satisfaction.

As I drifted in and out of my conscience, I strived to wipe the minstrel show away, but I could not overcome my thoughts. My love of history, and my studies were burning the letters from the books I had read in my brain. The detail was so real, and my reading comprehension brought it all to life in living color. My pulse must have risen, and I wished for morning to come sooner than later.

I woke up from my slumber as the sun shone like a laser through a crack in the window curtain. It reminded me that I had to go the bathroom in a bad way. I peeled back the covers, jumped out of bed, and made my way into the bathroom. As I stood over the toilet relieving myself I did not bother turning on the light. I just relaxed and waited until I was finished with my business. It felt like I took a twenty-five-pound weight off my stomach. I guess the beer I drank with dinner last night stayed with me.

After I was done, I turned to face the sink, and wash my face. I flipped on the light, and then saw my reflection in the mirror. I started to stagger backwards and caught myself from bouncing off the back wall of the bathroom and falling. What had happened to my face? What had happened to my face? I replayed the last twenty-four hours in my mind, and in an instant I remembered putting makeup on my face the night before for my acting debut. The blackface I had put on was waterproof, so I splashed a little water in my eyes, and brushed my teeth. I had shaved the night before, so I moved out into the bedroom area and starting dressing in the new old clothes for playing my new part in the play of my life. It consisted of dungarees and a woodcutter's flannel shirt, red and black in color. I took my wig off the holder, and then put on old shoes. I stood there for a few seconds modeling my outfit and rehearsing my new lines to impress.

I packed the rest of my belongings in my bag and then I scanned the room to make sure I did not leave anything behind. I left the key on the main bureau so I would not have to see the desk clerk again, since my appearance had changed. I stepped out into the hallway and made my way into the elevator on the second floor. An older couple were already on the car and when I stepped in, I gave them a nice smile. They frowned and moved as far into the corner as possible. I turned to face the doors and looked up at the floor numbers, wishing to be in the lobby in record time.

As the doors opened, I made my way across the lobby and out into the parking lot. My yellow Chevrolet Vega stood out like a sore thumb. As I came around my car and got ready to stick the key in the lock, I heard a voice in back of me. I turned quickly, and noticed the hotel security guard chasing after me. Forgetting about my appearance, I faced the man as he closed the distance.

"Can I help you sir?" I blurted out with a disarming quality.

"Sir, sir," the security guard responded. "Are you staying with us at the Holiday Inn?" He had a very serious look on his face, and as I looked him up and down I noticed he was wearing a firearm and had handcuffs also on his belt.

"Yes I am, sir. I stayed at your hotel last night. In fact, I liked it very much," I said in order to get on his good side, in case there was a problem.

"Is that your bag you have with you, Sir?" he spouted with no change in demeanor. "What room were you staying in?"

I thought for a minute, and then said, "Room 227, I believe." I looked him square in the face, and all I could see was contempt for me. I had not done anything wrong. What was this guy's problem?

"Do you have proof that you are staying with us?" he demanded. He stood very tall with his hands on his hips and did not change his expression one bit.

I pulled out my wallet and began searching for my receipt. My anxiety level was climbing as I scanned through the billfold. After what seemed like several minutes, I pulled out a receipt, and peered at it for a second. It had the Holiday Inn logo on it. I handed it over to the white security guard, and he looked at it very carefully. He looked me up and down for a few seconds, and then handed the receipt back to me.

Suddenly he said, "I hope you had an enjoyable stay with us, Mr. McPherson. Come back and see us again when you are in the area." A smile came across his face, and before I could respond he turned and headed back to the lobby.

I got into my car, stuffed the receipt in my console, and turned the key in the ignition, thinking about what had just happened. As I adjusted my mirror, the answer came to me loud and clear. Staring back at me in the mirror was my Black face. I thought for a second if I had been a white man coming out of that hotel, would the security guard have approached me?

As I drove out of the parking lot I took a quick left, and then asked for directions to 749 South Warren Street at the local gas station. I turned perpendicular to the main street and started driving west. As I made my way to the destination at hand, the neighborhood was getting worse, and the structures became more dilapidated. I passed several people who looked to be walking to work, mothers pushing old baby carriages, and old model cars, some that looked broken down and had not been driven in years. It was a mix of multifamily brick and wooden dwellings, and most were in need of repair. Most of the residents were Black and working class. I saw a few men on the corner who were standing around smoking cigarettes and flipping coins off the granite edging on the sidewalk.

As I made my way down the street, I strained my eyes to see the next street sign. It was very faded green with white lettering. The glare of the sun was impeding my vision, but as I fixated on it, it read South Warren Street. A wave of calm came over me as I turned the corner and made my way down to number 749. Just as I counted my way down my heart dropped. On the side of the road was crime scene tape, and the chalk outline of a body. This was the same location that was on the eleven o'clock news from the night before. I flashed back in my mind to form a picture of the two devastated Black family members who had just lost their son. I rubber necked the chalk outline, and as I looked up I saw the Salvation Army shelter on the left side of the road. I pulled a U-turn and parked my car. I pulled my bag from my backseat and then took one last look across at the crime scene. A thousand thoughts were racing through my mind. It was a wakeup call that I had entered another world.

I peered up at the Salvation Army sign on the entrance to the building and thought back to what I had read about its long history. The charity had started in London in 1878 by William and Catherine Booth who were Evangelists, and wanted to help those down and out, prostitutes, drunkards, and gamblers. They gave them a safe place to rest their head, and in exchange they tried to convert them to Christianity. They called their converts a volunteer army. Hence, the military titles were given to different levels of workers in the operation. They had done so much good work over the years, and I was glad this was my first stop on the tour.

As I opened the door, a few younger Black men who looked disheveled were coming out. They were complaining about something, but I could not make out what they said. I waited for them to pass and then stepped into the lobby. I scanned the lobby and looked at the office doors. The lights were off in most of the rooms, so I made my way down the hallway where I saw people coming and going. I figured with so much activity happening it must be the cafeteria. As I looked down at the old white and black tile floor, and up at the vaulted white plaster ceilings, I noticed the different rooms and titles stenciled on the doors as I walked. At the end of the hallway, I saw a lot of commotion. Several men were standing at a big mahogany door smoking a cigarette, and each holding a cup of coffee. They held the door for me as I tried to squeeze past them with myself and bag. I asked one man who was dressed in normal street clothes, and looked like a volunteer, where the head man or woman was? They both looked at each other.

"You mean Vernon?" the other man said. He pointed to the right side of the room, and a big Black man was sitting with what looked like some homeless veterans. I thanked them for their time and stepped into the big room. On the opposite wall was a serving area, with all kinds of breakfast items, and behind that was a kitchen, and a big man peering through the opening. He had a chef's hat on and a big smile with shiny white teeth.

I stepped down one step, put my heavy bag down on the tile floor, and began to meander over to the veteran's table. As I approached the men, they looked like a conglomeration of World War II, Korean, and Vietnam veterans. They all wore their uniform tops, and had their badges and metals showing. Back where I came from, most Vietnam vets stored their uniform in a trunk as soon as they were discharged from the military, since a lot of military draftees were not held in high esteem by the public. As I gazed at these downtrodden veterans, I'm sure this was the last materialistic thing that they could grab on to validate their own self-worth, since most of them looked like they had fallen on hard times.

I stood in back of a few men, and a few more looked up from their conversation. I cleared my throat to get Vernon's attention. After a few seconds Vernon turned to me, focused his eyes on me for a split second, and said, "Can I help you son?" with a slow voice and a slight southern drawl. Then the conversation went silent, and all faces turned to me.

"Yes, sir," I responded with as much confidence as I could muster on short notice. "I was told you were the man in charge, and I just got into town, and was looking to volunteer here."

Vernon sat there for a minute pondering the thought, and then pulled his chair back, stood up, and walked around the table towards me. As he approached, I stuck out my hand, but he did not meet it. Instead, he put his arm around me, pulled me tight to him, and said "What is your name son?" with a slight chuckle.

I said, "Jimmy, sir." I made sure I did not tell him my last name since most homeless people did not deal with last names. I gave him a nice smile back, and we started walking arm in arm back up the way I had entered the room. I picked up my bag on the way by, and we continued to his office down the hall.

As we entered his office, he flipped on a light since it was a cloudy day out, and not much sunlight was flowing in. He stepped around the gray metal desk and settled himself into an old comfortable chair with a ripped cloth seat. He then put his hands behind his head and settled back.

"Well Jimmy, what brings you to our fine establishment this morning?" he bellowed, then smiled.

"Well sir, I am from Boston, and have fallen on hard times, and I'm looking for a place to live for a while. I am willing to work for my room and board, and don't expect any favors," I told him, with an air of depression in my voice. I had practiced this line many times in my mirror at home, but this was my debut.

He looked through me with laser focus for a few seconds. He picked up a pencil out of his round leather holder and started tapping the end of the desk, making a rhythmic beat. "Well Jimmy, people come to us for many reasons and many circumstances, and we are not very judgmental. We do not ask a lot of personal questions. The only thing we require of our employees is sympathy and understanding for the people we are taking care of." Vernon looked out the window and stared off into space, and then turned back. "Well son, you have arrived at the right time. As it turns out we are in need of volunteers, and we do have a room you can stay in for free as long as you work for your keep." He settled back into his chair and stared right back at me for a response.

I stumbled as the words came out of my mouth. "That sounds great, sir, sir." I stuttered. "I appreciate the offer, and I will not let you down."

"Jimmy, call me Vernon," he said with a smile. "I will take you up to your room and you can unpack, and then you will be my guest for lunch, and after you can meet the rest of the staff. They will be glad to have you. By the way, how did you get here this morning?"

"I have my car out front, Vernon."

"Well son, pull it around into our side lot, or you will not have a car in the morning." He chuckled, then bellowed, "You are in the bad part of town now, and car parts are at a premium."

Vernon showed me to my room on the second floor, and then I secured my car in the side lot. The chain link fence was so high, and at the top was barb wire. As I left the lot, I pulled the gate across, and put the lock back into place, making sure it was not locked. Many staff in the area would come and go during the day. Vernon would make sure the gate was locked before night fall.

I LAY ON MY bed looking around the room after I had unpacked my bag. I set my clock by my bedside and set the time. I put a few paperback books on my nightstand and stowed my suitcase in the closet. The bedroom was sparse with only a four-drawer bureau, a nightstand, single bed, and a wooden chair in the corner. The walls were wood paneling, with white plaster ceilings and off-white tile floors. I looked out the window, and then back at the ceiling. I pondered who might have lived in this room before I got here. Was it a volunteer or was it a homeless person looking for a place to rest their head for a night or two. I was in the hood now, the economy was bad, and many people on the lower economic scale had fallen on bad times.

I laid in bed daydreaming, and picking up my books flipping pages, when I heard a rap on the door. I said, "Who is it?" with as much confidence as possible.

"It's Vernon, son. It's time for lunch."

I popped out of bed and he was standing right there as big a life looking down at me with his signature smile. I stepped out of the room, and he threw his arm around my shoulder and we began walking down the corridor to the stairwell. He started talking about the Salvation Army, its long history, this shelter, and all the inner workings. I listened to every word he had to say since this road trip was a fact finding mission, and I wanted to learn as much as possible in a short time.

Down in the kitchen area I was introduced to a few men and woman, and the only names I could remember on first pass was Lloyd, and Rose. Lloyd was a smaller man of sixty with a weathered face, big muscles, and dressed with a white chef's outfit. Rose was in her fifties with a large build, brunette short hairdo, and a jovial disposition. She usually coordinated the serving of the food with the other volunteers. Lloyd was the head cook, and he directed all the other assistants, and gave them suggestions to make them more efficient. Especially when things got busy around dinner times. Lloyd took me under his wing and started showing me where everything was, like the storage closet and the pantry, and then gave me a few cooking lessons based on the menu of the day and night. I followed his instruction with all ears, since I knew there was a lot to learn. Then a feeling of guilt started setting in, since I knew I would only be here for a week, and then moving on to my next destination.

The dinner crush was brutal. The homeless and hungry poured into the cafeteria and stood in line. The people were an assortment of men, woman, and a few children with their mothers. They all looked downtrodden and some looked very dirty. I suppose I could not blame them especially if they were living on the street. Rose grabbed me and had me stand behind the serving tables and spoon out macaroni and cheese on to the customers plates. As they passed me by, they all gave me a look of thanks, even if their face was pasted with a sad look. A few of the older gentlemen were dressed up in what would have been nice clothes for the forties, but now they were out of style and very old. The drug addicts and alcoholics were up and down, and several were having a conversation with the voices in their head.

I went about my work with vigor and enthusiasm, and I think Rose was happy with my performance. She was very comfortable talking to the patrons, and treated each person with respect, even if a few were in a bad mood or having a bad day. I thought to myself that if I was in this circumstance, I would be in a permanent bad mood.

After the dinner hour had passed, several other volunteers took a head count of who would be staying overnight, and then they were escorted to the gym area where several hundred military cots were spread out. Most of the women and children would stay for the night, and some would go to school the next morning, as the mothers foraged for things of value to trade, or bring to the pawn shop for money. Most of the men did not want to stay inside overnight in the summer, and usually found space in a back alley or an abandoned car to rest their heads. It was all very depressing, and something I had prepared myself for in the prior week. But nothing really could get me ready for the reality check I was witnessing.

We were all sitting in the cafeteria area at one table when Vernon came down around the corner and stopped at the head of the table. He asked several questions of us as to how the dinnertime had gone, and if there was any trouble. Based on the majority of the volunteers, it had come off according to plan. Once he was satisfied with the responses, he dismissed the staff, except the volunteers that would stand watch over the gym for the night. They would not go home until morning. Everyone over time would have this shift, including me. The job was to keep the women and children safe and secure in case a homeless man stepped out of line. Most of the residents staying overnight were Black.

Vernon escorted me back to my room and showed me where the bathroom was down the hall, and then thanked me, and gave me a wakeup call for seven o'clock the next morning. I washed up quickly and then returned to my room, pulling out my notebook binder, and pen, and began to write down my observations. It was day one, and I had already accumulated so much information in my mind, and I wanted to remember it all. It was all very heartbreaking but thrilling at the same time. I was opening my mind to a world I had never seen before.

As I sat there writing I thought about the goodnight conversation with Vernon. He had looked me up and down, like he was trying to read my mind. I was starting to get myself paranoid. Was Vernon looking through my makeup, and realizing I was not Black, but really white? Had he seen my whiteness in my mannerisms or the way I talked? I had been around enough high school and college plays to master the part of a young Black man, but maybe I had been overconfident. I went to bed with this thought on my mind.

I WAS TOSSING AND turning in my bed, drifting in and out of deep sleep. I had a million dreams cascading through my mind from my college years, my trip to Syracuse, and all I had seen and heard since I had been here. It was like a movie being played back in my mind. I thought about my experience in the cafeteria, and all the volunteers and patrons that crossed my path. It was a cross section of all kinds of people. Some were short, tall, thin, fat, female, male, children, and most were Black. I was playing back in my mind if I had gone to a poor white section of Syracuse, would I see as many people coming into the shelter, and being served food? I kept that thought in my dream, when all of a sudden my mind switched to a Black man, sitting at a lunch counter in Greensboro, North Carolina. He was a Black student at one of the local colleges and had entered a Woolworth Five and Dime store on the main street. He was accompanied by three of his friends. After shopping for some merchandise, they sat at the counter to get something for lunch. As the dream unfolded, I could see the faces of the employees behind the counter, and in the kitchen. They looked very uncomfortable, and were talking in low voices on how they should handle the situation. They looked over and pointed to a standup area in the corner that was for Black people or whites. The mood was tense, and the manager of the store walked over to them and asked why they were sitting at

the counter. The man by the name of Clarence spoke up, and said he and his friends would like to order lunch. The manager looked back, perplexed at the request. This young college student must know this was a segregated lunch counter.

I began to roll back and forth in my bed as my inner tension grew. I felt uneasy inside as I focused on my dream, and it became more clear. The mood in the store was tense, and the manager had never had this situation happen. He was clearly out of his league. He pleaded back and forth with the customers to stand in the corner area, and he would be more than glad to serve them. They sat at the counter, and looked back and forth with each other, and then shook their heads in a negative way. They were not having it. The manager stood there looking at the other customers and shoppers who had stopped to view the confrontation. He began to break out in a sweat and kept adjusting his tie. Finally, he picked up the phone in front of all the people and called the police.

The crowd grew in the store after the police were called, and the tension also rose. The white housewives in their fine dresses, with child in hand, stood behind the men at the counter, in a show of support. The food staff were lined up on the other side next to their manager and tried to stare down the men sitting there. They kept flipping their menus, and continued talking to each other like it was just another day at the office. I rolled in my bed deep in light REM sleep, but uncomfortable with my subconscious.

Suddenly two police cars pulled up in front of the building and the patrons divided like the Red Sea. The police walked through the crowd. The head officer with a tan brim hat and sunglasses looked very ominous. His three deputes followed close behind. He walked up and stood right behind this Clarence fellow, and stared at the manager, and said, "What seems to be the matter my good sir," with an air of authority. The mood immediately got very tense. The crowd held its collective breath.

"Well, Officer," he spouted back, these four men have decided to sit at our lunch counter and order some food. I have told them I would be more than happy to serve them at our stand-up counter, but they insist on sitting."

The officer put his hand on Clarence's shoulder, and said, "Sir, can you stand up, and face me, so we can discuss this in a reasonable manner?" he spoke with a calm tone.

My dream had my body floating right over the scene looking down. I could see all their faces clearly and their body language, too.

All of a sudden, all four men stood up, turned, and faced the four police officers, and the crowd that had formed inside. Even the cashiers had left their post and walked over to see what was going on. The other three deputies pulled out their black night sticks and began tapping them into the palm of their hands in a threatening way.

As the leader of the group stood, and turned he was nose to nose with the officer. He did not give any ground to the police. It was four on four, and nobody wanted to give an inch. I thought back to the racial division I had read about in my classes that happened in the past, and my blood pressure was rising as my dream state continued.

It was clear from the mood that this situation could escalate in a bad way very quickly, and the officer knew that the Woolworth manager and shoppers would not appreciate it. A lot of the patrons disagreed with segregation, and several of the white patrons had friends or helpers at their houses that were Black. Over time whites and minorities had crossed the racial barrier, and civil society had just not caught up with the process.

The officer spoke to Clarence in a low voice, and said, "Sir, you and your friends cannot be served at this counter. This is clearly displayed in this sign here." The officer reached down and picked up the sign and held it to his chest. "I must tell you, if you and your friends do not either stand over at the other counter or leave the store, we are going to have a problem."

Clarence looked at the police, looked at the crowd, turned and looked at the kitchen staff, and then said, in a confident manner, "Common boys, we have made our point." A big smile came across his face. The four men started moving toward the front doors. The police and the crowd parted, with a low murmur cascading through the crowd. The men walked out slowly, and on to the sidewalk. A big crowd had grown outside, and the newspaper and television stations had reporters everywhere, and cameras were clicking and rolling. This would play on the nightly news for days on end.

Low and behold, Clarence said years later, this event had been staged to bring the subject of segregation front and center in the eyes of Americans everywhere. He and his friends had targeted Woolworths since it was a national store chain, and this would not only be in the Greensboro newspapers but leak out across the country.

They had started the ball rolling, and went back to the store the next day, and the day after, and the day after that. Due to their efforts, the store lunch counter would become integrated six months later.

My heartbeat and anxiety dissipated in my body, as the dream streamlined out, and the danger had passed. I rolled to one side, and all my muscles relaxed as I drifted into a deeper sleep.

THE ALARM CLOCK FLASHED red, with its obnoxious beep over and over. It woke me out of the deep sleep. I focused my eyes on the screen of the clock, and it said six o'clock. I looked up and scanned the interior of the space I was in and did not recognize it. My mind raced as I dug down deep to unlock the clue as to where I was. After a few seconds I recognized my location. I was at the Salvation Army shelter in Syracuse, New York.

My pulse lowered since I was getting acclimated to my new space. It looked sparse, but it got the job done. I jumped out of bed and grabbed my toothbrush, paste, and towel, and opened my door, and headed down the hall. I arrived at the men's room door and gave it a knock. I heard a faint voice from inside say, "Just a minute."

I was bouncing from foot to foot since I needed to relieve myself. I had held it all night since the bathroom situation was so inconvenient. As I tried word games, and any other games to take my mind off the bladder pain I was feeling, I turned and looked out the smoky second story window to the alley below. I had a great view down into a big blue steel dumpster when I focused in on a man on top of the pile, sleeping on a cardboard mattress with a silver reflective blanket. My mind jumped and I became alarmed as to why this man was there sleeping in a dumpster instead of downstairs in the gym area? Were they at capacity last night, and he was turned away, or was he like a lot of homeless people, where he felt most comfortable in the outdoors. I pondered the thought for a few seconds when the men's room door flew open.

A tall man of medium build, clean shaven, stepped out and said, "Good morning," and then said, "Excuse me." I gave him a quick smile and responded with a hardy, "Good morning." I remembered him from the kitchen area yesterday. He was cranking out food like a short order cook. I stepped to the side as the man walked away and closed the bathroom door. I rushed over to the toilet to drain my bladder. As I was standing there passing the time, I almost fell asleep. I snapped out of it, almost missing my target.

After I finished my business, I stepped over to the sink, and was momentarily taken back by what I saw in the mirror. There was a Black man looking back at me. My mind adjusted to the mystery for a split second before I remembered my mission, and my disguise. I was here undercover to document the plight of the Black person in America, and I was under deep cover. The thought bounced around in my mind for a few seconds, and I was feeling very altruistic. After freshening up, I got back to my room, got dressed and reported down to Rose in the cafeteria area.

She looked different from when I had seen her yesterday. She looked bigger, with a nice floral dress on. Her voice and demeanor were very bright and uplifting, and she was a beacon of light for the downtrodden, coming in to put a little food in their stomachs. She conversed with the customers in an easy, non-threatening voice and tried to make them forget about their plight for a while.

I stepped behind the long row of tables and began receiving large steel trays of scrambled eggs, bacon, toast, home fries, and pancakes. It was about seven o'clock, and there was a big rush at the beginning. The line was stacking up, with residents pouring out of the gym, and many people coming in the front door tattered, dingy, and hungry. My heart sank as I saw the line form, and most people were obedient, courteous, waiting their turn. My heart went out to all of them thinking about each person's history and what brought them into this circumstance. I scanned the room looking for Vernon and found him at the same table with the veterans, holding court, and making them feel at home. The coffee was flowing, and they were all talking about the news of the day, and the plight of the Vietnam veterans.

As the serving continued, I began to shoot the breeze with the man next to me. He was small, maybe five foot six, with a small afro, dark complexion, and perfect white teeth. He had a blue work shirt with dungarees, and light brown work boots. At first, he was a little stand offish, but after ten or fifteen minutes, we were good buddies. We went through all the small talk we could think of. Some of the customers said good morning to him, since he must have been a regular employee who had been here for some time. After a while, and with the line diminishing, I asked more probing questions of my neighbor to my left to ascertain what his life was like, and how he ended up here. The more I asked the less explanation I received. You could tell after some time that he had issues, and had overcome them, but felt embarrassed as to his background.

As the morning passed the numbers got lighter, and then Vernon yelled over to the servers to fill our plates and join him at his table. Most of the Veterans had gone outdoors to walk the streets, panhandle, or do some drugs or drink liquor. Some of them looked lost, and just wanted to get through the day. Some others were just angry at the United States government for sending them to Vietnam to fight a useless war that did not accomplish anything. Most Veterans coming home after the war ended in 1973 were received with disparagement from an American public who were war weary, and saw all the bad stories on the nightly news.

I set my tray down as the rest of the workers joined us, and we began to chow down. I sat there and ate thinking the less I said the better. It would be more beneficial to listen to the morning banter and pick up as many facts as I could. Most of my coworkers looked worn, but happy. I think the shelter management tried to instill in them that if they had a positive outlook, then this would rub off on the homeless.

After sitting at the long table for some time, I felt a tap on my shoulder. I craned my head around and there was Rose looking down at me. She had on her usual big smile, and then said, "Jimmy, can you come with me. They need help on the other side, and we need a young man like you to help."

I gave her a cheery "Yes," and stood up to follow her to the other side of the building. Rose walked ahead of me, and I followed along. There was no time for small talk or questions. As she proceeded, things that stuck with me were how people greeted her, and she knew everyone's name. Even homeless people who had been coming here for a while. The conversation was always tailored to the individual, and I was astounded with the memory she had for people who society thought were so insignificant.

As we walked, we passed through the gym area where two hundred cots had been set up the night before, and now they were miraculously gone. In their place were some inner-city young people playing pick-up basketball, with an older man dressed up in a red and white sweat suit giving them instruction on the game. He had a big silver whistle around his neck, and he would blow it to stop play when he wanted to make a point or give some instruction. The kids were young, but they responded to his guidance, and seemed to take to him like a father figure.

After we crossed the gym, Rose opened a door which led to a huge warehouse located in the back of the building. The floor was made of cement, with big blue and white aluminum walls, and a roof which was thirty feet above. As I peered around, I could see sorting tables for clothes, and several massive commercial washers and dryers in the corner of the room. To the front were several people tagging merchandise, and then a customer counter, which connected to the other side of the building, and the parking lot.

Rose told me they sold clothes at a very reduced rate to the public, and people who could not pay were given a free new change of clothes every once in a while. Several sneaker and clothing companies donated shoes and socks, because this was a significant problem with the homeless. Their shoes would wear out, and then the socks would wear, causing cuts and bruises which could turn into a bigger affair if left untreated.

I followed Rose over to a long wooden table with several pieces of clothing. Two young girls standing there were focused on checking sizes and folding washed outfits into piles and placing them in different shelves behind them. They looked up when they saw Rose, and said, "Good morning, Mama," with a smile in their voice, and a spring in their step. She introduced the two girls as Sarah, and Melba. They were each seventeen years old and attended the Catholic school down the street. Their families were from meager means, and they volunteered to give back to the community. Most of the families in the area were lower middle class or poor. The lucky ones knew that they could be here as a resident if their families luck ran out due to the economy or social problems.

I thought to myself why are they calling Rose Mama? After a few moments I realized this was a nickname for their leader. I introduced myself to them, they giggled, and then Rose left, and they instructed me on my duties for the rest of the day. The warehouse was a flurry of activity, but everyone knew their job, and it was like an automobile assembly line. The girls pretty much stuck to their selves, and my job was helping fold, and then unload the wooden bins, and once and awhile walk the stack of clothes to a tagging area in the front of the building. The clothes were priced, put on hangers, or left folded, and brought to the public area for shopping and buying. There was another counter there with several cash registers, and women standing there to cash customers out. The shopping area had several people looking at the garments, and there were some homeless people meandering around looking like they were very confused. Some were killing time before they headed out to the streets again.

I thought back to my life in Massachusetts, and my home, and it became apparent I was so lucky to have a safe, secure home, and loving parents. For these people who had fallen down, the world could be very cruel and lonely.

After my day's work, Vernon came back and retrieved me, gave me an early dinner with other workers, and said I could retire to my room for the rest of the night. I welcomed the rest, but had a million thoughts racing through my mind. I wanted to document what I had seen, and what I had learned that day. As soon as I got back to my room, I freshened up, set my alarm for the next day, and started writing in my journal at a feverish pace. My brain was like a sponge and a Polaroid picture at the same time. Things kept popping in my mind, and I could not write them down fast enough. I tried to slow my pace of writing and reflect on all I had learned and seen to put it in perspective.

The pictures of the workers, residents, and customers cascaded through my mind, and I started daydreaming on what I would see or encounter the next day. I felt fulfilled, but hungry to learn as much as I could about the plight of people.

As the week wore on, I met so many hapless people, and many people who had fallen on hard times. I felt terrible for the clients and volunteers. The thing I took away from the week so far was these volunteers at the shelter were beyond loyal, and hardworking, they were creating a safe secure space for the residents where they could feel like things were normal, even if it was just for a meal, overnight rest, or clothes shopping. I was impressed and tried to learn everything I could about the homeless, economically disabled, and the forgotten. They came in all shapes and sizes, and my heart went out to them.

I peered down the lunch line looking to see when it would end. Today we were serving sandwiches and tomato soup to our customers, and homemade chocolate chip cookies for dessert. The room was only moderately filled today since the sun was shining, and a lot of the homeless would walk the streets this afternoon and wait until dinner to have another meal. There was the normal buzz in the air with volunteers talking to people, and the patrons gulping down food, and talking and ranting in their normal manner. It was a conglomeration of broken toys all trying to get back in the game of life.

As I served the resident standing in front of me, I heard a load thud, and then the sound of food and silverware crashing on the tile floor. I looked down the line and saw an older man, shabbily dressed in green trousers, blue shirt, and a brown overcoat. He was out cold on the floor and had hit his head on the serving table on his way down. There was a slight cut on his head, with blood pooling across the floor. I stopped what I was doing and ran around the tables to pick the man's head up off the floor. Just as I was closing in on his body, a wave of urine and alcohol smell hit me right in the face. The man's clothes were very dirty and had not been washed in weeks. His personal hygiene was not up to speed. He had clearly been on the street for a long time and was just living day to day with minimal care for his body.

I got my hand and forearm under his head and lifted it. I put my finger into his curly hair and felt around to see where the cut on his head was, and how bad. As I looked closer, Rose was standing over me with a cloth diaper from the clothes department, and handed it to me. I gave her a quick smile of concern and applied pressure to the cut. It looked to be a small wound, and the compress was working to clot the blood. As I looked down at the man's eyes, he was starting to come out of his daze.

Once I looked back to Rose, I saw Vernon standing beside her advising me to keep comforting him, and once he was composed, the volunteers would lift him into a chair. By this time, I had a circle of bystanders, mostly volunteers from the clothes side of the house. Most of the residents didn't break stride in their mission to get a meal and feed themselves. They were used to seeing passed out people on the streets, and for the most part, if you were alone, and not part of a group of street people, no one was going to pay any attention to you.

The longer I kneeled on the floor, cradling the vagrant's head, the more my stomach began to get upset from the man's smell. I tried so hard to look down on him with compassion, but the smell was starting to overcome me. I signaled to Vernon that I was in trouble, and he quickly knelt down and scooped up the man's head from my hand, and I slipped out of the way.

I ran full speed down the hallway until I saw the men's room door. I grabbed the doorknob, but it was locked. I couldn't believe it. My stomach was in full retreat. I turned and continued down the hallway at a rapid pace and went out the front doors. Two men were standing there having a cigarette, and I threw myself over the railing and blew my lunch. It was projectile vomiting, and they both jumped back and looked at me like I was possessed. After I was finished, I pulled a handkerchief from my pocket and wiped my mouth. I sat there for a few minutes, gathering myself and breathing in some fresh air. The men kept asking me, "Are you alright man?" with an air of sympathy in their voices.

I looked up and gave them a head bob in return.

After a few minutes I saw one of the custodians come around the corner of the building with a hose and hook it up to an outdoor outlet. He started watering down the vomit all over the bushes. He looked very intent, and professional in his rounds, and I knew he probably cleaned up a lot worse accidents inside the building.

I eventually came back into the building, and Vernon dismissed me for the afternoon, and asked if I could report at five thirty to help out with dinner, and I gave him a half-hearted "yes."

The rest of the week went well with a lot of observation, writing and documentation for my thesis. I felt bad that in a day or so I would be leaving. I had come up with a cover story in my mind; I would tell Vernon my mother was very sick, and I had to go home to Boston to help my father take care of her. I knew this excuse was unfair to the Salvation Army volunteers that would miss my services, but I had a time schedule to keep, and it was the only way to accomplish my task.

I WAS TIPTOEING DOWN the empty hallway at five in the morning, trying to be as quiet as possible. My time in Syracuse had come to an end. I took off my makeup last night before bed to give my skin a chance to breathe after a week of blackface. I would go back to my old self for the next twenty-four hours before I got to my next stop on the tour.

I kept looking around corners and out windows to make sure I did not run into anyone I knew or otherwise I would have a lot of explaining to do. I knew they had a skeleton crew in the gym to keep an eye on the overnight guests. I finally got to the front door and looked through the thick doors to the outside. As I peered through, the coast was clear. I pushed down on the brass bar, and popped the big panel door open, and stepped out.

As I looked around, you could hear a pin drop. The June morning air was cool, and in the distance, you could hear the faint noise of a dog barking. I dragged my bag down the cement stairs and headed down the sidewalk to the chain link fence that protected the parking lot. I pulled out my penlight, and flashed it on the combination lock, and began spinning the tumblers. I tried it once, and no luck. My blood pressure started to shoot up as I pulled a crumbled piece of paper out of my pocket with the correct numbers. I could not afford to stay at this fence too long as the local police were always patrolling this area, due to crime, and drug dealers. I also did not want to run into one of the volunteers coming to work to cook food in the kitchen for the breakfast shift.

I focused on the combination and dialed to the right, back to the left, and then back to the right. I prayed this would be it and pulled the lock down. It sprang open and I took it off the gate, then slid the chain link fence across to make the opening.

I briskly ran to my car, popped the hatchback, and threw my bag in, and tried to shut it without making a big thud. I opened the driver's door, jumped in, put the key in the ignition and fired up the engine. It came to life with a roar, and I put it in drive right away. I pulled to the outside of the lot and then jumped out to put the lock back in place. In split time I was making my way out of the ghetto and back to the Syracuse campus on the main street.

I breathed a sigh of relief as the city lay behind me and I got closer to the highway. I saw a couple of fast-food joints on the strip and pulled into the takeout area and ordered a cup of coffee and a breakfast sandwich. As I was driving, I took a big sip of coffee and let it slide down my throat. It felt so good, and the caffeine would bring my tired body back to life for the long drive.

I kept following the Route 90 signs until I got to the highway, stepped on the accelerator, and put my radio on a great local rock and roll station, and started to cruise. I daydreamed about my week at the Salvation Army shelter and all I had seen, and learned, about the disadvantaged, drug addicted, and the forgotten citizens of this fair city. The very limited view I got so far was heartbreaking, and the faces and stories felt like they had been stamped in my mind. Fortunately, I had documented everything, my disguise had worked, and I had gotten away without a trace. I had a pang of guilt in my heart for running out on these fine people, but they would find a worthy replacement in no time. I was very impressed with the volunteers and workers I had met, and was so proud of their commitment to the downtrodden of our society.

Chapter 8

I LOOKED TO MY right and saw the skyline of Cleveland, and Lake Erie in the background. I had been driving for many hours and my mind and body were tired. It was a beautiful day here, and the city looked more inviting than I remembered it being in some travel guides I had flipped through to read up on the sites and the history.

It looked like a midsize industrial city with a normal downtown area, a large shopping area on the Great Lakes, banks, theaters, and many manufacturing companies as you got away from the downtown area. I hit the ramp down off the highway and cruised to the bottom. I quickly looked at the tour guide for the hotel I would be staying at tonight. As I collected myself and looked around, I realized the town was very run down with abandoned factories and panhandlers roaming the streets. I put my finger on the street name and went to the closest gas station to get directions. The man pumping gas was very helpful, and said the hotel was right down the street towards the nicer section of town.

I pulled out and meandered my way down a few blocks. The buildings got more modern and reminded me of any city in America. From the news, I knew the Midwest had not fared well in the recession, and many people had lost their jobs; the manufacturing had gone somewhere else due to excessive union wages and cheaper help down in the South.

As I drove, I saw the familiar site of Howard Johnson's. It brought back memories of many family trips down to Florida when I was growing up. I had a flashback of driving down South with my parents and haunting them to find a motel that had a pool with a diving board, so I could swim after a long day's ride. My father favored Howard Johnson's and Holiday Inns because he knew they were clean and had decent food in their dining rooms.

My mind also flashed back to the chain gangs I had encountered in the deep South as we drove down old Route 1, and Route 301. It always troubled me to see those poor Black people on the side of the road picking up trash or doing construction work in the hot summer sun and humidity. You would see the prison guard sitting in his air conditioned car or sitting on the hood, drinking soda pop. The men's faces always had a look of despair, and I tried to imagine in my own mind what their offences must have been to end up in that place.

I pulled into the hotel parking lot, popped my hatchback, and started making my way to the lobby. There seemed to be a lot of people coming and going, and I wondered if I had wandered into the middle of a convention in the city. It looked like all men in expensive suits, and some were dressed in casual clothes, while others were in pool outfits, carrying mixed drinks.

I stepped up to the counter and gave the nice counter person my name. She pulled my reservation and said, "Nice to have you with us, Mr. McPherson," with a nice midwestern drawl in her voice. I filled out the registration card and gave her cash for the room. Before I knew it, I had my room key and was making my way over to the elevator, which would bring me to the second floor. As the doors opened a few convention attendees jumped out of the car, back slapping each other about how great they were, and looking somewhat intoxicated. It was about three o'clock, and I figured I could rest up in the room, watch some television, and then get showered for dinner. The long day of driving in the summer heat had drained me of my energy, and I wanted to recharge my batteries. I knew it would be another long week tomorrow of playing a Black man in the game of life. I pondered in my mind how things would unfold for the next week.

I WOKE UP EARLY the next morning and decided to try an experiment before leaving to travel to the local homeless shelter. I decided to put on my makeup, and then go down to the lobby to have a cup of coffee and a muffin before heading out. It was a beautiful day in Cleveland, and I watched the local news as I finished dressing in what I thought would be cool to wear as a modern day Black man. The colors were bright, and the pants had bell bottoms, with a matching soft cotton shirt with long sleeves.

I grabbed my room key and wallet, stepped in front of the bathroom mirror for the last time, and then moved out into the hallway. I yawned a little as I was walking. My neighbor next door had an informal party in his room to about three in the morning, and even though I was sleeping, I could hear the noise in my subconscious. I stopped in front of the elevator bank and pushed the button. After a few seconds the doors opened, and I stepped in.

There were two men standing there all dressed for a meeting with nice colored dress pants, clean white shirts and madras dress coats. Both were sporting mustaches with slicked back hair. It smelled like Brylcreem. They immediately gave me a look up and down, and then retreated to the corner of the car and stopped talking. I stood at the front of the car and waited for it to descend to the first floor.

When the doors opened, I worked my way across the lobby to the buffet table, picked up a coffee cup and saucer, and started to fill it with coffee. I quickly added cream and sugar, and then made my way down to the muffins. The two men in the elevator were breathing down my neck to get their coffee, and really looked put off wondering why I was there. I think they thought I was reporting for work in the hotel, versus just staying overnight on my way to somewhere else.

I heard them whispering under their breath, and when I turned back to face them, the chatter stopped, and both their heads faced down towards the table. I scooped up a muffin and then made my way to a nice table, with a picture window overlooking the pool. I noticed a few guests with children outside getting some sun and chaperoning their children. As I gazed out the window, I could see the two men congregating with some of their convention buddies at a few tables in the corner. I could tell I was the topic of conversation, and finally I pulled my room key out of my pocket and put it on the table. Once they spotted the room key, the conversation on the other side of the room came to an end. They realized I was not just some street tough stopping in for a free breakfast, but I was really a patron.

After about a half an hour, I finished my breakfast, and walked by the men's table. I gave them the peace sign and kept walking. I quickly went up to my room, packed my bag, and made my way downstairs into the parking lot. This time the security guard only followed me to the front door, and then stopped outside, lit a cigarette, and kept his eyes glued to me until he saw my car keys come out, and go into the hatchback lock, and pop it open. He was a fifty-year-old white dude, with a Howard Johnson's uniform on with the logo on the chest. He looked like a retired cop. As fast as he came out, he threw down his cigarette, held the door for a young couple coming out, and disappeared inside.

I pulled out on to the main street, and headed back to the same gas station as yesterday to fill up my tank and ask directions to 5310 Carnegie Ave. The gas station owner was a brother, and as soon as he heard the address, he knew it was the City Mission homeless shelter. He said, "Man, you look too well off to be checking in to the shelter, man," in a slow city street dialect.

I smiled back at him and told him I was going to be working there as a volunteer for the summer. When he heard that, he came to life, smiled, shook my hand, and sent me on my way. I motored down the street at a slow pace with several cars blowing by me on the left, went under the interstate, and kept driving. The downtown city district soon changed into a run-down industrial area, with several factories, abandoned warehouses, and pawn shops. Vagrants walked the street with their backpacks and shopping carts. These contained all their worldly possessions.

As I was counting down the numbers, I noticed Carnegie Avenue changed from industrial to run-down two and three decker homes in all shapes and sizes. Some had metal clapboard, and some had asphalt shingle. The porches all looked rickety and unsafe. On the front steps were young women with kids playing in the streets. On every corner there were men talking and playing cards or flipping coins towards the curb. The sidewalks were littered with trash, and empty wine and beer bottles. I came to the end of the street, nervous that I was lost, and then I looked up and was staring at the front of the City Mission with its religious logo. It looked like an abandoned warehouse that was reconstructed into a men's shelter. I peered to the right of the building and saw a fenced off lot. I pulled my car in.

I walked up the stairs and opened the large front door. It creaked open, and I stepped inside. An older Black man was standing there, picking up cigarette butts from an aluminum ashtray that was attached to the wall. He poured the contents into his janitor's barrel and then turned towards me. He had a stern look on his face until I asked him where Cecil Washington's office was. He was the head of the homeless shelter, and I had called ahead and told him I would be coming. As soon as he heard that name, a smile came to his face, and the man said, "You know Cecil?" with an enthusiastic voice.

"Nah," I responded. "I am here for a job interview, and I was told to speak to him."

The smile never left the man's face, and he turned up the stairs and said, "Follow me."

The office was on the first floor, with a nice view of the parking lot through barred windows and wire mesh glass panes. They were dirty and hadn't been cleaned in years. As I came through the door, the janitor told Cecil my business, and then Cecil thanked him, and he was dismissed.

When he stood to shake my hand, I was amazed. I was looking at a huge Black man, with broad shoulders, muscles bulging, and medium length hair. In the background, I could see a big picture under glass of an Ohio State Buckeyes football player running through a line of other players. To the right of that was another picture of Cecil with his parents, standing with the coach in the middle of the football stadium. I gazed at these pictures a little too long, and then I heard the man clear his throat, and looked back at him quickly.

"You must be Mr. Jimmy McPherson. How are you doing?" he spouted with an air of confidence in his voice. "I heard you were coming to do some volunteering for the summer. Well, we can use the help since business is booming." He chuckled again. He pulled a pencil out of an Ohio State pencil holder and began tapping it in the palm of his hand.

"I appreciate the offer, Mr. Washington. I wanted to do some volunteering before I enter the real world," I stated as intelligently as I could.

He laughed. "This is the real world, Jim. The street is the real world. Corporate America is for the white boys, and pencil pushers." He then started pushing the pencil around his desk until he got a smile out of me.

I asked him how a big star from Ohio State ended up in a place like this. He went on to tell me in a few minutes that he had graduated from South High in Columbus, Ohio, and got a full ride for football to Ohio State. His parents were so proud of him and dreamed about bigger things. After four years, and many yards, and Big Ten championships, the NFL came calling. He was drafted in the second round by the Cleveland Browns and would be playing at the "Mistake on the Lake," which was the Brown's home stadium, and home of his hero Jim Brown. He looked at me, and sighed, and then told me in his second game as a pro he got broadsided coming through the line and the helmet hit destroyed his knee. After that, his career was over before it started. He tapped the pencil a few times on the wooden desk, and then said, "I should have studied in college, Jim. If I had,

I would have landed on my feet." He paused for a few more seconds and he rolled his eyes up, and looked at the pictures, and then back at me. He went on to tell me about college and all the perks, car keys under his pillow, all the women he wanted, spending money, and free dorm food. "Of course, I had a graduate student who did all my homework, and then taught me how to write and type. That was a struggle, but I graduated even though I had not learned a thing."

He stopped for a few minutes, went over to the corner of the room, and filled up a paper cup from a bottled water cooler. He walked back behind the desk, sat down and continued.

He then told me how he spent all his bonus money from the Browns, moved in with his friends from high school, got a blue-collar job in a factory not far from City Mission, and then got into drugs and booze. It was your typical downhill spiral, and it ended on the street, and the last stop on the tour was the Mission. Here, the volunteers picked him up, dusted him off, taught him about the Lord Jesus, and he made his way back into society.

I felt so bad for him, and I asked him where his college diploma was? He looked out the corner of his eye, and I could see a reflection of a tear, and then he said, "I did not deserve that diploma. I think it's up in my parents' attic," he said, with an air of shame in his voice.

I quickly changed the subject, knowing I had struck a nerve, and was sorry after it came out of my mouth. We stuck to business, and he filled me in on the history of the City Mission, what services they offered, and what my duties would be. After about an hour, he showed me to my room, and then showed me the floor bathroom. Everything looked pretty much the same as Syracuse, except this building was a little more run down.

As we walked and talked, several volunteers and patrons walked by, and they all knew Cecil and called him by his first name or his last. Some slapped his hand going by or just smiled and gave him a head bob. I could tell he was the king of the hill and commanded respect. He not only cared about his employees and residents, but he was one of the biggest football stars to ever come out of the state of Ohio. He had become a happy man after he gave his soul to Jesus. He felt so secure in his beliefs, and it gave me a boost of confidence just viewing his body language.

IT WAS JUST AFTER lunch time the next day. I had my room assignment, got settled, and met the rest of the staff. They were very similar to the group I had met in Syracuse. It was a conglomeration of college educated social workers, ex-drug and alcohol addicts, and religious people who wanted to give back to their community. Some of the stories were heartbreaking, and I could sympathize with all of them, but there were so many stories they all blended in together. The great thing about City Mission was most of the people here either grew up in Cleveland or they grew up in the blue-collar suburbs right outside. They were very comfortable with the clientele at the Mission, and gave the residents what they needed to get through another day.

As I was shuttling trays of food and utensils back into the kitchen, I saw Cecil heading towards me in a stern manner. Tagging behind him was a younger Black man who was about five foot eight inches with short hair and built like a beanpole. He had a smile from one ear to the other and it contrasted Cecil's serious outlook.

"Hey Jimmy," Cecil said, "this is Emmitt Smith, one of our helpers, and I need you and him to set up beds in the warehouse for the night." He stopped and pondered the thought. "I need about sixty cots set up in the next few hours. The weather is going to turn bad, and some of our regulars will be coming in early."

The young man stepped from behind Cecil and stood at his side. He looked like a midget standing next to such a big hulk of a man. He stuck out his hand and grabbed mine, and said, "Nice to meet you, Jim," in a high-pitched voice.

I grabbed his hand back and gave him a formal handshake. "Nice to meet you."

With the smile still evident on his face, he turned and stood beside me facing Cecil. He was full of piss and vinegar, and you could tell he loved being there. That gave me an added boost.

"Listen," Cecil pitched, "you guys set the beds up, make sure you sweep the warehouse before you start, and clear any debris out of the area. I don't need anyone tripping in the middle of the night finding their way to the bathroom!" he bellowed, then cracked a slight smile which took the pressure off both of us. I think Emmitt knew when Cecil was serious and also when he was trying to be coy or funny. "Also, after you finish that task, you are both dismissed for the afternoon. I need you two for watch in the dormitory warehouse. Make sure you are down here around nine o'clock to report for duty."

After Cecil moved on to another group, Emmitt and I made our way to the other side of the building, and then over to the opposite side of the warehouse. It was a huge area that was vacant of all the industrial machinery it had once had. The walls were made of steel, with big windows at the top with wire mesh running through them. They were very dirty, and you could hardly see out of them. Some sunlight was breaking through even with the fog of dirt over the glass.

As we policed the area, Emmitt kept peppering me with questions in his funny way, and I tried to stick to my cover story of graduating from college and wanting to travel to cities that needed volunteers in shelters. I tried to limit the discussion to this city, since I did not want it to get back to Cecil that I would be leaving in a week. I looked down at my watch to check the time, and noticed the date was July third. The last week and a half had gone by so fast. I was enjoying the work and the challenge and was learning so much about a culture I had never been exposed to.

Emmitt and I were like two helpers in Santa's workshop. We were whistling while we worked, setting up the beds left and right. It seemed the young man was asking all the questions and when I turned the conversation around, he would always defer or change the subject. I suspected he had some uncomfortable things in his background, but I could not imagine what since he was so happy go lucky. At about four o'clock, Cecil was proven correct about the weather. The low-pressure system was passing through the area, and the heavens opened up. Many of the street people were streaming in and putting their sparse belongings on their bed, and then heading to the cafeteria for a hot coffee before the dinnertime started. Some of the men would come up to us and tell us where their bed was, and to watch their stuff. We said we would reserve their cot for them, but we were going off duty. The beds would fill up fast on a night like this, and no one wanted to get left out in the cold rain.

After a few minutes, two older women relieved us, and we made our way back to the cafeteria to grab a bite, and then returned to my room. Emmitt and I played cards and talked about baseball, since it was in season. We both tried to top the other's story about the Boston Red Sox and the Cleveland Indians. Both teams had not won a World Series in many years, but to hear Emmitt talk about players and batting averages, it sounded like his team was right on the cusp, even though they were not in contention, even though the midpoint of the season had not come yet. I loved baseball and played it from when I was young up and through high school. I could not get this young man to admit he ever played the game.

As we were jibber-jabbering back and forth, there was a rap on the door, and then nothing. I looked at my watch and it was straight up nine o'clock. We knew what that meant. I opened the door, and no one was there. I looked both ways down the hallway, and it was vacant. I looked at Emmitt and he said it was Cecil and he did not want to get into a long conversation since he was probably on his way home for the night. Both of us collected what we would need for the overnight shift, and relieved the two women down in the warehouse. They both looked happy to be going on their way.

After we got the residents settled down and answered all their questions and complaints, we sat down at a steel table in the corner of the room next to a steel support beam. This table gave us a bird's eye view of the whole floor to see if everyone was okay. The low murmur of people talking drifted away after a while, and then Emmitt and I resumed our card game and baseball talk.

All of a sudden, I heard a crash and a yelp from someone. I pulled my head off the card table, and quickly looked at my watch. It was four o'clock in the morning. I must have fallen asleep. My eyes were foggy, and I adjusted them to the dim light cascading across the warehouse space. I quickly looked to my left and noticed Emmitt still was in la la land with his head on the table, snoring.

I quickly stood up and made my way down the long corridor of cots, and walked carefully, to not trip over a bed or someone's belongings. As I got to the end, I peered to the other side and saw an old man lying on his side next to his bed, moaning and asking for help in a low, muffled voice. I picked up speed to get over to him, and then knelt next to him. His eyes were shut, and I looked him over to make sure he had not hit his head falling. He looked like an older man in his seventies, with scruffy facial hair, tattered clothes, and dark socks with several holes in them.

I scooped my arm under his head and lifted it up and tried to have the man sit up. He came to life, and opened his eyes, and asked if I could walk him to the men's room. He became very coherent, and it was almost like he was just resting on the floor until someone could come to rescue him. I talked to him in a low voice and then leveraged him to his feet. Then I let him put his arm around my neck to walk, so he would not stumble in the dimness. Once we got to the toilet, he said he could handle it from there. I waited outside until he finished his business. To and from the bathroom we talked in low voices to each other, and he told me a *Reader's Digest* version of his life that he had probably told many times before. You could tell he was very well educated at some point in his life and was up to date on all things political happening in the city. I wondered to myself if he went to the local library or read discarded newspapers to keep up with the news.

Once morning came, and the residents had gone back to the food hall or back into the streets, Emmitt and I broke down the beds, got something to eat, and then I retired to my room and Emmitt went home to his house, which was not far from the shelter. It had been a good night, and we had no altercations with our overnight guests. Most of the men had gotten a good night's sleep before they hit the streets for another day in the humid heat of the city.

I WAS STANDING IN the food hall peering at all the people coming through the line with a little bit of confidence in their step. It was July fourth and a beautiful sunny day outside, and Cecil was standing at the entrance of the hall giving out red, white, and blue hats, streamers, and other prizes. It was whipping everyone into a great mood and there was no absence of patriotism. The Vietnam vets coming through the line had an especially good outlook on things, as this was one of the special days of the year America thanked them for their service.

Emmitt and I were ladling out the macaroni and cheese, and further down there was a station for hot dogs, hamburgers, and homemade beans. At the end of the line there was an ice bucket of Coke, ginger ale, and orange aid. Both of us were exchanging pleasantries with the residents and in between we were talking about whatever came into our mind. Emmitt loved talking baseball, and what was happening on the political scene. I was amazed he knew so much about what was happening in town, but he freely admitted to me he was sort of an egg head.

After there was a dead space in the conversation he blurted out, "Hey man, what are you doing later?"

I turned my head and said, "What do you mean, later?" with a perplexed look on my face.

"I mean what are you doing around nine o'clock tonight?"

"I have no plans except go back to my room and read a book," I admitted sheepishly.

He looked over at me and smiled and said, "Why don't we take your puke yellow Chevy Vega down to Gordon Park and watch the fireworks display. It's the best in the city."

I thought about what he said for a split second and responded, "That sounds nice, Emmitt. I would like that."

The smile on his face got bigger and wider. "My grandmother used to take me down to that park since I was a little kid, and also to the fourth of July fireworks. I have so many good memories of that place."

I asked him if he wanted me to drive his grandmother to the park with us, and his shoulders slumped. He indicated she had died of pancreatic cancer a few years before. I could tell from his reaction that they had probably been very close, and dropped the subject immediately.

After dinner was over, Emmitt gave me a piece of paper with his address on it and said to come by at eight thirty. The venue was just three miles away and they had a big parking lot in the park. I was just glad to be doing something different, and the thought of July 4th brought back memories of all the fun I had with my family going to our town celebration.

It was about seven when the dinner hour was finished. I transferred the serving dishes and tray back to the kitchen for Floyd, the cook and dishwasher, to wash and put away for the next meal. I dashed back to my room to change and then made my way to the community restroom to freshen up, check my makeup, and brush my teeth. The makeup was holding up well, and since I was going to spend a lot of time tonight with Emmitt, I worked on my street accent to make sure he was not suspicious that I was a suburban white boy. I practiced a little slang I had learned around the Northeastern campus, and was satisfied once I had practiced for a while.

I headed out to the shelter parking lot, dialed the combination of the parking lot lock and pulled back the gate. My car had been sitting for a few days and I prayed the battery was juiced. I jumped in and turned the key, and the little four-cylinder engine fired up. I idled the car for a few minutes, and then collected all the eight track tapes and put them in the holder box and locked them in my trunk. I knew if Emmitt got a load of my musical taste, he would know something was up.

I pulled the piece of paper out of my pocket, looked at the address, and studied it. The address said 52 Daniels Street. Emmitt said it was right off Carnegie Street, which the shelter was on. I went down the dark street looking for the intersection to take a left and noticed many people hanging out on such a beautiful night all dressed in their patriotic colors. Some were playing games, stickball, drinking liquor, and the mood of the city was in high gear. I was daydreaming for a second when I saw the street sign, pulled a left turn, and started checking the apartment building numbers.

As I ventured further down the street, I heard the sound of a bottle breaking in the distance, and then I looked up and saw Emmitt standing on the curve with a red, white, and blue hat, and a noise maker. His smile was infectious, and as he jumped in the car, the tall hat spun off his head, and he grabbed it. He told me during the ride that his grandmother had bought the hat for him a few years back.

We jumped into a casual conversation and then he had me turn around, and then guided me the four miles to get to Gordon Park. He started telling me the history of the park. From what he said the name of the park was after a local philanthropist by the name of William Gordon. The park was located at 8701 Lakeshore Boulevard on the shores of Lake Erie, near the end of the Cuyahoga River. The land was given to the city of Cleveland in 1892, and the park was opened in 1893. To the edge of the park was the Doan Brook, which dumped into the lake. It was a beautiful park back in the day and was a favorite place to walk, fish, picnic and do some boating. It used to have a big pavilion for social occasions or to change your clothes. Over the years the I-90 superhighway had split the park in two, and the water had become polluted by the industrial waste upstream from the many industries. Also, the iron ore boats filled up their cargo to sail across Lake Erie to the other side, which was

Canada. Unfortunately, William Gordon had died before the park was finished and open to the public.

Emmitt kept me entranced with all his stories, with the times he spent at the park and his grandmother. You could tell she had a big influence on him and made him the person he was today. So far, he had not mentioned a mother, father, sister or brother. I did not press him for details, since I didn't want to tip my hand that I was pumping him for information.

Once we got to the park, we parked the car and as we got out of the car Emmitt pulled out two Stroh's beers, each with its own brown paper bag. I grabbed one from him and you could still feel a chill coming though the bag. We cracked the beers open as I thanked him for his hospitality. As we walked from the lot across the nice green grass, we could see the water's edge up ahead with hundreds of people from all walks of life lined up. Children were running here and there with sparklers, enjoying the night's activity. There were several soft drink and ice cream vendors pushing their carts around the park. People were lined up to buy their wares, and keep the small children happy.

I followed Emmitt, who obviously knew his way around. He meandered through the crowd and ducked under a piece of wood that was nailed on a small dock to keep the general public off of it. I looked at him for a second, and he assured me it was safe. The public works crew was just being super careful due to a few rotting boards. I walked to the end of the pier, and it gave a beautiful panoramic view of the harbor and Lake Erie.

As we stood there, I jumped. An explosion went off about two hundred feet above our heads. Emmitt laughed in his funny way, and then a cascade of color burst above us in red, white, and blue. The crowd cheered and the little ones screamed with delight. Now I knew why he wanted to be here. We were so close to the fireworks overhead that you could reach out and touch them. Emmitt's eyes lit up with delight and I knew he was thinking about his grandmother and all the good times they had shared. My heart went out to him, and I thought back to my own family and my life.

After the festivity was over the crowds broke up pretty fast, and people started to retreat to the parking lots, or public transportation. We made our way to the lot following the well-lit asphalt walkway. Emmitt was silent for a few minutes and when he opened the passenger side door, he pulled out two more beers, and we sat on the hood of my car with the radio playing the latest top forty songs. You could hear other people further down the lot doing the same thing. The conversation between the two of us was easy and unguarded as the beer was going down. After a while, we started hearing the sounds of broken glass, and kids screaming, and decided to get in the car, and make our way home.

I dropped him at 45 Daniels Street and made my way back to the shelter to get some sleep. It was going to be an early morning and I knew I would need to be at my best.

THE MORNING SUN PEERED in the next day and blinded me for a split second. I was just about to roll over and look at my clock when I heard a rap on the door. I then heard what I thought was Cecil's voice requesting me to report to the cafeteria. I jumped out of bed and put on my clothes, checked my look in a handheld mirror, and grabbed my shaving kit. Then made my way to the community bathroom to freshen up before reporting for work. I washed my face, brushed my teeth, and then stared into the mirror at my look. I had totally transformed myself from a white suburban kid, into a Black inner-city volunteer. It gave me a slight sense of satisfaction thinking about things, but that was crowded out by the embarrassment that I was doing this to write a thesis paper in order to graduate from college. This was because I was such a screw up.

I daydreamed too long, and heard another rap on the door. I raced out of the bathroom and ran down the hall to drop off my shaving kit, and continued to the cafeteria. It was ten minutes after seven and people were streaming in from the warehouse, and the streets, to fill their stomachs with nourishment.

I took my station in the serving line standing next to a girl with a mild complexion, straight black hair, and medium build. I could not tell if she was a college student, a working girl, or a reformed drug addict from the street. This place had all sorts of volunteers from all walks of life.

As I looked around the room, I could see the usual cast of characters of all ages. Some were dressed in tattered clothes and others had nice hand me downs from the charity clothes store down the street. This facility did not have that option, but the City Mission did buy clothes from them to hand out to people in an emergency, or if they soiled themselves while they were in our care. I was bantering with my neighbor and serving food as fast as I could when I saw Cecil headed towards me with a serious look on his face. My heart dropped for a moment, playing back in my mind if I had done anything wrong or broke any of the house rules.

He walked right up to the table and stuck his head out and whispered in my ear. "Can you go back to my office and wake Emmitt up and tell him we need him to clear tables for an hour or so?"

I was taken aback, thinking, "Why would Emmitt be in Cecil's Office?" I had dropped him off at his house last night and as far as I knew he had today off. I looked at my boss, nodded yes, and made my way out from behind the serving table as Cecil jumped into my spot and continued serving.

I briskly walked across the room, getting a few back slaps from some of the regulars that knew me, and liked my upbeat manner. I jumped up the stairs and headed down the hallway to Cecil's office, going over in my mind what — if anything— happened last night. Was Emmitt an alcoholic and I had helped get him drunk? He is the one who brought the beers to the July fourth celebration, though. He looked fine when I dropped him off. Had he sat on his steps and indulged some more? A million thoughts were racing through my mind as I opened the door and walked into the office.

At first, I did not see anything. I looked to my left, then behind Cecil's desk, and then turned to the right. There in the corner was a cot set up with a person neatly tucked under a wool blanket with his back to me. I stood there for a minute, getting my bearings and then started moving towards him slowly. He looked sound asleep. I knelt and put my hand on his shoulder and shook him ever so gingerly. There was no movement, and I started to get nervous. Was he okay? Why wasn't he moving?

All of a sudden I felt him move, and then turn towards me with a groggy voice.

"I'm okay Mr. Washington," he said with a raspy voice. He opened his eyes as he turned, and our eyes met. He abruptly turned back the other way so I would not see him. Unfortunately, I *had* seen him. His face looked like a punching bag with a cut and bandage over his right eye.

I tried to pry his body back towards me, and then I said "Emmitt, it's okay." My heart sank after the words left my mouth. "What happened?" I blurted out. "Who did this to you?"

As fast as I said the words he jumped up from the cot and rushed by me out the door, headed towards the men's room. I thought for a moment if I should go after him, but then decided to retreat to the cafeteria and resume my duties. As I was serving food, I kept a lookout for Emmitt. After several minutes he appeared, and Cecil intercepted him, steering him towards the kitchen to help the cook clean dishes. I tried to collect myself and resume my conversation with the nice woman to my left, but I was in a fog, stunned by what I had just witnessed. As the line progressed and the serving slowed down, I started daydreaming about all the possibilities of what had happened to my new friend. Had he got jumped after I dropped him off? Did he hang around with some bad actors and got in a gang fight? Why hadn't he gone home to his house?

After the dust settled and our morning visitors were taken care of, I dismissed myself and walked to the front entrance of the building. I wanted to get a breath of fresh air to clear my head. I came through the large aluminum and glass door, and a few of the residents parted as I sat down on the granite front steps. I put my hands behind my head and looked down at the ground pondering what I had seen, when I felt a tap on my shoulder, and looked back up, and over.

The sun glared in my face and then I saw a man standing there that looked ten feet tall. As I adjusted my eyes, I could see the familiar face of Cecil. I gave him a halfhearted smile, and then looked back at the ground. I could feel Cecil edge his way beside me and sit down. I scrunched over a bit, and then he put his huge arm around my shoulder in a supportive way. I did not look at him.

"Sorry man," Cecil said with a tinge of embarrassment in his voice. "I'm sorry you had to see that, but you would have seen it eventually." He stopped talking for a few seconds collecting his thoughts. "Emmitt is such a good kid, and was dealt a bad hand, Jimmy."

"What do you mean, boss?" I blurted out. I regretted the tone as soon as the words left my mouth.

"Well, Jimmy, Emmitt is your usual poor Black urban story. The boy was born into a family with an alcoholic father who likes to gamble, and a very loving mother who is scared to death of her husband. Emmitt's mother used to be the punching bag until Emmitt became a teenager, and then he defended his mother, and now he is the one his father takes out his frustration and abuse on."

I collected my thoughts before I spoke and looked at Cecil. "That is so unfair, sir." I sat there, upset, with a million thoughts racing through my mind. I had never experienced this before and never experienced any of my friends going through something like this.

"Jimmy, life in the ghetto is hard," Cecil continued. "He is one of so many heart-breaking stories. We have too many kids out on the streets trying to get away from just this kind of violence. It's the economic cycle, mixed with drugs, alcohol and gambling. Many of our citizens can't shake the Devil's voice, and give in to its downward spiraling direction. Once the kids are on the street, they are lonely, scared, and hungry. Eventually they get drawn into bad behavior and become the next generation of despair." He looked out for a few moments and looked like he was going to keep going, but then stopped, and stood up, and patted me on the shoulder, and then disappeared into the building.

I sat on the steps waiting for Emmitt to come out to go home or on his way, but he never came out. I'm sure Cecil was letting him stay there for a few days until his father sobered up, and then his father would apologize for the hundredth time and say it would never happen again. I daydreamed for a few minutes, thinking about if I was in the same predicament, and my heart started racing, and I began to perspire. Then I stood up, walked over to the side of the building, jumped in my car and listened to my eight track.

I LAY IN MY bed tossing and turning. The day had been long and hard, and I was mentally exhausted from seeing and thinking about what Emmitt had gone through, and what his childhood and teenage years had been like. My heart went out to him, and there was nothing anyone could do about it. I'm sure he was torn and wished he could move out of the house to avoid the violence, but he did not want his father to turn on his mother. It was a real dilemma that I'm sure he agonized over and over in his mind. It was just too much for a teenager to be put in this position.

I was in a deep dream state, and when my mind became clearer, I flashed back to my sophomore year in college. I was sitting at my desk, cramming for a test on slavery and abolitionists. The book had a picture of Harriet Tubman, who was a famous abolitionist. She was born into slavery and then at some point escaped and became an abolitionist, and helped slaves escape and use the underground railroad to bring them up north to freedom. Over her life she helped seventy slaves go north to freedom.

All of a sudden, my mind darted to a picture I had seen in the lobby of the City Mission. It was half picture, half sculpture of a woman by the name of Sara Lucy Bagby. She was an escaped slave from Virginia, and made her way north through Beaver, Pennsylvania, before reaching Cleveland. There was an abolitionist sentiment in the city, and the underground railroad going through university circle. The escaped slaves hid in the bell tower of St. John's Church, then when the dust settled, they were loaded on a steamer, sent on to Sandusky and moved into Canada.

The person who took her under his wing was a Chas Storrs, who was the president of Western Reserve College, and started the Western Reserve Anti-Slavery Society. Sara got a job with him as a domestic servant, and did her abolition work on the side.

My mind drifted in and out and I could see Ms. Bagby so clearly, I could almost reach out and touch her. Suddenly, a man's face flashed in my mind. It was her owner from Virginia, Mr. A.G. Riddle. He and his henchmen captured her and loaded her on the local train in Cleveland for the long journey back to Virginia and the plantation. My anxiety level rose. I was tossing around in my mind. How could they do this to a free woman in a free state? It was not fair.

My thoughts started to become clearer. I was on the train sitting in a seat, looking right at Sara. She was dressed up so nice. Her boss in Cleveland treated her so nice, and paid her well enough to afford nice clothes. I gazed into her eyes, and she looked so despondent and sad. The congressman and guard had her packed in so tight, she could never get away. I heard the train whistle, and then the brakes of the train were being applied, and we were slowing down from top speed. I started thinking it might be a mechanical issue.

I stood and looked out the window, and I saw several hundred anti-slavery protestors lined up, and across the tracks to stop the train. Several people had signs with abolitionist sentiment, and were cheering that slavery was wrong and should be abolished. The train conductor knew if he stopped, this was going to turn into big trouble. A.G. Riddle became very agitated and sent one of his henchmen to the front of the train to talk to the conductor.

The congressman had his wrist handcuffed to Ms. Bagby, and wedged her further into the corner of the seat, pushing her against the window. The protestors saw her face and went wild. The crowd shifted to the side of the train and started chanting their anti-slavery platform. The crowd was being worked up into a frenzy, and the other passengers started to get nervous.

The train edged at five miles an hour and parted the crowd standing in their way. Eventually the sea of people spread apart, and started throwing rocks at the train. The conductor accelerated the engine and pulled away into the distance. Sara's heart sank when she knew that was her last chance for freedom. Now she would be back in Virginia as a slave, and treated harshly for trying to escape to the north, and assist in the abolitionist trade.

I was so nervous. My mind was weaving in and out of consciousness as I looked down at my book on my desk. My roommate was stirring in his bed. I tried to be quiet, and flipped to the last page of the chapter. There it said Sara Lucy Bagby was freed during the end of the Civil War by a Union soldier by the name of George Johnson. They ended up falling in love, and after the war ended, they moved to Cleveland to live out the rest of their lives.

My mind settled down and was at ease. Another person released from bondage. My mind was more relaxed. My labored breathing settled, and I drifted into a deep REM state. It was such a great feeling.

Chapter 9

I WAS WEAVING IN and out of traffic on I-75, headed towards Toledo, Ohio. It was a beautiful, warm summer day and the sun was shining. The music on the radio was a mix of top forty to teeny-bopper music. As I moved down the highway, I checked my mirror, and noticed I had left my makeup on since I was nervous about leaving the homeless shelter in Cleveland and running into someone. This would create another series of problems once I got to Toledo, but I would cross that bridge when I came to it. I had learned a lot at my prior location about the ups and downs of the Black experience. My heart went out to all the homeless people I met. My hat was off to the volunteers and helpers trying to help them, and put some sunshine into their lives. I was feeling better about my experience, and documenting it would imprint all I had leaned into a permanent record.

As I sat relaxed, cruising in my car, my food alarm started going off. I checked the time on my dashboard, and it said twelve-thirty PM. I started checking the signs as I was driving along, looking for a food stop and gas station. I was out in the wide-open spaces of Ohio, and the scenery was flat, but beautiful. It was filled with many farms and small towns, right out of a magazine cover.

All of a sudden, I saw a highway sign with a restaurant and gas station advertised. It said two miles up the road. I started playing over in my mind what I would order. The thought of it only made me feel hungrier.

I stopped at a local gas station and filled up, and then pulled into a parking space for the restaurant. I jumped out of my car and started up the walk. I was taken aback with the name of the establishment. It said Sambo's Restaurant, which was a chain group of restaurants across the country. Then I peered down and saw a statue of a small Black boy holding a lantern, with a big smile on his face. I was appalled when I looked at this person. We did not have any of these restaurants in my area outside Boston, and it seemed very callous.

As I walked through the front door, the sign said, "Wait to be seated." I looked around and waited for a server to approach me, and the dining room looked busy, even though there were plenty of empty tables. It seemed like I had been waiting there for several minutes and no one was paying me any attention. I decided to seat myself at the counter, where many people were sitting and shooting the breeze with the waitresses. Everyone one looked to be in a good mood, bantering about the news of the day.

I grabbed a menu and began to scan it for a luncheon item. The pictures on the page looked enticing and only made me hungrier. I picked a cheeseburger, French fries, and a coke. I looked up and tried to flag the waitress, but neither of them was looking in my direction. It seemed they were attending to everything and everyone but me. I started getting a complex because of bad service when I looked straight ahead, and saw my reflection in the mirror, and then it all made sense. I was a young Black man with an afro in a white man's world.

My patience started to grow thin. Finally, as I saw the counter person walk towards me, I waived the menu in front of her, and said I would like to order food. It was a middle-aged woman, with short blond hair, average weight, and her name pin said Tammy. She stopped in front of me, looking a little bit put off. I decided to take advantage of my opportunity and told her my order. She took out her notepad, and wrote down the selections, and then started adding the cost up, and quoted me a price. She said she would need the payment in advance before she submitted the order.

I was fuming! This was not how you treated a customer. In my peripheral vision, I could see a couple of good old boy truckers with a smirk on their faces. I dug into my pocket, pulled out my wallet, and paid the lady. I was not happy, but I was really hungry. I had already decided she was not going to get a tip for her service, and mood.

After I had inhaled the food, I decided to go to the men's room, and take off my makeup. I grabbed my carry bag and made my way into the lavatory. I put my bag on a sink and stared into the mirror. My reflection said it all. The room was empty, and I started applying the makeup remover, then wiping it off with paper towels. I was working as fast as I could to avoid detection, but then a few customers came in to relieve themselves. Most people tried to look disinterested, but I could feel many eyes on me wondering what the hell I was doing. A few minutes, and many paper towels later, I had transformed myself into a white man's look. A sense of calm entered my body as I exited the room.

As I turned to walk through the dining room and out the door, I eye-balled the counter, and my waitress. My original seat was open, and I decided to do a little experiment. I sauntered over and sat myself down, and my bag down behind me, and grabbed a menu. I couldn't have looked over the choices for more than a few seconds when Tammy descended on me, and asked me what I would like to order in her midwestern drawl. She had a nice smile on her face that was very welcoming.

I ordered a piece of blueberry pie, and a glass of milk. She wrote down my order, and within a minute had the food and drink in front of me and said, "Let me know if you want anything else, darling." She did not put down a check or ask me for any money. That said it all. It was like black and white, literally. I ate my dessert, and drink, asked for my check, and paid the hostess at the front desk on the way out.

As I walked through the parking lot to my car, the sinking feeling of being a Black man in a white man's world started to sink in. Even with all the progress we had made in civil rights, there was an undercurrent of distrust based on your color.

I CRUISED OFF THE I-75 ramp at full speed then let my foot off the accelerator and drifted down to a stop sign intersecting the main street. I turned down my eight track to think about where I was going.

Toledo was an average size mid-western city with a small downtown area consisting of a few high-rise buildings, many low-rise businesses, and a large commercial and manufacturing district, which outlined the city proper. It looked just like any other city, with people coming and going on their way here and there.

I fumbled with my map for a few seconds while waiting for the light to change. I had decided to stay at a local motel near the Toledo Gospel Rescue Mission on Jefferson Avenue. This was my next stop on the tour, and I needed to save some money to get through the rest of my trip. Budgeting and accounting were not my strong suit, and the last thing I needed was to run out of money and have to look for paid work to get through my summer project. My anxiety level increased a little with the thought of money, and not knowing where I was going. I had talked to Reverend Jason Williams at the mission from the road and told him I would be reporting for duty the next morning, and went over a few particulars about my job. I mentioned I would see him at nine o'clock, and he had a nice sincere voice on the call.

I moved through the traffic light and pulled into a vacant parking lot to study the map. I was only two miles away from Jefferson Avenue, and the tour guide mentioned a small family-run motel on the same street. As I started to drive, I daydreamed about my journey so far, the things I had learned, and what lay ahead. The possibilities were unlimited, as well as the pitfalls. The shelters seemed to have more minorities than whites, which indicated to me that Black people fell into poverty faster than whites when the economy turned for the worse.

As I drove down the street, the buildings and the area started to deteriorate with many run-down businesses and multi-family dwellings. I could see several people of all ages meandering around aimlessly, going here and there, but never really getting to their destination. I saw a few young mothers pushing baby carriages, several men sitting on front porch steps, and kids playing stickball in the street. I saw no old people on the street, but saw a few peering through open windows as the morning heat started to rise.

As I progressed down the avenue, I looked for the lodging I had booked the day before. I slowed to a near stop to ask some young men where the motel was, but thought better of it. The look in their eyes was threatening, and I realized I did not have my blackface makeup on yet.

After a quarter of a mile, I saw the lodging on the right and pulled into the lot. I regretted my decision as soon as I parked my car. The motel looked dilapidated and rundown. I saw several drunks sleeping in chairs outside their rooms, a few younger guys in their twenties who looked like they were closing a few drug deals, and other men who were walking around talking about something. I sat there for a few moments to collect my thoughts, and then pulled my car back out onto the street. I headed to McDonald's to apply my blackface for another day and night.

I felt I would be more accepted if I joined their culture for the next week. The last thing I needed was trouble to start off my week. I would pick up some food also while I was there to get me through dinner. I accelerated back down the street, dodging several potholes and baby carriages.

A LOUD THUD SHOOK the wall behind the head of the bed. I awoke from my slumber to faint screaming and yelling. As I turned towards the window, I could see the radio clock on the nightstand. The hands of the clock said 4:05 and the face of the clock glared back at me as the only light in the room.

I turned my body and sat on the bedside to get my bearings. Then I stood on my bed and put my ear to the wall. As I listened intently, the only thing I heard was the muffled voices of a man and a woman. I could tell they were arguing, but as I strained to hear the conversation, I could not make out what was said.

After about ten minutes of listening to the voices, I heard the door in the next room open and close with a thud, and then the female voice was raised; it sounded outside instead of coming through the wall.

I turned back from the hotel wall and saw the shadow of a figure through the window curtains walking quickly by. The female yelling persisted and became louder. My curiosity got the better of me and I made a stupid move. I jumped off the bed, took the chain off the front door lock, and turned the knob and opened the door.

As I peered down into the lot, I saw a large man getting into an older Cadillac and starting the engine. It was a beautiful candy apple red, and it had a nice wax shine reflected by the streetlights in the parking lot. The man in the car was looking up to the second level where I was standing, and shaking his fist out the window, and letting out a number of four-letter words.

Before I knew it, I heard a female voice just to my left screaming out a volley of four-letter words right back at the man. She was going on about how the man did not pay her enough for rough sex, and she was not that kind of girl. As I turned my head, I saw a middle-aged Black woman in a very sheer powder blue house coat with the top open, and her large breasts cascading out into the night. There was a slight chill in the air which made her nipples hard, and stand out. You could see her beauty that had been worn down by her occupation, and life.

I stood in the doorway for a few minutes, watching the back and forth, and before you knew it the car backed out of the parking lot and accelerated down the street. I must have turned back to the woman next to me, because I heard her raise her voice. "I hope you got a good look sunny. If you stand there any longer, I'm going to have to charge you for the peep show."

My eyes dilated and snapped me out of my dream state. I looked up into her eyes, and she looked at me, and gave me a disgusted look, and then stepped inside and slammed the door. I was embarrassed, to say the least, but as I looked down into the parking lot I noticed two guys standing by my car. They were not paying any attention to me or the lady of the night.

I stepped back into my room, shut the door, and locked it. I immediately went over to the picture window, sat on the floor, and pulled the shade back ever so slightly. Looking down towards my car, I could see the two men leaning against to the side of my car. I strained my eyes to figure out what they were doing.

A wave of panic came over me as I sat on the floor. Suppose they were stealing my car? Would they try stripping my car for parts? Either scenario did not sit well with me, since I needed my car to get around, and continue my journey. As I watched both men carefully, I noticed a small plastic bag of something passed from one man to the other, and in return money was exchanged. My blood pressure started to lower as I felt better about a drug transaction taking place in lieu of a stolen car. Then I saw the other man pull out a couple of GIQ beers in brown paper bags and pop the aluminum tops open, and they meandered over to a curb and sat down.

They were talking and laughing together, and looked like they were having a good time. I sat there for a while making sure that the men did not get any other ideas after they finished their night out. I kept thinking to myself "I need some sleep before I go to the Gospel Rescue Mission in the morning." I drifted in and out of sleep for what seemed like forever, and tried to stay focused on my wheels.

I heard the thud of a door slam and saw a shadow of someone marching down the outdoor hallway to the parking lot. There was a cold feeling coming over me when I realized I had slept on the floor next to the picture window with no blanket over me. I looked back at the radio clock, and it was early morning. The sun had come up, and it felt like the cold night dew would wear off, replaced by a hot humid day in the city of Toledo.

As I stood up, I could feel a pain in my shoulder blade from resting on the floor for the night. I bent my body numerous ways to try and work the kinks out of my muscles. I bent over and touched my toes a few times, and then pulled the shade back to see if my car was still in the lot. The morning sun reflecting off the bright yellow paint job of my Chevy Vega was a sight for sore eyes, and I turned and strutted back towards the bathroom with a new sense of confidence.

I flipped on the light, and jumped back, thinking a Black man was hiding in my bathroom. My heart jumped out of my chest until my mind caught up with my body and realized I was looking back at myself. I was the Black man, and then I turned to relieve myself, and catch my breath. I started to think about my day, and what new people I would meet, and what activities the good Reverend had in mind for me?

I sat in Reverend Jason Williams's, office looking out the window at the alley next door. It looked like any other alley with trash barrels, abandoned items, rats, and grime. I fixated on the sun glaring in the window spraying sunlight around the room. I could see particles of dust floating in the air, and eventually settling back to earth.

I had caught Mr. Williams at a bad time, since he had just wrapped up breakfast at the Gospel Mission, and was now in the middle of choir practice with his congregation. The building I was in was one stop shopping for the homeless. They had a church, lodging, drug and alcohol counseling, a clothing store, and a cafeteria to feed the hungry. The complex was large with tan brick, and was in reasonably good shape for being in the middle of a rundown part of the city. The staff I met were friendly, and the head man walked me to the Reverend's office. He made it clear in my telephone interview that I would be teaching some homeless residents job skills, resume writing, and interviewing techniques. I was intrigued by the thought of working with people one-on-one to try and help them get gainful employment.

As I was daydreaming about my future role at the shelter, the door flew open and a large man in religious garb came into the room, smiled, and stuck out his hand. "Nice to meet you, Mr. McPherson. I'm so glad you were able to join us today."

He broke away from me, and walked around his desk, parking himself in a big brown leather chair. It squeaked as he settled back, setting his eyes on me and sizing me up. He was just about to speak when the door opened and a young Black man in his twenties came into the room, looked at me, and then sat down in another chair right next to me. He gave me a disarming smile, and then looked back at the Reverend.

"I'm glad you could join us, John. This is Mr. James McPherson from Boston. He is here to help us with the job service program and see if he has any creative suggestions to help advance it," he finished.

"Hi. My name is John Janes James. Nice to meet you."

"Nice to meet you, John," I said, with as much enthusiasm as I could muster on short notice. The man smiled and turned back to his boss.

"Well James, your job this summer will be to work with our homeless, and try and give them some job skills, and other things that would help them gain steady employment. We are trying to make this place one stop shopping to getting our homeless, and drug addicted, back on their feet," the reverend said. "After we finish, John will give you a brief tour, and introduce you to the staff, and then show you to your room. You can get settled, and come down for lunch, and then John will work with you this afternoon on what you need to know, and meet with some of the residents who have shown interest in getting a job."

I asked the Reverend, and John, several questions, and tried to get a flavor for the shelter, and their philosophy on helping the homeless and the drug addicted. The Mission had a good reputation in the community, and the neighborhood treated the people, with respect and dignity. I felt good about my new role, and we wrapped up our meeting, and I left with John to go on my tour.

I SAT AT THE Reverend's desk, and was playing around with his stationary supplies, and was thinking about going through his drawers. My curiosity was getting the best of me when Reverend Williams came through the door with another man who looked about forty years old. He had a tattered pair of black pants on with a brown flannel shirt, with black shoes that looked like they were never shined. He had a two-day growth of facial hair, and a forlorn look that really brought my enthusiasm down. He kept looking at the Reverend, and then back at me, looking for direction.

"Well, James, this is Mr. John Carter from the neighborhood. He is a Vietnam veteran, and one of our frequent flyers. John is a good man, and looking for a job," he preached. "I told him you were going to help him get ready to find out what kind of opportunities are out there."

I stuck out my hand and looked for his. He looked me up and down, and then back at the Reverend for approval. He nodded, and then the man's hand was extended. I shook it with a firm grip, and felt his firm handshake coming back my way. I looked into his eyes, and smiled, trying to improve his mood.

Suddenly, I heard a raspy "Nice to meet you, sir," come out of his mouth.

"James, I want you to give Mr. Carter the red carpet treatment, and all the skills he will need to gain useful employment."

I nodded, and welcomed Mr. Carter to sit down in the chair before him. As fast as the man sat the Reverend was gone on his normal daily rounds.

After we were alone together a wave of anxiety came over me. Here I was, halfway across the country, in a homeless shelter giving employment advice to a man who could be my teacher or boss in another life. I started to fumble with the generic employment application when I thought about designing a resume first. I pulled out a blank piece of typewriter paper and fed it into the old Smith Corona machine. After that, I adjusted my seat, so I was not facing the man, and then asked with my head turned towards him his full name, and date of birth. Then I asked his address.

Mr. Carter sat there for a few moments thinking, then gave me the information. His address was, of course, the homeless shelter. I thought the good Reverend said he was from the neighborhood. I guess that is what he meant. I then went through his high school years, his Vietnam service, and his honorable discharge. He then strung together a number of menial jobs that covered the spectrum. As I looked at his face and body language, I could see it was like I was trying to get blood from a stone. This man was struggling to get through this interview, and I worried that even with my help and guidance his chances for gainful employment were slim at best.

I decided to have a conversation with him to lower the wall that he had built around him. "Hey John, where did you grow up?" I asked with as much of a smile in my voice as I could muster.

He sat there thinking about it for a few seconds and pointed out the window. His face twitched just a little, and then he said, "Third Street," with an air of embarrassment. "I grew up right down the street from here." His confidence came back a little after that.

I decided to segue into his high school years and Vietnam service. I regretted that right away. It was filled with one sad story after another that left John a broken young man. Then he documented his employment history, drug and alcohol abuse, and this story had continued up until six months ago. It seems he overdosed, and ended up in the hospital. His parents, who were God-fearing people begged the good Reverend to let John live at the shelter, and participate in a detox, and AA program to try and save him one more time.

After it was all over, I tried to remain composed and give him the impression I had heard this story many times, but the truth was I knew this story existed in the lives of many people, but I had never known anyone who had befallen such bad luck. I knew people in high school that had been drafted, but most of the kids had gone off to college and avoided the whole sorry war. There were rumors around town of people who knew people who went into the war and came back changed forever. I let my thoughts drift until I heard John clear his throat and look at me with more life in him than I had seen yet. I tried to have a normal conversation with him, and as he talked, I typed his resume and then formatted the highlights on to the generic employment application, then I tried to fine tune it to look as good as possible. As we conversed, I could tell this man had a lot on the ball, and street smarts that could translate into some sort of gainful employment. His facial expressions looked me up and down, and his trust in me as a helper increased with every word we exchanged.

After we were finished, I looked at my watch, and it was close to dinner time. I asked him if he would like to join me for dinner, and we continued our conversation about what he was interested in doing, and employment opportunities in the area.

After a few days of working and coaching John, we narrowed down some jobs which he seemed to think he could handle. Reverend Williams gave John a new used suit, shirt, tie, and shoes from the clothes bank, and when he was cleaned and shaven, even I did not recognize this man I had met only a few days before.

As he walked up to me in the hallway, I almost walked by him. He stuck out his hand and said, "Nice to meet you, James," with an air of confidence in his voice. I gave him a second look before I realized it was John and not an employee from the shelter. "John," I said, "you look like a million dollars."

A smile came to his face. "Well, Jim, I am ready to go on my job search," he chuckled. I couldn't believe my eyes. He looked like any corporate executive walking down the sidewalk of any U.S. city.

After my shock wore off, I told John I would go grab my car keys and then we would be off to the employment agency.

THE MIDMORNING TRAFFIC WAS manageable as I dodged people going to work, shopping, and getting to where they needed to go. I was still on the western part of town where the shelter was, looking for the local employment agency. John was sitting in the passenger seat of my car, directing me here and there. We were having a last-minute conversation about interviewing skills, and I felt comfortable that John was going to do well once he got seated and comfortable.

All of a sudden John said, "Pull over here."

I pulled into a parking space and as I looked up, I could see the sign for the agency. There were a few men standing in front talking to each other, smoking cigarettes, and looking like they were more interested in having fun versus finding a job.

John twisted the mirror, checked his appearance, and seemed satisfied with his looks. He then said, "Wish me luck," in a confident manner. He grabbed his folder off the seat and opened the door, gave the men standing there the head bob, and disappeared inside. I pushed in an eight-track cassette of Elton John and sat back and relaxed. The men on the sidewalk gave me a few looks, and then went back to their discussion. This part of town looked a little better than Jefferson Street, even though we were only a few miles away.

A short period of time went by when I was awakened by a rap on the passenger window, which woke me out of my quick nap. I looked over and saw John standing bent over, looking in at me. I checked my watch and noticed it had not been long since he entered the building.

I reached over and flicked the door lock to the up position, and he hopped in the car.

"How did it go?" I asked with as much enthusiasm as I could muster. He looked serious for a split second and my mood was turning stale. Then a smile came to his face, and he gave me a fist bump and said he had an interview at a machine shop not too far from where we were located. I asked him if he had some experience, and he slid out the resume and pointed at a previous job he had many years ago that had the same experience this company was looking for. I started the car and pulled out. John gave me a weird look when Elton John came on the eight track, and I ejected the tape and stuffed it under the seat. He reached over and started adjusting the radio to the local Motown station, and then Stevie Wonder came blowing through the speaker. He sat back in his seat, and we took a short cruise a few more miles down the road and located John's next interview. He proceeded to tell me that as soon as he looked at the job board this machinist job just jumped out at him. As he described his duties the confidence in his voice took over. I would have never imagined that John had just got out of rehab a few months ago. I prayed this would work out for him.

After John disappeared into a small commercial building called Acme Enterprises, I kept watch on the people walking around, all looking like they had no place to go. We were in a heavy commercial district, and I couldn't understand why people would be around here unless they were working. I watched people come and go and tried to get their drift. They came in all shapes and sizes, and they looked very suspicious. After some time of observing I realized some of the men were doing drug deals, and looking to break into cars. The police came by all of a sudden, doing their rounds, and everyone scattered. The police did not stop, and just gave them the look. After fifteen minutes, all the people reemerged and went back to their business.

I was keeping a close eye on all of them when I saw John come out the front entrance of Acme, and as he closed the distance to the car, a big smile came across his face. My blood pressure lowered as he jumped in and said he aced the interview.

"Well, Jim, they liked my experience, but they loved the resume you designed for me. They said most applicants don't come in with something like that." He chucked in a low, soft voice. "They were looking for two machinists, and my previous experience matched what they were looking for. I took a short test in HR and then as soon as the manager interviewed me, he knew I was the real deal."

I looked over at John while I was driving and said, "I knew you could do it, John. You have a lot to offer. When do you start?"

"Monday morning. They provide a work outfit, and boots, so I don't need to buy any additional clothes. I also get health insurance after ninety days. Can you believe that?" he laughed.

As I was driving, I saw a local bus drive by in the opposite direction and felt confident he could get to his job from the shelter, until he saved some money for his own place. We talked nonstop on the way back to the shelter, and John opened up more about his life in the military and on the street. I was really taken aback by his stories, and knew as a white kid from the suburbs I had no clue to how hard people had it in the inner city.

JOHN AND I WALKED up to a second-floor flat in a working-class district of Toledo. It was filled with many multifamily dwellings and was not too far away from the downtown area. John's mother had invited him over for dinner after he conveyed to them his good fortune of getting through rehab and obtaining a job in the city. Even after all his ups and downs in life, his family had never abandoned him. The only stipulation they had was he could not live at home. They did not want to make him feel too comfortable since they felt it could contribute to him falling off the wagon. They had always rented, and even though both his parents worked full time jobs, their income was not enough to buy a home of their own. The banks in the inner city required a twenty percent down payment, and certain areas were not even available for mortgage loans.

As we approached the front door on the second level John turned and said, "My mother's name is Mildred, and Dad's name is Clayton. Please don't talk to my father about unions. It is a sore subject and really gets him worked up," He had an air of concern in his voice. "I want this visit to be a good one since I have not seen my parents since before I went into rehab."

I agreed with his suggestion and gave him my affirmation. He proceeded to wrap on the door. His mother answered after a few seconds and gave a hearty "Hello" to both of us.

"John. I'm so glad to see you, honey." She gave him a warm embrace and kissed him on the neck. As she did, she was looking me straight in the eye and gave me a wink.

I smiled. John let go of his mother and introduced me. She was wearing a medium length print dress and had an apron on. Her hair was short to her head, with blue eyes, and radiant features for a lady her age.

"Mom, this is my friend Jimmy from the shelter. He is volunteering there for the summer," John said with a smile in his voice. "He helped me with my resume in order to impress my new employer."

"Oh, John, I'm so glad Jimmy has lent you some assistance. God knows it's hard enough to obtain employment in today's economy." She reached out to me and shook my hand and then cupped my wrist and looked into my eyes like she was reading my mind.

"I didn't do that much John. You are the one who had to interview," I replied with a knowing voice.

"John, come in and introduce your new friend to your father."

We stepped across the threshold and entered the home where John grew up. It was filled with nice worn furniture, and had different designs of wallpaper depending on what room you were in. From what I could see, it looked like a three-bedroom flat with a small living room, dining room, and an outdated kitchen. The floors were made of hardwood and covered with beautiful braded rugs. As I looked over the wall, I could see many interesting paintings, artifacts, and family photos. The house had a warm feeling, and I could tell John felt at ease being here versus the mean streets of the city.

John steered me into the living room area, and I saw an older man sitting in a nice worn stuffed recliner. He looked to be about sixty years old, heavy set, with short cropped black hair. He was smoking a pipe and reading the local paper. He had his reading glasses halfway down his nose and looked up as we entered the room.

"Sir, this is a friend of mine, Jimmy McPherson. He is visiting Toledo this summer and works over at the Gospel Mission. He is from Boston."

His father looked me up and down, and then stuck out his opposite hand and shook mine with a very firm grip. "You must be part of the Black Irish from Boston." Then he let out a low-key chuckle.

I got the joke as soon as he said it, and then gave him a smile back, and said how glad I was to meet him, and be at his home. We sat down, and as fast as we hit the couch, John's mother came back into the room with a soft drink for us both and said dinner would be ready in fifteen minutes. John and his father started bantering on his newfound employment, and he asked me questions about my college days and what I was going to do with my life. I could tell from his line of questioning that he was a no-nonsense guy who came up the hard way, and had worked for everything he had in this world.

John and his father started talking about the Owens Corning company in Toledo, and from what I could take from the conversation, the father had worked there his whole life as a ceramics engineer, and was a foreman of an assembly line, making many fabricated things that were sold by the company. He seemed to suggest he was a shop foreman for the union, and the company was hitting some hard times due to the economy. I found the conversation very interesting and wondered how John knew so much about the company and what his father was doing. Then it dawned on me that I had noticed on John's resume that it indicated he worked there several years ago. I started pondering why he was not still there, since his father was a higher up at the company? How had he fallen on such hard times?

We were served a beautiful pork dinner with mash potatoes, green beans, and homemade applesauce. We were just settling in for dessert and Mrs. Carter served a tasty blueberry pie, with ice cream. The coffee she served was strong, but good. The conversation meandered from current events, the economy, family, to what was happening in the neighborhood. I listened intently and as I gazed across the table, I noticed some family pictures on a mahogany table, on a white doily. It looked to be a nice man, about eighteen years old, dressed in a high school graduation outfit, holding a diploma in his hand, and giving a beautiful smile to the camera. As I scanned the other family photos, the young man was in every picture. I listened to the conversation, trying to learn as much as I could about John, and how he ended up in such a dark place, since it seemed on the surface that he came from such a loving family. I knew drugs and alcohol were a scourge to the Black community, but I had no barometer to measure it from my life and friends that I knew. To see John in his home environment, and remember the man I had meet just a few days before, it seemed like a different person. I enjoyed my time there, and after several hours we were on the road back to the Mission.

As I drove back across town, John was settling into the passenger seat, and looked to be in a deep state of thought. I was listening to the radio when I just came out with it. "John, who was that man in all the picture's in your home?"

He seemed to snap out of his relaxed state and looked over at me. A few seconds went by as he seemed to pause to think about what he would say. "That was my younger brother, Malcolm," he said with an air of depression in his voice.

I waited for a few seconds, and wondered why he was not continuing to fill me in about his brother." My curiosity got the best of me. "Where does Malcolm live now," I asked?

John looked out the window for a few moments and then back at me, and in a low voice said "He died in a car accident, not long after he graduated from high school."

I regretted asking the question right away and let the subject drop. I did not say a thing for a few minutes, and just listened to the radio, and meandered my way back to our destination.

All of a sudden John burst out, "Full of personality, and a good student too. He was going places until the accident."

I stopped at a red light, and was pondering if I should ask any more about the subject when John continued.

"He got in with a bad crowd the summer before he went to college. His friends stole a car and ended up on I-75 going too fast with the cops chasing them. The car went out of control, and my brother was killed." An exasperated exhale came from his throat, and he looked back at me. "My parents have not been the same since, and I have not been any help, and caused them so many problems. They still can't fathom that I not only lost my brother, but my best friend. It hit me like a ton of bricks, and I could not be there to comfort my parents."

Out of my peripheral vision, I saw him brush a tear away. The rest of the way home we did not talk. I knew I had touched on a sore subject, and I didn't want to upset John any further since this day was to celebrate his good fortune.

I WENT TO BED early Friday night. It had been a long week at the Rescue Mission Shelter. I had met many new people and a lot of downtrodden citizens of Toledo who were looking for direction in their lives. Some were just trying to get through one day to get to the other. My mind was bouncing around from one subject to the next, and I had learned so much so far on my journey. I wrote down my notes every night on all I had observed, and learned, and it was like another world, and one I was not familiar with. There were so many people of color, young and old, who had such a hard life, and it seemed like the progress made in the early sixties had been left far behind. With the 1973 oil embargo, and the recession, many jobs had been lost, and the manufacturing jobs had started to leave the Midwest, and head for the South or overseas. I pondered the thought for a few moments.

I drifted into a deep sleep, and as I dreamed, I formed a picture of myself sitting in a comfortable chair in the Northeastern University library. I was reading a textbook on Reconstruction in the South right after the Civil War. The North had won the war, and the Emancipation Proclamation had been signed by President Lincoln, and now could be put into effect to free so many slaves that had been held captive for so many years. It was an exciting time for the Black race, and also a troubled time. People who were used to being told what to do, where to go, and how to do things now had their own destiny in the palm of their hands. They could make decisions for themselves, and chart a new path for their families. In many cases slaves were afraid to leave the plantation because their own family had been broken up, and they wanted to wait to see if family members would find their way back to the plantation they had started at or been born into too.

Plantation owners in some instances had never worked their own fields and crops before, and only served in a supervisory role, and ran their businesses from their office or home. The end of the war and all the Confederate dead and wounded had created a significant manpower shortage, and Reconstruction had only contributed to it. The owners of all the farms tried to guilt the slaves to stay or tell them they could never make it in the outside world. Some were sharecroppers, but the plantation owners charged the ex-slaves such excessive fees for the farm supplies and seed that they could barely squeak out a living.

My mind was awash with information and then I saw a person in my mind. It was a Black man, his wife, and family somewhere in the Low Country of South Carolina. His name was Clayton Carter. He had come from one of the bigger plantations near Dreyton Farm, near the Ashley River. They had grown rice for so many years, and a year or so ago the Freedman's Bureau had given them a forty-acre parcel of land that was confiscated after the war. The nickname for the land was Sherman's Land. The men worked the land and planted food crops and tobacco to support themselves. New wood structures and barns were built, and the ladies raised the children or worked in the homes of their old slave owners if the price was right. Clayton and his friends started some fraternal organizations and churches to build a community for themselves. Everyone worked together to make a success of their newfound freedom. Having a strong community was what Clayton needed, since many white Southerners who had not fared so well after the war lashed out at Black people, and blamed them for their downfall. They had been lucky that many schoolteachers from up North had come to the South to teach in Black schools and educate the children, who in return taught their parents how to read and write.

As I looked at the text of the schoolbook, my eyes jumped to the next paragraph. It seemed that Southern citizens where not happy with the Freedman Bureau and the Federal Government. They wanted their land back for the white people of many Southern states. The politicians in Washington wanted to mend as many fences as possible in order to have the South come back to the Union way of thinking as fast as possible.

My mind jumped to the Carter family loading up a couple of wagons, and all the family members had a dejected look on their faces. The government had broken their promise of a new life for the Black citizens of the South. It took the land back and kicked the new residents off. Clayton looked at his family and his heart broke. All they had built in the last four years was for nothing. They had to leave their old friends and community to venture one hundred and fifty miles southwest to the county of Edgefield District. An old friend of Clayton had gotten word to him that a company called Wilson Potteries was starting a training program with fifty former slaves to learn the ceramics craft, and it was an opportunity that he could not turn down.

Who would have known that several generations later the Carter family would migrate north to follow the ceramic and glass industry to its new home in Toledo, Ohio. It was the year 1938, and two huge *companies had just merged. One was called Corning Glassworks, and the other was Owens-Illinois. They made bulb-shaped encasements for Thomas Edison's glass globes for railroad signals, and lanterns that were heat resistant. The new company was called Owens Corning, and the Carter family would have a craft and a prosperous life in their new home called Toledo. They had left slavery and the South far behind and were now part of the industrial revolution. They felt like they belonged and were part of the American dream. The hard work and sacrifice of their forefathers had paid off.*

Chapter 10

I was cruising down I-75 towards Detroit, Michigan, heading to my next stop on the tour. The traffic was light, as the rush hour had gone by, and everyone was at work doing their little jobs. I was listening to Led Zepplin on my eight-track player, and had it cranked up to the moon. My speed as I looked down was sixty-five miles per hour, and my Chevy Vega was gliding down the highway.

I was thinking about my prior week, and then the phone conversation I had just had with my parents at a pay phone a few exits back. They said they missed me but then started peppering me with questions about my journey and what I had been up too. I tried to be forthcoming, but I could not divulge my true mission and that I was by myself halfway across the country. As the conversation continued, they wanted to talk to Willie Shaw to see what he thought about the cross-country trip. I lied and said he was in a gas station bathroom relieving himself. I made up some interesting stuff about tourist attractions we had passed along the way, and scenic landmarks we stopped at to view. I felt bad about lying to them about my trip and its purpose, but after the summer was over, I would come clean and tell them all about my make up assignment, in order to graduate.

As I was meandering down the road, I looked at some of the billboards and the advertisements that were pasted on them. One was for Interstate batteries, and how dependable they were, and another was for Stroh Brewing Company. I was getting thirsty just looking at the highway ad and decided to order a beer tonight at dinner after I checked into the Holiday Inn. My skin had a bad rash on it from putting my makeup on and taking it off so many times. In my training, the only solution for this was to not put on the Black salve for a few days and let my skin rest. I would kill some time at the hotel rewriting my rough notes and observations, get some rest, and sit around the pool and see if any pretty girls were visiting Detroit at the same time.

I was feeling good about what I had seen so far, and the people I had met, but some melancholy seeped in, due to so many people who lived in such desperate circumstances, and just to get through the day was a major event. I started to feel guilty because I had such a nice upbringing, and even though I had to work for what I had in life, I always had that sense of security due to the home my parents had provided for me. The people I had seen and observed along my trip either never had that opportunity, or had a decent upbringing and then fell off the apple cart later in life for some reason. I thought about the Civil Rights Era, and all the legislation signed in 1964 in order to alleviate the roadblocks for people of color, and level the playing field to give everyone equal opportunity. Why were so many citizens struggling to live the American dream? It had been ten years, and as I toured these upper-Midwest cities it did not look like much had changed.

I FINISHED MY DINNER at the Holiday Inn and headed up to my room to apply some salve to my body to clear my skin before I headed out to my next destination in the morning. The hotel was close to downtown Detroit and my room had a nice view of the city and the General Motors towers. As I stepped off the elevator to my floor, I heard a few people's voices echoing down the hallway. It sounded like someone was having an argument. I was wondering what all the fuss was all about. As I turned the corner, I saw a person in a hotel uniform berating another man who looked to also be an employee. The superior was talking about getting complaints about the rooms not being cleaned up to the company's standards, and if the employee would like to keep his job things needed to change. The man getting scolded had his head down and looked embarrassed. The manager was white, and the other man was Black.

As I approached them, the manager stopped talking and a smile came across his face.

"Good evening," he said to me. He glared at the other man to do the same, but the man just smiled at me as I passed and said nothing. I bid them both goodnight and made my way to room 322. My stomach was full, and I looked forward to taking a shower and relaxing on my double bed to catch up on my television. My body and mind were tired from the long ride and whirlwind journey through the Midwest.

After I showered and put the healing cream on, I sat at the hotel room desk and started my notes. I tried to tell my story up to this point, so I would not have as much work to do once I arrived home after the summer was done. As I wrote my notes into full sentences, a story formed in my mind, and it was not good. The people I met, and the stories I heard, were heartbreaking. I had interacted with so many people in the last month, and the minority community had been left behind. I knew the economy was not good since the oil shock of 1973, but Black people seemed to be affected more than other groups. I went over in my mind how this could happen, and why more inroads had not been accomplished since all the civil rights legislation of 1964. I pondered the thought and still had a hard time wrapping my head around it.

After I summarized my notes and flopped on to my bed, I turned on the TV and settled in to watch a few programs. My body relaxed, and I went into a deep sleep. It seemed like hours, and I was in a trance like state when I heard gunshots. It shocked me out of my rest, and I sat up fast. I ran to the window to see what all the commotion was. As

I scanned the area, all looked calm. Then I realized the gunshots were coming from the eleven o'clock news. According to the news anchor, there was a man holed up in his house who was shooting randomly into the air. The Detroit police were there and had the area closed off and were trying to get the person to drop the weapon and come out peacefully. The scene was going back and forth for a while and then they cut back to the news for the weather and sports. The scene was erased from my mind in a few moments as I was still groggy and decided I needed my sleep more than zoning out to television.

The next morning, I grabbed a quick continental breakfast set up in the lobby and went back to my room to apply my makeup and get ready for the day. My skin rash had cleared up a little and I decided I would need to take my black face off more often. This would help my skin breath even though I had to worry about blowing my cover. I pondered the thought for a few minutes and then grabbed my bag and headed down the hallway to the elevator.

Once the elevator doors opened to the lobby, I ventured by the check-in counter and flew through the gold revolving door. The parking lot was big, but my yellow Chevy stood out like a sore thumb. I opened my door, put my seat forward and threw my bag in the back and jumped in and started the engine.

I reached over and opened my carrying case for my eight-track tapes and pulled out Jethro Tull. I was just about to put it into the player when I heard a rap on my window. I jerked my head back and saw a big guy dressed in a security uniform from Holiday Inn, and I realized he was carrying a big black flashlight that looked like a Billy club. I rolled down my window and asked the man what was on his mind.

"Sir," he said. "Could I have your hotel key so I can give it back to the front desk clerk?"

I had to think for a moment what the man was talking about. Then it came to me. I had my hotel room receipt slipped under my door, but I had not given the key back to the clerk. Sometimes I left them in the room, but this time I had not dropped it off with the front desk.

I fished through my pocket and found it. I handed to the security guard, he smiled, and then walked away.

I sat there for a few minutes getting my Jethro Tull tape going when it dawned on me, how did that security guard know I did not leave my room key in my suite? As I adjusted my car mirror to pull out, I noticed my reflection and saw that I was a Black man once again. It all started to make sense to me. That security guard had no idea that I had not left the key in my room. He was making sure I was not ripping someone off in the hotel and stealing the car. I'm surprised he did not ask for my license and registration. As I thought about it more, I started to get mad.

I CHECKED INTO THE Pope Francis Center on St. Antoine Street in Detroit. I met Father Clarence Mitchell who ran the church and the homeless shelter. It was a beautiful complex, with beige brick on the outside and with many stained-glass windows in the church and rectory. On the back side of the complex was a soup kitchen, homeless shelter and used clothing store. He introduced me to their great staff that consisted of nuns, high school students, adult volunteers, and former clients that wanted to give back. They were all so cheerful and helpful, which reflected Father Mitchell's personality and work ethic.

Once acclimated with my surroundings, I unpacked my bag and headed down to the cafeteria to help with serving dinner to about one hundred and fifty people who would cycle through over a two-hour period. My job for that meal was washing dishes in the kitchen and shuttling cooked food out to the serving tables to be distributed to the hungry patrons.

The kitchen was hot, but there was an air conditioner in a back window that gave some sense of cooling. I met a nice man in his fifties named Gus. He was a former resident from many years ago, and worked as a paid cook for all three meals of the day. He had been a cook in the army in Korea, and hit hard times when he returned with shell shock. After he slid down the scale of life, he ended up at the Pope Francis Center. A priest named Father Fred took him under his wing and taught him about God and salvation. He was eventually able to get back on his feet and gave his life to the Lord. After that day, he never looked back, and was so happy with his life and giving back to his fellow man. He went to Mass every morning before breakfast and said his rosary before Mass started.

Gus always had a smile on his face, even when the kitchen got hot, or there were calls to speed up the cooking and serving of the mass-produced meals. He told me he never had a complaint with his food or service in four years in Korea. He would always laugh with his slight mid-western twang after he said something.

After the dinner time, and most of my dish and pot cleaning duties, were accomplished, he gave me a wave that indicated I was dismissed and could go about my business until the morning. I washed my face and hands in the industrial sink and was drying myself when I heard a sweet sound of a guitar playing folk songs in the cafeteria area. I ventured out and saw a young man in his late twenties sitting on a table, strumming good old folk songs and gospel songs to about twenty employees and homeless residents. He was dressed in some bright colored Caribbean clothes and had a small Afro.

He was playing one song after another and some of the people were singing the words and the rest were just swaying to the melody. After a few minutes, he looked at me, and gave me an inviting nod to come over and sit beside him on the table. I was a little apprehensive to put myself out there, but then I figured, what the hell? I jumped up beside him and when he finished a sweet, serene gospel song, he introduced me to the crowd and said I would be helping out at the shelter. He actually said my name, which surprised me. The group of people clapped and gave their recognition and then he went back to his set.

After about an hour, the man stopped playing and said his goodnight to the crowd. He stayed behind as the rest of the people drifted out of the room. Some going home, and others retreating to the shelter connected on the other side of the complex. After we were alone in the room, he introduced himself as Josh Reed. He was a public school music teacher, and volunteer at the Center. I shook his hand and introduced myself again even though he knew my name from before.

He was such a nice person and knew so much about music. I was a big fan of music, even though I could not play any instruments. My mother always wondered how I could be in and working in so many theatrical performances and not have any musical ability. I always appreciated music and attended many concerts at Northeastern University, Boston Garden, and other venues. I loved rock and roll the most, but appreciated all genres of music and instruments.

We talked for an hour about music, artists we liked, people, and places. He was such an interesting person, and I was drawn to his mystique. After we talked about life, I retired to my room to get ready for the next day and think about the day, and what tomorrow would bring.

LATER THAT WEEK, I was cleaning the rest of the lunch dishes, and busing a few tables in the cafeteria. It was a moderate-sized lunch crowd and afterwards everybody left to go back to what they were doing on the streets. Gus was jibber-jabbering about anything as he finished up cooking and cleaning and I dismissed myself.

I had learned so much during the week and met so many nice volunteers, of all shapes and sizes, that took good care of the downtrodden of society. The more I travelled and visited towns, the more I felt sorry about all the people who had been cast aside and for some reason missed out on the American Dream. My parents had taught me the steps to a successful life and for some reason, so many other people missed that opportunity. It made me feel bad and I felt helpless in some ways on how to help fix this national problem. The way the volunteers felt was to just help one person at a time and don't be judgmental.

As I pondered that thought I felt a tap on my shoulder and turned. It was Josh with a big smile on his face.

"Hey man," he spouted. "Do you want to go on a little field trip downtown? Since you are a music lover, I wanted to show you something that you might appreciate."

I looked him up and down, trying to think what he was talking about, and he was not giving an inch as to what it was. My curiosity got the better of me, so I said, "Yeah. You're on. Take me on your magic carpet ride to wherever."

Before I knew it, we were in my car driving down I-75 into the downtown area of Detroit. I could see the city skyline with the big glass General Motors towers in the distance. The automotive industry was in a slump with the recent gas crisis and the invasion of Japanese compact cars. It reflected in the community as many blue-collar workers with good assembly line jobs were unemployed and blowing through their savings. I'm sure some of the people we had seen in the homeless shelter could have been some citizens who got caught up in the layoffs.

As we were cruising down the highway, Josh told me to take the next exit, and then take a right. The area was very poor and looked like a combination of older homes and industrial sites. They were all in disrepair and a lot of them had been burned out and not ever built back up. It seemed to go from block to block and as I looked over at Josh, he already knew what was on my mind.

"Too bad Jimmy. I know it looks like a warzone. This is what is left over from the race riots in 1967. It was happening in many major cities in the U.S. As the heat and frustration got to people, the Black area of Detroit boiled over and burned. The National Guard was called in to quell the situation, and as fast as it ended it started up again in 1968 after Dr. King was killed. He was our last great hope and after he was gone, Black people just gave up in despair. Major businesses started leaving the city for the suburbs and no one had a job in order to start to rebuild." Josh sat there for a moment and exhaled slightly and then sat back in his seat and looked out the window.

We drove for a few minutes, and I tried to draw a mental picture in my mind of those two events and all I could see was what was on the national news at that time. The police were pushing back large crowds of Detroit citizens with Billy clubs and fire hoses. Buildings were burning in the background, and it looked like utter chaos. It was a distant memory, and I'm sure the news reels of the Vietnam war every night on the news overrode my memory at the time.

We kept driving down a long main street that led out of town and then Josh said to turn on West Grand Boulevard and drive slower. This looked like a nice, working-class neighborhood with one and two family houses, and small, well-manicured lawns. I saw people walking up and down the sidewalk getting exercise, pushing baby carriages, and kids riding bikes and having fun. I was really taken aback by how fast the real estate went from bad to good. My blood pressure was coming down now that we were out of the bad areas.

Josh started waving at me. "Man, pull in there." A smile was plastered across his face.

I hit the brake, pulled in the other lane, and then took a right and drove into the driveway. There was an older model Buick parked in front of me. I turned off the radio and shut off the car.

"So here we are Jimmy. We are home," Josh started to laugh. "This is where I live."

I gave him a suspicious look. Did he just trick me for a ride home?

"Don't worry man. This is just the start of our little tour. I only take special people on my magical mystery tour." He began to laugh again, and his smile was two feet wide.

I smiled back and opened my door and got out. I started walking towards his front steps and then I heard his voice again.

"Where are you going? We are going this way." He started walking back to the sidewalk and I ran to catch up. He put his arm around my shoulder, and then we meandered two houses down. I stopped in my tracks with my mouth open. I could not believe what I was looking at. It was a single-family home painted white, with blue trim, and written across the top it said, "Hitsville USA." This was Berry Gordy's home and the headquarters of Motown Records. My pulse had elevated, and elation took over. This was where so many dreams had happened, and unbelievable music was made. This was where the music that made the sixties had been produced. I had to pinch myself to remember I wasn't dreaming.

Josh looked at me and smiled. As we walked up the front walk, we took a little cement walkway around to the back yard and went over to a big oak tree with a boxing punching bag hanging from a huge branch above. It was held on with silver chains to make it strong.

I looked back at Josh, and I said, "Don't you think the people inside will get mad if we're trespassing on their property?"

Josh looked at me and burst out laughing. "Man, do you think I would come over here if I was not welcome? These people are my second family. I grew up over here. The Gordy family are my neighbors and friends." Josh started punching the bag and it swung back and forth. "I'm going to tell you a little story that will answer all your questions."

I reached over and held the punching bag as Josh punched it in rhythmic time, and began his story.

"One day, when I was younger, we moved into our new house right over there, and the first thing my old man made me do was cut the lawn. I remember it was a hot day and I started arguing with him, but there was no getting out of my chores. It was one of those old push mowers with no power. I remember going back and forth, and back and forth.

After a while, I got lost in my own thoughts and remember getting pushed down from behind. I turned around, ready to yell at my father, when I was staring at five or six teenage boys riding their bikes away down the sidewalk. They started yelling at me, and said I better stay off their turf. They didn't look that tough, but I was the new kid on the block and did not want to start trouble. My ego was bruised pretty bad. As I started pushing my lawn mower, I heard a voice yell to me, and I looked up. It was a nice man two doors down waving me over. I dropped what I was doing and ventured over to see what was up." Josh paused for a moment, then continued. "As I walked over to the man, he stuck out his hand and said, 'Hi I'm Berry Gordy, your new neighbor.' Well, I almost fell over right there on the ground. The head of Motown Records was here talking to little ole me. He was the nicest guy you would ever want to meet. Well, he took me over here to where we are standing right now and said, 'You need a few boxing lessons.' He taught me how to box and defend myself. He also said he needed a landscaper and asked me if I wanted the job. Well of course I took the job, and this became my second home."

I stood there, amazed. I could not believe what Josh was telling me. He had been here for it all. The music that had been made, and the history that had been made here in the sixties and beyond. I was star struck, and this was just the beginning.

We made our way to the front of the house, and walked up on a nice stoop, and Josh knocked and stepped inside.

He yelled, "Esther!" in a friendly sort of way.

Out of a side room that looked like an office came a nice woman who said "Josh honey, it's so nice to see you. It's been too long, and who is your nice friend?"

Josh introduced me, and then they had a little small talk and he asked her if he could give me a tour. She gave her approval and then said she had many things to attend to and raced back to her desk.

I waived my goodbye to her as she turned to leave.

Josh said, "Follow me, Jimmy. I will take you to where it all happened."

We walked to the back of the house and on top of a doorway it said "Studio A." As we walked through, we were in the control room with all the electronic equipment. It had everything you would need to produce a record and mix it properly. There were several chairs there, and a big glass window separating this room from the recording room on the other side. It had a piano there, several guitars, amplifiers, and microphones. Dust had collected on the equipment since the studio had not been used for several years. I remember reading in *Rolling Stone* magazine that Motown moved to Los Angeles late in the sixties because that is where the music scene was headed.

Josh walked into the studio and picked up one of the guitars and began playing it as if he was recording. I sat down in one of the control room chairs and gave him hand signals like we were really recording a jam session. He started really strumming the notes and broke into a medley of Motown hits even though the sound was muffled playing an electric guitar without being plugged into an amplifier. My keen sense of hearing picked up all the cords and it sounded familiar as to the 45s I listened to in the sixties. He seemed to know them all. I was very impressed. I gave him the cut sign and he started to laugh. He put the guitar back on its stand and came out and plopped himself in the seat opposite me and exhaled.

"Wow man, that brought back a lot of memories," he said with an air of satisfaction in his voice. "So many great times happened in this house and studio."

"Who did you see Josh, and what type of music did they play here?" I said, thrilled and full of questions.

"Oh Jimmy, I saw it all. We had Smokey, Marvin, The Supremes, Stevie Wonder, The Temptations, The Jackson Five, and so many more. They played gospel, pop, rhythm, blues, jazz, and doo-wop. It was unbelievable."

I sat there looking back at him. "Josh, how did Motown start?"

He paused as I looked at him for a few seconds, and I could tell he was collecting his thoughts to let it all spill out.

"Well Jim, Berry was interested in the business, and worked a lot of jobs that just didn't interest him. One day, he decided to get a loan from his family and set up a business where people of color could come and try and make their dreams come true." He started to laugh. "It was one stop shopping man. You came here with your music and tried out in this here studio and if Berry thought you had what it takes, he would bring you into the organization and develop you as a recording artist and star. He did it all from A to Z." He paused for a second and continued. "I remember coming over to cut his lawn on a Saturday and seeing a line of people standing from the front door to the sidewalk to get their turn to show him what they had. I didn't even realize it at the time that I was witnessing music history."

"Wow, that is something man," I responded. I sat mesmerized, hardly believing what I was listening too. "Tell me some more."

"Hey man, have you got a few days to sit here and listen?" He laughed in his jovial manner. "Well, I'll tell you about Stevie Hardaway Judkins. I was kicking around the house one day, listening to a few tryouts, when a kid came in with his father and wanted to gig. Berry didn't like to have kids here and parents, because he felt uncomfortable if the kid was terrible, he would have to kill the parents' dreams. Well, this kid was different. He played the piano and everything else and wrote a few songs to show Berry what he had. As soon as it was over, a smile came to Berry's face and he told the father, 'You need to keep bringing this kid over here after school, but drop him off and pick him up.' The parents agreed, and after only a short period of time he knew this kid was destined for great things. One day, Berry and a few people were kicking around what to call this special kid. As they brainstormed a few ideas, Esther came out of her office and said, 'That Stevie is such a wonder.' Everyone laughed and then Berry said, 'That's it. We will call him Stevie Wonder.'"

I almost fell off my seat. This guy knew it all. I needed to hear more. I felt like pinching myself to make sure it wasn't a dream.

Josh got up, and we made our way past Esther's office. We said our goodbyes to her and stepped out to the porch. Esther told Josh to stop by more often when he was in the area.

Out on the porch, Josh turned to the right and went over to a large wooden porch swing suspended by two chains. He sat down and pulled a pack of cigarettes from his top pocket and held the pack out, offering me one.

I took one to be polite, and he lit us both up.

"I remember when I was sixteen, I was sitting here, and Smokey Robinson was standing right where you are. He offered me my first cigarette and I nervously turned him down, fearing what my parents would say if they saw me. I remember him harassing me for what seemed like forever before I gave in. He said he would stand in front of me, so my parents couldn't see me from the porch."

"That is so cool, Josh. How was he as a person?" I asked. "How did he treat you?"

"He was smooth as silk man. Everything he did and touched turned to gold." Josh pondered the thought for a few seconds. "Except playing cards. He was awful. I remember him trying to get into so many card games with Berry and his friends. Berry would always shut him down, saying he did not want to steal his money. Smokey would get so mad even though he knew he was right."

I stood there puffing on my cigarette, feeling a little dizzy since I wasn't a regular smoker. I usually just smoked at parties and other social gatherings.

Josh sat there rocking back and forth with a content smile on his face, and then blurted out, "Do you want to hear the story of The Jackson Five?"

My jaw almost dropped. I began giving him hand signals "Yes" while I was exhaling a drag of my cigarette.

Josh continued. "Well, I remember hearing a lot about this family band from Gary, Indiana. Berry was really excited after he got back, but said the father was the manager, and he was impossible to work with. He decided to talk the father into letting them come to Detroit and move in with him and he would be responsible for their care and safety. The old man went for it, and the buzz started around the house. These guys had it all. I was lucky enough to be hanging around the first week they were here, and I was able to watch them in the studio. Little Michael sang his songs with his sweet voice and boy did he have all the moves. He bounced around that sound stage like he owned the place." Josh looked down at his watch and then said "Oh man, I need to go. My parents are expecting me, and you need to get back to the shelter to serve dinner."

As he stepped off the porch, I looked back at the house and the sign on top. I tried to make a mental picture in my mind that I could blaze there for eternity. "Josh, how long has Berry been gone from here?"

"Oh, ah, ah about five years. They picked up the whole operation and moved out to Los Angeles with The Jackson Five, and The Supremes. That is where the music scene was going, and he also wanted to chase Dianna out there. He was very taken by her voice and beauty." He looked at me with a sly smile, as if he was telling me some secrets out of school.

He walked me back to my car, said his goodbyes, and gave me directions back to the shelter. As I was driving back to the other side of town, I went over what I had just heard and witnessed and was so excited to get back to Boston to tell my friends that I had been at the heartbeat of music history.

I LAY AWAKE IN my dorm room at the Pope Francis shelter, thinking about my week's activities and the people I met, and the heartbreaking stories I heard. They were always the same. The social ills of society had left people behind, never to catch up. Why had so many people been left behind and missed out on a good life? As I came into the suburbs and the city proper it looked like the houses were nice, the businesses were thriving, and people looked happy and prosperous. As I got deeper into the city and the other part of town the buildings changed, the people changed and the expressions on their faces went from happiness to desperation. I was always an upbeat person and tried to look at the world through a lens of optimism, and the last several weeks had worn that sense down to a grinding halt.

The students of color on the Northeastern campus looked happy and well adjusted, and I assumed they came from all over America including the cities, suburbs and rural areas. I never thought to ask since most of my friends were white and lived in the areas around Boston.

As I lay in my bed, I kept following the path of a small fly that was taking laps around my room. He was going here and there, and then landed on the window. He then started to walk up the glass and stop on top of a round hole in the window that was covered with a piece of masking tape. I peered at the hole, and then thought it might be a bullet that made the indentation. I got out of bed and kneeled next to the tape and tried to trace the direction of the bullet as it came through the window. My eyes scanned the ceiling up by the light fixture to see if another hole was in the ceiling. I saw nothing, but my nose picked up the scent of a new paint job. The thought came to me that maybe the hole was filled in by spackle or paint. My knee started to cramp so I retreated to my bed and lay there for what seemed like an hour.

I was then awakened by the sound of a cat and some other animal in what seemed like a fight to the death for control of the discarded food in the dumpster outside my window in the alley. I was too lazy to get out of bed and yell at the two animals, so I lay there and waited for the fight to end.

As darkness fell over the city, and the quiet quelled the city sounds, I drifted in and out of sleep. A picture in my mind formed of the EL Center cafeteria at the University. I was looking down a long cafeteria table at my college friends having lunch. They were scarfing down cheeseburgers, fries, Cokes, and anything else they could get their hands on. They were all living in the dorm rooms on campus and had a meal plan. This meant they could eat twice as much food as they normally would. I heard of the freshman fifteen, but these guys broke all the records.

As I peered at them in my dream, I was jolted back to looking down at my textbook on music appreciation. This was a gut course I was taking with a Professor Javitts who had a reputation for hard quizzes but an easy essay final.

I was really just up on rock and roll stars. I forced myself to look down at the text since next period would be a quiz on jazz and ragtime music. All my fellow students thought the test would concentrate of Duke Ellington and the roaring twenties, but this professor was tricky and always tried to outwit the smart-ass students taking it as a gut course. I remember a few classes ago he touched on a Black ragtime musician named Scott Joplin. He mentioned it in passing, but went back to it twice which was unusual, since we had not gotten to that period in time in American music. I decided to throw all my chips in superficially and study ragtime but concentrate on this Black composer and musician.

I screened out the background noise from my friends and zoned in on the chapter on Scott Joplin. He was born in 1868 during the Reconstruction period after the Civil War. He lived in Texarkana, Texas, and his father worked building the railroad west. In the Houston and Galveston areas Black people found inroads in civil rights. This gave little Scott a chance to have a normal, free life. His mother played the banjo and taught him plantation songs from river boat country. At his church at Mount Zion, he was in the choir and sang many inspiring Baptist songs.

Scott's parents divorced when he was young, and his mother bought him a piano and gave him the opportunity to learn music and play songs. She knew there was an opportunity for Black musicians to become successful in East Texas playing at church socials, school functions, and dance halls.

After he grew older, he played the "Maple Leaf Rag" in Texarkana and could play from memory with no sheet music. His mother sent him to a music academy in Sedalia Missouri. He trained as an itinerant musician and travelled the Southwest. In 1893 he played in Chicago at the World's Columbian Exposition. He met people there and formed a band that included a cornet, clarinet, tuba and Briton horn. They went on the road and played in Saloons, Cafés, and Bawdyhouses.

I looked up and thought what I had just read and wrote down notes at a furious pace. I needed quick simple sentences so I could refer to them right before I went into the quiz.

I looked back and read some more. In 1900 ragtime was becoming a national craze. The "Maple Leaf Rag" music took off and sales increased because F. W. Woolworth sold Scott Joplin's music at all their stores around the country. In 1903 Scott formed a drama company and toured on the road, which was also a huge success. In 1907 he came back to his roots in Texarkana and was advertised as a hometown boy that made good. He made a huge contribution to make ragtime a mainstream music in America.

My friends were walking behind me and slapped me on the back as they passed. I got up from my seat and followed them to my next class. I felt confident that this would be a good day for me. My mind drifted as I slept not knowing what was a dream and what was real.

Chapter 11

I stopped at a red light on Michigan Avenue in Chicago. I was driving north on the Magnificent Mile. It was so overwhelming with the buildings, the high-end shops and the people going here and there to accomplish their daily tasks. I looked to my left and saw a yellow cab with a taxi driver with a big stogie hanging out of his mouth trying to keep up his conversation with a passenger. I looked quickly to the backseat area and the man sitting there was looking very bored.

As I looked around the city, I could not forget all the history of the big midwestern town and its place as a great American city. It was the home to Al Capone and his gang, and Mayor Richard Daley and the Democratic machine. This city was a center for manufacturing, commerce, finance, higher education, religion, sports and many other activities. It had very strong family roots from many European countries that settled in the area. Large numbers of African Americans migrated from the South post World War 1 to take advantage of solid job opportunities. Unfortunately, deindustrialization had hurt stockyards, steel mills, and many factories across the area.

As I was driving further down the long street, a reflection of sun hit me in the face from one of the high-rise buildings in the city. I flipped down my visor to block the sun, and then I looked back to see where the brightness was coming from. I stuck my head out the window at the next stoplight and peered up into the sky. The majestic building was taller than any of the surrounding structures. I knew it must be the Sears Tower. I read about it in *Time* magazine back a few months ago. It was advertised as the tallest building in the world and would be one hundred and ten stories by the time it was finished. The construction time would be three years and employ thousands of local construction workers. Once finished they said it would be the jewel of the Chicagoland skyline. From what I heard on the national news last year, the building was finished in May of 1973. I thought to myself, "I wonder what the rent was in a building that nice and big?"

Out of nowhere I heard the honk of a horn. I looked into the rearview mirror and saw a taxi driver in back of me shaking his fist. I looked forward and the light was green. I floored the accelerator and peeled out. As I started to move out of the city proper, I saw Lake Michigan to my right and my first thought was it did not look like a lake, it looked like an ocean. I skirted by a few parks that were near the water and saw many mothers with their children playing and having fun.

Going further into North Chicago I noticed the housing and the businesses were getting more run down and the people looked more lower class or destitute. My heart sank as I saw a homeless man pushing a shopping cart with all his worldly possessions. He looked maybe forty-five years old, had a week's worth of beard stubble, and wore tattered clothing and black shoes with many miles on them. As I passed him, he was yelling something at an invisible nobody. My heart went out to him and thought he probably needed help from a mental health professional, but nobody was looking out for him.

I made my way down the main street leading to the north end of town. I was looking for 1230 North Larabee Street. It was the address of the homeless shelter I would be working at for the next week. I had stayed at a highway motel on Route 94 the night before and had changed my makeup, had a good meal, and sleep. I was ready for action. I looked down at my map on the passenger side seat and made sure I was headed in the right direction. Before I knew it, a vast housing project appeared from nowhere.

It looked like a city within a city since it was so big. I could not believe it. Some buildings were low rise and there were a few high-rise buildings. As I drove on to North Larabee Street a sign appeared that said Cabrini Green Housing Project. The man I would be reporting to was in Building 28. He had sent me a brochure about the neighborhood. From what it said, the housing was built over time from 1941 until 1962. It was designed by the Massachusetts Institute of Technology urban planning department to house a post-World War II population in need of a place to live. It was a neighborhood ahead of its time, and it worked well for the families getting home from the war and saving money to buy a house and be part of the baby boom.

I remember what Mr. Lewis, the homeless coordinator, said on the phone about what happened after Martin Luther King was killed in 1968. He said all hell broke loose and people got scared and moved to the suburbs. The businesses left and the amenities were gone. In 1970 the federal housing reforms kept the units for very poor families, and single mothers on welfare. Another building was converted to a homeless shelter and then things really went downhill. The reduced rental income was not enough to maintain the buildings and move the trash. As the neighborhood became more blighted, the drug dealers moved in and prayed on the youth and the gangs took hold. It was a shame that such a magnificent experiment had gone bad.

As I turned my way into the main road, I began looking for the shelter. The buildings were a maze, and my directions really did not narrow down where I was going. I shut my eight-track player off, popped out the tape and put it back in the carrying case. I did not want some nosy resident tempted to break into my car and steal my prize possessions. I continued to meander down the road and saw groups of Black residents standing around talking. Some were listening to music on a transistor radio. They looked to be in their thirties and forties. I wondered why they were not at work. It was a weekday, and the city was booming with commerce. All I could think of was with the downturn of the economy it might have affected minority groups more than other people. I pondered the thought.

All of a sudden, a teenager no more than sixteen came out from behind a building carrying a rifle. He looked at me for a second and I stopped the car and froze in my tracks. What did this person want? He did not look at me twice and crossed my path, headed over to a dumpster that was overflowing from the recent garbage strike in Chicago. It had gone on for a month with no end in sight. The union was strong, and they were looking for an increase in pay and better subsidized health insurance.

I followed the person's path as he made his way towards another building and stopped at the dumpster. He stood there for a moment bouncing from one foot to the other. The young lad looked a little like Michael Jackson. He was a good-looking kid and seemed pretty comfortable in his own skin. I focused on him and watched his every move.

After several minutes, he marched closer to the garbage and a huge rat came out from behind the blue metal container. He held up the rifle and fired at the rat and kept firing. The rat spun around and frantically tried to retreat, but the young boy was at point blank range. That is when I realized he was shooting a BB gun, and not a rifle. He must have pumped ten BBs into the animal when, finally, it lay still on the ground. As fast as he finished his task he turned and came back the way he came. I yelled to him to ask where the shelter was. He stuck out his left arm and pointed over about one hundred yards to my left where I saw a group of people standing in front of another beige three-story building. I thanked him and drove my car in that direction. I entered a chain link parking lot, parked, and got out with my duffle bag. I locked my car and made my way into the building.

As I approached the front steps, I could see a group of men standing around drinking coffee and smoking cigarettes and there were a few women with baby carriages bouncing around trying to get their babies to sleep and keeping up a conversation with the men. The girls were in their late twenties and good looking and the men were shucking and jiving and putting their best moves on the girls to get a late-night date after their family settled down for the night.

I walked past the congregation of residents, and they looked me over carefully. As I made my way into the building, I saw a sign on the wall that said manager's office to the left. I turned and walked down the corridor and then I knocked on the marked door and made the mistake of opening it before someone said come in.

The door was open about three inches and then I heard a man yell "Wait!" Then there was an explosion of glass. I waited another moment and then opened the door. Standing behind a nice wooden desk were two men. One was in his thirties, dressed in casual clothes and sneakers, and the other man was much older, dressed in tan slacks, white shirt, and highly polished brown shoes. He was sporting a small Afro and when his eyes met mine, he gave me a look of fright. The other man smiled and came around the desk and said, "Watch your step, man. We did not know anyone was coming in." He started to chuckle and then the other man waved me in and said to shut the door.

I introduced myself to both of them and explained why I was there.

"Hi. My name is Amos Lewis Bell," the older man said. "This here is Kenny Harris. I run this fair hotel for the homeless and Kenny is my main man." Kenny smiled and opened a closet in the corner of the room and pulled out a dustpan and broom. He picked up a picture on the floor and gave it to Amos and began to sweep up the glass on the floor and put it into a metal wastepaper basket on the side of the desk. I caught a look at the picture. It was Richard Daley, the mayor of Chicago.

Kenny picked up what looked like a paperweight and placed it back on the desk and finished up cleaning the shards of glass off the wooden floor.

Amos directed me to a chair which faced him, and as I turned to watch Kenny and noticed two more pictures the same size on the wall. One was of John Fitzgerald Kennedy and the other was Pope Paul. As I sat, the two men were bantering back and forth and finally

Kenny finished his task and settled into the chair next to mine. He stuck out his hand and shook mine.

"Nice to meet you, bro. I hear you're going to be helping us around here the rest of the summer?"

I gave him a smile and a nod of my head to indicate he was right and faced Amos. He was big and strong, and I saw a tinge of gray hair mixed in around the edges of black.

"Well Jimmy," Amos said. "What's a good Irish Black man like you doing out in these parts?" He chuckled and was very pleased with himself. "I'm sorry for the introduction." He held up the picture of Mayor Daley and dropped it into the trash can to his right. It landed with a thud. "That son of a bitch cut our funding in half because he is having so called budget problems. Can you believe that guy? He has more hack employees on his payroll than I have cockroaches in my apartment."

Kenny burst out with laughter, and I gave a small chuckle to be one of the boys. I settled back in my chair, and Amos started to explain the inner workings of the shelter and what my duties would be. Both these men were on the city payroll, but they were committed to taking care of their flock and making sure the homeless were fed, clothed, and had a place to rest their head in a safe, secure environment.

After some discussion with the men, I found out that Kenny had a second job as a gas station attendant at night. I asked him why, and as I asked, I regretted the question since it was no business of mine. He was proud to respond. He had a sister that lived at Cabrini Green, and this helped with the food and rent, since she was a single mother of two children.

We wrapped our conversation and Amos gave me the twenty-five cent tour and then took me to my room. It had stuff already laying around and clothes in the closet. I looked at Amos with a questioning glance and he said I would be bunking with Kenny due to lack of space. He indicated that Kenny lived here to be closer to his job and save more money for his family. I was impressed with his sense of family and commitment. Amos parted by saying I could report to the cafeteria mid-afternoon, and the people down there would walk me through my duties.

After the door shut, I put away my stuff and lay on the other bed and pondered how the week would unfold. I had applied my makeup prior to arriving in Chicago, but the constant on and off with the black paste was wreaking havoc on my skin. It looked like a good case of acne. As I lay on my bed, I began to count the holes in the ceiling tiles and think about what laid ahead. I would try to learn as much as I could about the disadvantaged, and I hoped I could add something positive to someone's life this week.

AS THE WEEK WORE on Kenny and I got closer. Amos was always busy and stand-offish and paid attention to business and making sure the shelter, cafeteria, and used clothes facility ran like a clock. I figured he was an ex-military person because of this fact, but Kenny said he never was in the military. He came from humble beginnings in the Chicago area, and felt it was his duty to look after his flock. People respected him and even the alcohol, drug addled, and mentally ill would listen to him when he spoke.

I was assigned to the food line in the cafeteria and sorting clothes in the store area on the other side of the complex. Kenny hung out with me and introduced me to all the volunteers. Kenny and a few others were salaried employees and had a lot more responsibility. We both had a love of sports, and we had many discussions about the Chicago Cubs and Bears, and I countered with all I knew about the Boston Red Sox, and Patriots. We kept going back and forth about the teams, players, championships and what team had a greater history. It was good-natured banter, and it made the week fly by. I knew I would be leaving after my shift on Friday and had second thoughts to stay an extra week. I knew this was not in the cards, since I needed to stay on schedule and visit all the cities I had mapped out for my journey.

I asked Kenny if he wanted to go out after work and hang out, and he said he couldn't. He always went over to his sister Adrian's house on Thursday to have dinner and visit with his nieces. I was disappointed and then he turned and said, "Why don't you join me for dinner at her place and I can introduce you. I know she would love to meet you, and I have to tell you she is a good cook."

I thought for a moment and knew it was a good idea, and I would get a good home cooked meal. The food at the shelter was good, but it came in large quantities, so it lost a little luster. I agreed, and I told Kenny I would meet him on the front steps at the designated time, and we would go.

KENNY AND I WERE walking across a big expanse of paved ground with not a blade of grass in site. Cabrini Green was such a huge piece of land and it all looked like a barren wasteland. People walked around who looked like they had no destination, kids roamed the area with their friends, some people played basketball on the courts in the area, and cars were strewn around the acreage. They were all older cars, and I could tell which were owned and running and which were abandoned. As I walked past a few, I could see some homeless people made one their home for the time being.

As we walked, Kenny knew all the players. It did not matter how young or how old the person was. He knew who they were, what their story was, and where they lived. Most people gave him an upbeat look, a handshake or a nod. It was a comforting feeling, since the crime in the area was heavy, and I was not the most street-smart guy.

We continued to make our way to his sister's apartment. After a few minutes, we were there. I was staring up at a high-rise project building in very dated shape. I tried to imagine how nice it looked when it was built, but I could not envision it. Kenny pushed a few shopping carts out of the way, and we walked up cement steps and into the lobby of the building. I saw the elevator banks and a few homeless people sleeping on a couch against a wall in the corner.

We turned and faced the two elevators. One said out of order, and Kenny pushed the button and as it lit up, I looked at the numbers on top, and saw the car was at the eighth floor and was coming down. It seemed like ten minutes before we heard the familiar ding and the doors opened. We both stepped in, and my new friend pushed the ninth-floor button. The car jerked into motion, and I stared at the city inspector's certificate encased on the wall above the display panel. The car had not been inspected in three years. The car creaked along, and my hands started to perspire from stress and anxiety. I looked over at Kenny, and he gave me a look back like he knew what I was thinking.

As the car approached the ninth floor, I heard what I thought was someone crying, and then when the car reached the floor and the doors opened I not only heard crying, but someone in severe distress. It sounded like a woman, and I hoped we did not stumble across a mugging. I knew this was not the best part of town and the police never came down here unless there was trouble. This sounded like trouble for sure. I turned the corner and Kenny went right behind me and what I saw made my stomach drop.

Down the long corridor I saw three Chicago cops. Two were male and big, and the other was a female and small. They all had on their famous checkered hats. The female officer had what looked like a six-month-old baby in her arms that was crying. The other woman was in her thirties and was kneeling on the floor with her hands wrapped around the female officer's knees. She would not let go and one of the other officers had a hand on her shoulder and was ordering her to get up. She was screaming like a crazy person not to take her baby away. My eyes were transfixed on the commotion.

Kenny stopped and pulled me face to face.

"Listen man, just keep walking and don't say a word to anyone. This woman is my sister's neighbor and has an asshole boyfriend who comes up here when he needs money or is drunk. He is trouble and

I know he smacks her around if he is in a bad mood. The last few times I have run into her in the hallway, I saw a few black and blues on the child." He finished with a knowing stare to make sure I got the message.

My stomach started turning inside, and the closer we got my ears started ringing from all the noise. The cops were trying to diffuse the situation, but this woman was not going to let the police take her baby away. As we walked closer, I began to worry. Did we have to pass them? I hoped not.

Just as we were about to intercept the hysterical group Kenny stopped, and I walked into his back and stopped. He pulled a key out of his pants pocket and threw it into the door lock. He put his arm around my neck, and pushed me through, and proceed to slam the door and flipped the lock. The noise instantly lessened but was still there. As I looked up, I could see straight into the kitchen where a woman in her thirties, stood at the stove with a ladle in her hand.

Kenny kept pushing me along towards the woman, and said "Hey Adrian, this is the man I have been training all week. Jimmy, I would like you to meet my sister Adrian. She is my younger sister, and the best cook in the world."

She smiled and stuck out her hand to meet mine. She was meek and mild and soft spoken, and I could tell from Kenny's body language that he adored her. I could hear the drone of the commotion in the hallway, and Adrian mentioned there had been a lot of trouble with the neighbor's boyfriend, and the welfare authorities were putting an end to it.

I kept playing over and over in my mind how anyone could harm a woman or abuse a helpless child. I was learning so much about a world I had never seen, and my heart went out to the people who became casualties. I looked over at the stove and I saw a pot roast, gravy, potato salad, and carrots. It looked good, and my appetite alarm was going off. Adrian shooed us out of the kitchen and then we made our way to the dining room with place settings for five. At the end of the table, I saw two young girls with pigtails, dressed up in what looked like Catholic school uniforms, doing their summer school homework at the table.

On the way over to Adrian's apartment, Kenny had told me the story of him and his sister growing up in a blue-collar household with hard working, loving parents, and not having much. They had each other, and learned respect and decency. When his sister was in high school, she started dating an upper classman, who sweet talked her and turned her head. Kenny was concerned, since she was a good student, and a good athlete and was worried she would be taken advantage of.

Kenny was right. Her marks went down, she dropped out of team sports, and she started to spend more time with her so-called boyfriend. He was a smooth talker from the public school down the street from the family house. She would meet up with him after school and hang out. After Mr. Wonderful graduated from high school, he got a job at a record store and moved into an apartment with a few of his buddies. Adrian began to skip school and frequent there.

Kenny said he was torn. He and his sister were so close, and he knew she was headed down the wrong path in life, but he did not want to tell her how to live. One day they meet after school at the local malt shop to catch up, and after some generic conversation she broke down and told him she was pregnant. He was shocked and told her not to tell their parents until she was further along in her pregnancy.

After months of hiding being in a family way with baggy clothes, the day of destiny finally arrived. She needed obstetrical care, and doctor visits, and that only meant one thing. She would have to tell her mother and father what was going on. Kenny said he remembered it like it was yesterday. They were all sitting around at Sunday dinner, and Adrian just came out with it.

"I remember looking over at my father to read his expression. He put down his fork, and knife on his plate, pushed back his chair, and went back to the parlor, and shut the door. Our mother sat at the other end of the table, stunned by the news. She did not ask a lot of questions but tried her best to be concerned for her child's welfare. I tried to run interference for my sister, but my parents would have none of it. They were devout Christians, and this was embarrassing news to say the least."

After a few days of walking on eggshells, Kenny's Father packed Adrian's bag and told her to move out, and that she was no longer welcome in his home. It was shocking and bewildering to Kenny that his parents would ever turn their backs on one of their children. When the final day came, he helped his sister move into a home for unwed mothers on the other side of town, and said if she needed anything to contact him.

"When her boyfriend heard the news, Kenny continued, "he started distancing himself from Adrian and offered no emotional or monetary support to help with the expectant baby. After high school, I got a job with the Chicago housing Authority. It was entry level, but as I moved my way up the money became better.

"To our surprise, my sister delivered twin girls on Super Bowl Sunday, and I remember the doctors, nurses, and orderlies were trying to pay attention to my sister's labor pains and watch the football game at the same time! My two nieces were born healthy, and on time. The home for unwed mothers let her come back with her new additions for only so long. They told her she would need to make other arrangements. I was able to arrange for her to get a rent-controlled apartment at Cabrini Green, and apply for welfare to help support her young family."

He went on to tell me that his sister had done such a great job raising her two daughters, and keeping them on the straight and narrow. Kenny blushed and said his nieces treat him like a father and an uncle all at the same time. They realized he had been there for them through their young lives, and he was determined not to let them become casualties of the inner city.

As I looked around the dining room, this sparse little apartment on the bad side of town was so warm and welcoming. I knew it was because all the love and caring that was expressed by all concerned.

I knew Kenny worked hard to make it all happen, and his sister appreciated it down to her inner core.

The meal was great, and after a nice visit Kenny and I negotiated our way back to the homeless shelter. We finished settling down the residents, who had come off the mean streets of the city to try and have some peace, and sleep.

I lay in my bed, reading my latest paperback novel, and started to think about how many obstacles people of color had to grow up with in a harsh environment and make their way in the world. The further I got into my cross-country trip, this was reinforced over and over again. I knew the deck was stacked against people in the inner city, and I still had no answers as to how anyone could make the situation better.

I WAS DRIFTING IN and out of deep sleep. I felt my body moving around the bed as I was unsettled, but I stayed in a subconscious state. My body seemed to be floating over a city. I tried to wake up and sharpen my focus to know where I was. I could see cars, buses and streetcars going up and down the busy avenue. Across the street were many buildings with a sign that read Northeastern University. As I looked to my right there was a small Pub that was down under on the other side of the street. It said Caskon Flaggen Pub over the top.

My body floated down the stairs and into a small booth in the corner of the room. It was midafternoon and not many people were attending the establishment. No one looked at me and no waitress came to take my order. It was like I was invisible.

I opened my school backpack and pulled out some research books and my notebook. Today I needed a quiet place to write an essay on slavery in America. For weeks, the professor had been going over information with us on the roots of slavery and how it started, and its ramifications for people from Africa. I wanted to concentrate on a place where this business was concentrated, and felt Charleston, South Carolina, was the epicenter of that trade. I flipped through the book to the index and found the correct pages to focus on this area.

The text indicated the slave trade in South Carolina was very lucrative and fetched higher prices because Negroes were not worked as hard as other areas of the South. In return, they were in better shape to be a productive member of any household or plantation. The progression of slaves came from the natural increase from procreation instead of replacing worn out slaves with new people.

I need a five-hundred-word essay and my professor was a stickler for detail and accuracy. I heard stories from other students of the teacher giving back research papers for some people to do over. The reason for most of the returns were footnotes. I was going to make sure I had all my ducks in a row to get this done, get a decent mark, and move on to the next assignment.

The book mentioned the Old Vendue House on Tradd Street. It showed an advertisement from a local paper for twelve valuable plantation Slaves. Credit for one year or longer will be given, if desired paying interest, with approved security. On Tuesday the 24th slaves will be sold at public Venue at the usual place in Charles-Town.

I was writing down information in rapid succession to complete my task. As I was working in my little alcove, a bunch of first-year students marched in for a late lunch. The roast beef sandwich at this establishment was the best in the area. They were loud and very jovial. I prayed they would not sit in my area and break my concentration with the assignment. I held my breath until they made their decision. They moved to the other side of the room and found a booth in the opposite corner and a waitress meandered over to hand them menus and take their drink orders.

I went back to the text and focused on pulling more information out of this book. I drifted off to a woman standing beside her husband at the auction. They were well dressed, and as rumor had it, they owned one of the better plantations in the Low Country on the Cooper River. They were here today to find a new housekeeper and cook to take over the kitchen in their home. Their previous maid and cook had died from *a sudden heart attack and the household was spinning out of control. The wife, Harriet, was putting pressure on her husband to fill the void in the household.*

This auction hall was one that people of the Charleston area liked to attend because it was out of the way. Many people of means in the area did not want to be spotted trading, buying, or selling slaves. This was because many tourists from up North were travelling down to the South on vacation and did not like to see this fabric of Southern society. The more it was hidden the better it was.

As the auction started, an old, burly man stepped up on a stage in the front of the hall and introduced himself and instructed people how today's proceedings would go. He was gruff and had a thick southern drawl, and his clothes were new and looked to be expensive. He waved to another man on the side of the stage and waved to the man to bring out the first group of slaves to be sold.

There was a Black woman in her thirties with beautiful skin and features and she looked healthy. In tow were two children of the ages of five and seven years old who looked to have features like their mother. They were dressed in beautiful dresses that were bought for them to wear at the auction and would be returned once they were sold and brought to their new owner's residence. The three slaves looked scared and unsure of themselves. They were far away from their native Angola and had been snatched up by local slave hunters in Africa. The voyage to the new world had broken them and taken the life they had out of them. The slave company had spent many weeks nursing them back to health to make them presentable for today's activity.

The auctioneer came to life and read off the background of the three slaves and what they could offer to a prospective buyer. The bidding started and the man on stage started talking in a fast-paced manner. People kept raising their bid cards, and the man pointed and locked in their bid price and kept going. Harriet's husband kept bidding, and they argued that they just needed the woman and not the kids. The husband raised his hand and after a few moments the auctioneer stopped what he was doing.

"My wife and I would like to buy the woman and not the kids," the man asked. "We do not want the two children as part of the package."

The wife looked at her husband with a dirty look and said in a disgusted voice, "What are you doing? We cannot take the children away from their mother."

The husband ignored the wife's concerns and the auctioneer said he would agree to separate the two parties. The man on stage stood in between the mother and the two girls and the young children looked scared to death. They did not know what was happening and clutched on to each other. Their mother looked over to them with worry in her eyes and the auction started again with the mother only. The price changed to a lower amount and the bidding started again.

Harriet was furious. How could her husband do this? You should never take away children from their mother. It was a natural instinct to protect your offspring. She kept looking around the hall to make sure none of her friends were there to see this spectacle. The bidding went on for several minutes and the husband kept upping the ante as other plantation owners and citizens kept driving the price up.

Harriet's husband locked in the final bid and the auctioneer slammed his gavel on the podium and awarded this woman to them. As they paraded the slave woman off the stage, she became enraged and started fighting her way back to the young girls standing on the other side. The auctioneer instructed two men standing to the side of the stage behind a curtain to come out and take this woman to her new owners. As she was led away the yelping from the woman became so intense that the women in the crowd sneered at Harriet and gave her dirty looks.

The little girls, who were petrified, started moving towards their mother's cries and the auctioneer got in between them and the mother. The scene escalated into pandemonium and the men in the crowd stated yelling to continue the auction. The women kept turning from one to the other and let their disdain for this activity be known. Men of means in the community did not want to be associated with this barbaric activity and several parties left the hall.

The slave woman thrashed and broke free, blew right by the auctioneer and bent over to sweep the young girls up in her arms and squeezed them tight. They threw their arms around her neck and held on for dear life. The other two men came out on stage and started to intervene. The crowd started to boo and look at Harriet and her husband with disdain. They were upstanding citizens and had a long history in the Charleston area, and here were people in the community looking down their noses at them.

Harriet turned to her husband with a look that could kill on her face. He knew he was in trouble and as much as he did not want to buy anymore slaves today, his wife's wrath would be much harder to overcome. He left his wife's side and moved to the front of the stage and told the auctioneer he would buy the two young girls for a fair price without further bidding.

The auctioneer responded that this was highly unusual, but due to the public altercation he did not want to let today's proceeding deteriorate into bedlam. The auctioneer turned and told the two men to leave the stage and the mother kept embracing the two young children. After a short discussion they agreed on a fair price, and everyone was reunited together behind the stage. Harriett embraced their new additions to the family and told them with hand signals that they would be coming home with them. Harriet figured she could find enough chores around the house and plantation to keep the little girls busy.

Chapter 12

I WAS CRUISING DOWN Route 55 when I saw the St. Louis Arch in the distance. It was a magnificent structure and one I had seen many times in newspapers and magazines. It was one of the biggest man-made structures in this part of the country.

My car was purring along, and I was listening to The Who on my eight-track player. The song "Won't Get Fooled Again" was blaring through the speakers and I felt relaxed and good about my trip so far. My notebook had many facts and figures of the plight of the African American community in America. It seemed the downturn in the economy hurt the community more than most and I kept wondering why hadn't people just worked their way up the ladder of success like many people in the county did? Was it schooling, good paying jobs, or discrimination? I pondered the thought for a few seconds.

All of a sudden, the guy in front of me locked his brakes up to avoid a hub cap that fell off a car in front of him. I hit my brakes immediately and cut into the next lane, barely missing the person in that lane. The guy laid on the horn and I tried to tell him with my hand that I was sorry. Before I knew it, I saw my exit come up for St. Louis proper and curled down the ramp.

It was a hot, humid day in the city, and I needed to stay at a local hotel for the night to get some rest and put my makeup on in the morning. The AAA guide listed some nice hotels to stay in and I finally picked a reasonable one and asked a gas station attendant for directions. I would ask for directions to East St. Louis and the Salvation Army shelter tomorrow. I kept dreaming of falling in the hotel pool and relaxing before another tough week dealing with the downtrodden of society, and trying to observe their plight. A sense of guilt set in as I was only staying for a week. The local people lived in poverty or on the street for long periods of time. I tried to block it out, but the depressing feeling kept seeping in.

I had a nice afternoon by the pool and had soaked in my bathtub to try and help the acne that was breaking out on my arms, neck, and face. The long periods of makeup being on my skin and the sweat from the humidity was wreaking havoc on my complexion. I kept using all my skin techniques that my mother had taught me. Nothing seemed to be working. I was so glad I was not home because no girls on the college campus would give me a second look. I would cross that bridge once I got home.

I was melting into the double bed, channel surfing. I was having fun with the remote control, which was a new adventure since my parents did not have one for any of their televisions. My father did not believe in them and always said to me he did not need one since he had kids to change the channel.

I flipped to the late-night news, and it showed the local police dealing with a domestic disturbance. It was a live shot from the local news and the reporter was trying to give a description of what was going on. I was fixated on the crowd gathering, and a man was on the sidewalk looking drunk with his shirt off. He had a knife in his hand and was waving it at everyone and telling the police to leave him alone. On the porch in the background, I could see a younger woman with a screaming baby in her arms. She was crying, with a black eye and blood streaming down the side of her face.

She was begging this man to come back into the house and stop causing a problem for the neighbors and the police. As the scene unfolded, the crowd became more agitated, and several policemen had to push back the crown while another group of officers came around towards the man on two sides and tried to out flank him. A senior officer was yelling at the man through a bullhorn and kept repeating for him to drop the knife and lay down on the ground. The angle the camera showed on the scene was a little bit obstructed due to several parked cars that were in the way. I was glued to the television set as things started to get tense.

Several of the police had their sidearms drawn and were creeping closer and closer to the man. He backed up to a chain link fence and kept screaming and hyperventilating. Suddenly, two of the police distracted the man, and then two more of St. Louis's finest rushed in and knocked him to the ground with Billy clubs. He went down behind a parked car, but I could see both officers winding up and hitting the person for several seconds. The crowd roared with indignation! I strained my eyes to see what came next.

The woman on the porch ran down, screaming to leave her man alone. A neighbor and another policeman stood with her and held her back. She was yelling and scaring the little baby into crying more. All of a sudden, the two police officers that were obscured from my view stood up with the drunk man. He was now hand cuffed, and they threw him onto the hood of a car. I looked at his face and he had cuts and bruises, a broken nose, and several missing teeth. He was bleeding heavily, and then the police told everyone to go back to their houses, and that the show was over.

In a matter of seconds, the police loaded the man into a police car, the EMT's retreated, attending to the woman. After ten minutes, only two officers were left, trying to comfort the woman. They kept asking her if she was okay and if she wanted to press charges. Then the camera cut away and back to the news station. I shut the television off, laid down, and pulled the covers up. The air conditioning was full blast, and I was actually cold. I stared out my picture window at the full moon, thinking about what I had just seen. The violence with families really took me by surprise and bothered me. Was it the heat, was it drugs or alcohol, or was it lack of money and opportunity that pushed people to their limit?

I pondered the thought, rolled around on my bed for what seemed like an hour, and eventually fell asleep.

I RAN UP THE front steps of the Salvation Army homeless shelter on west Page Street. It was a beautiful summer day in August, and I had cleared my head from last night's run in on the news. I was ready to give my full attention to the down and out residents of East St. Louis. The building had beige brick that was about three stories high and wrapped around to the back. The windows were smoked glass with wire mesh on the first floor and were normal metal sash windows on the second and third floor.

As usual, there were a cast of characters hanging out on the front steps exchanging war stories of how they had been worked over by the system and could not make it in an unforgiving world. I'm sure most of the reasons were legit, from the persons upbringing, to schooling, and then going out into the world to make a living. It seemed like a revolving door of bad luck, and disappointment.

As I entered the building, the sign on the wall said rest rooms and the office to the left, and the cafeteria to the right. I turned and went left and walked down the corridor until I got to the office. There was a window embedded in the door. I quickly glanced in, and no one was seated at the desk; the office looked vacant. I went the other way towards the cafeteria. The noise from the end of the hall got louder and louder as I made my way down the corridor. When I got to the stairs, I was looking over the cafeteria and it was filled with lost souls of all shapes and sizes.

I decided to play a game with myself and see if I could pick out Mr. Adam Bell before I had to ask someone who he was. I scanned the room, looking over people very carefully to see their characteristics and see if they had a look of management. I looked around from side to side and as I did a sadness filled my heart. All these people were God's children and had intrinsic value and something to offer the world. It was up to all the volunteers to bring it out and steer them in the right direction to find it.

All of a sudden, a big man with older features came out from the kitchen area and he spied me across the room. Our eyes met for a split second, and he could tell I was out of place. He started to walk towards me and as he did, I stepped down the stairs to meet him halfway.

As we met, he stuck out his hand and said "I'm going to take a chance. You must me Jimmy McPherson," he said.

I stuck out my hand and responded, "Right you are," with as much spunk as I could muster. "I talked to you on the phone a few days ago and you said you were looking for volunteers for the house?"

"You are right Mr. McPherson. We are always looking for good enthusiastic people to help with our homeless population. I'm glad you are on summer break and could help." A big smile came to his face.

A homeless man came up behind him, and interrupted. Mr. Bell turned and put his arm around the man and introduced him to me and then said he would talk with him later.

After some small talk and a few introductions, we made our way to his office, and I filled out an application. Then he assigned me a room on the third floor with a great view of the city. I also got my work assignment, and he said a man by the name of William Hill would be my mentor, until I learned the ropes.

THE WEEK HAD BEEN steaming along with my mentor and new friend William Hill. He was a young kid in his twenties and came from a tough background. He let out little pieces of his life to me when he felt comfortable and then drew back once I started asking some follow up questions for details. It was the same old story. His mother and father did their best to take care of him and his siblings. It was always a struggle and the economic opportunities for the family came and went. Like a lot of families from the inner city, the education and job prospects system had failed them which made a normal life a struggle.

After high school, William had taken several minimum wage jobs in many service sectors, but they all led to the same end. After moving up in any organization, you were dead-ended due to lack of education or circumstances. No matter how hard you worked or how hard you tried, the new job seemed to never work out the way you thought. After several years, the frustration grew to the point that William started to give up on life.

After several of his friends had taken the wrong path and paid the ultimate price, he visited his local church and poured out his heart to the minister. One thing led to another, and the minister introduced him to Adam Bell at The Salvation Army. The house manager had a similar upbringing and knew he could mold him into a good employee and one thing he knew from the first time they met, William had a big heart and cared about people. He got that trait from both his mother and father.

As the week rolled on, William and I would finish our tasks in the kitchen, the clothing center, or the cafeteria, and then retire to the back of the large tan brick building. Out back was a fenced in parking lot with a basketball court in the back corner of the paved lot. We would shoot around for a few minutes, play horse or one on one. William was a very good basketball player and had been brought up in the best leagues due to the fact his father ran youth programs in the city. William had every opportunity to excel at basketball and go to college, but just didn't have the drive. He was more of an intellectual type who loved to read books, but this never translated to going on to college or a higher education.

I peered out over the cafeteria as the breakfast meal was winding down and most of the people had finished eating. Most left to walk the streets or filled their coffee cup and broke off into smaller groups to discuss their plight or the news of the day. As I handed off the last of the dirty serving pans to Harold in the kitchen, Adam Bell walked up and tapped me on the shoulder. I turned and then saw that unmistakable smile stretched across his face. He was bigger than life and really cared for his flock.

"Jimmy," Adam said, "see that older man over there at the end of the table, could you meander over there when you have a minute and strike up a conversation?"

I looked over at Adam and wondered why. I looked back at the man, and he was at the end of the table, separated from the rest of the group. He had his head down and had his right hand wrapped around his coffee cup. The look on his face said it all. He came from the school of hard knocks and was down on his luck right now.

"Mr. Bell, what's his story?" I said in a compassionate way.

"Well Jimmy, my man Joshua's twin brother died a few weeks ago and he has been in a funk ever since. I need you to go over there and brighten his day. Do you think you can do that?"

I looked back at Adam and gave him an affirmative nod and grabbed a cup of coffee and made my way over and sat right beside the older man. He looked up for a second and then put his head down again, looking into his lap. I peered over to see what he was looking down at and saw a book of poems on his right knee.

I sat there for a few moments, looking up and down the table, collecting my thoughts and trying to kick off a conversation that would seem natural and not scare Joshua away. I waited for the man to look up from his lap and when his eyes met mine, I introduced myself with as much joy in my voice as I could muster. There was no response from the old man and as I turned my head Adam was looking right at me and gave me the sign to keep engaging him.

I kept talking to him and going on and on about anything that popped into my head. I covered the weather, politics, and sports. Nothing seemed to pique his interest. Then, out of nowhere I asked if there were any poems in that book written by Emerson. He was a writer and a poet from the early seventeen hundreds, and I knew superficially a few facts about him from class in high school.

As soon as I said his name, Joshua lifted his head and looked at me and at the same time raised the book of poems on his lap and flipped through the pages. He then flipped the book around and said how much he liked this poem. The name of it was "Give All to Love." I started to read it and realized the message was the power of love. It was a beautiful poem and I think this poem and many others in that book gave Joshua some peace.

After I finished the poem, I looked up and said "That's beautiful. That's what this world needs more of." As I turned my head to meet his eyes a smile came to his face, and he reached his hand over and put his hand on mine and started to pat it. I almost pulled it away since I wasn't expecting a show of affection like that from a stranger. I relaxed my hand and my mind, and it was just what he needed. The man just needed some sort of love or human connection. Even though he was hurting from the death of a family member, all was well in the world and the sun would rise another day.

For the next hour, I told Josh how I grew up only ten miles from Walden Pond, near where Ralph Waldo Emerson lived and wrote most of his poems and essays. I flashed back to when my father took me fishing there for trout and we had some father and son time. My mind wandered for a minute and then Josh squeezed my hand and started talking about other poems that he liked and had special meaning to him. I felt good about the connection, and I had made some inroads with this man, and it made my week successful and fulfilling.

THE DINNER HOUR ON Thursday had finished. I was not on the list of volunteers to chaperone the homeless shelter dormitory. I was up in my room resting on my bed, reading an old, tattered copy of The Catcher in the Rye, which I had found in the in-house makeshift library. It was just an empty room where some of the workers had put up some shelves and then moved in an old couch and a few chairs and transformed the space into a reading room. Some people would read, some would sit and talk, and some would use it as a place of solace, away from the hustle and bustle of other areas of the shelter.

I was flipping through the pages of the book and flashed back to my tenth-grade English class when this book had been assigned. Of course, back then I hated to read and ended up purchasing the Cliff Notes in order to write a book report and turn it in on time. Since that time, I had become interested in reading since I was a history major in college. When I was growing up my parents did anything they could think of to get me interested in reading and increase my reading comprehension. Over time my love of books grew. I knew the story of *The Catcher in the Rye* overall since I had the Cliff Notes, but as I read through the book now, I was getting so much more out of it. Holden Caufield was a young man who grew up in money and was in New York City trying to find himself. He was taking his ups and downs in the hard knock life of the city.

My body was tired after a long week of dealing with the down and out, but I was seeing myself as a Holden Caufield, driving across the country from city to city and experiencing how the real world was. I had such a different view of the world in my little suburban bubble, and this trip really woke me up that this was a beautiful world with a very deep underbelly of poverty, pain, and suffering. The longer the trip lasted, the more this point was being driven home.

Suddenly, I heard a knock on the door. My initial reaction was, "Did I have my makeup on and was there any part of my body that had exposed skin that would give away my skin color?" I looked over my body and then sprang to my feet to answer the door. "Who is it?" I asked.

"Hey man, its William. Can I come in?"

I opened the door and Will was standing there in a printed tee shirt with basketball shorts and beat-up Converse sneakers. He had a basketball in his hand, and he kept palming the ball as he stood there.

"Jimmy, I hate to bother you this late but one of my buddies and my ride crapped out on me for my pick-up basketball game. I was wondering if you want to play a game with some of my buddies over in the city." He gave me a cagey smile after he finished speaking.

William and I had grown closer as the week went on at the shelter, but I knew the only reason he was here was he needed a ride to his basketball game. I was just about to say no, but then I remembered that I was taking this trip to take in the full extent of the inner city and the people that lived there. I told William I would drive him to his game and be a teammate with him. I said I would meet him outside so I could get myself together. After he left, I checked my clothes and looked in the mirror. I was wearing blue jeans on a hot night in St. Louis and hoped this would not arouse suspicion. My arms were black as was my face, and the makeup was waterproof and would not run even after physical activity.

Before I knew it, William and I were driving in my car back over the main bridge into St. Louis proper and out of the ghetto. The windows were all down and the wind was blowing through the car. The eight-track player was turned up full blast with a tape of The Jackson Five, which William brought along for the ride. There was a stark contrast between the buildings and people as we left one world and drove over to the other. It reminded me of a castle with a moat around it to keep the peasants out.

As we drove, the bright lights of the city were beautiful, with people coming and going. In the foreground, you could see Bush Stadium and the lights were on, which meant baseball was in full swing. About a mile up the road, William tapped me on the should and pointed to the left. As I looked, I saw three basketball courts lit up on a beautiful summer night.

As we got out of the car, William reached into the back seat and grabbed the basketball and walked with me towards the crowd of men. The courts were in excellent shape, which I contrasted in my mind from what I saw back on the other side of the bridge. Two of the courts were in use, and there were a few guys shooting around on the other court. William introduced me to the guys, who were all white. I never questioned my partner how he knew these people. They looked like they were all in their mid-twenties, well educated, and drove nice cars. There was no ghetto slang and they treated William with respect. After a few minutes of conversation, we picked up sides and then I was on a team that was the skins and William team was the shirts. My heart dropped and I told the captain that I could not take my shirt off. Everyone stopped and looked back at me. My mind was going a million miles an hour trying to come up with an excuse.

William gave me a look like I was being difficult. I blurted out, "Sorry man, but I have a really bad eczema skin condition and am on medication for it. I need to keep it covered." I waited and prayed that they would take me at my word.

William jumped in and just said he would switch with the other team and be the skins. We started the game, and I never ran so much in my life. Even though I was young, I was out of shape after four years of partying and sitting in classrooms. I tried to keep up with William and his friends, but I was no match for these guys. After about an hour, another guy walked on to the court that they all knew and then I was treated as the little brother that nobody wanted around, but they had to humor me. I gracefully bowed out and went over and sat on a bench and drank some water out of a jug that we had brought.

I sat there for a while and observed the three games going on and saw how hard William was trying, and you could tell he loved being in this white world. I wondered if he would ever make it over that long bridge into that different life.

As the night wore on, the games started breaking up and the players said their goodbyes and went on their way. We started making our way out into the parking lot and talking about the next pickup game. As I opened my door, and started to get in my car, I noticed a St. Louis police cruiser go by and then make a U-turn and come back and pull into the lot. I closed my door, William jumped in, and I started the engine.

All of a sudden, the police unit pulled up right behind my car and put on its blue lights. I knew we had not done anything wrong, and

I looked over at William and we exchanged perplexed glances. Before I knew it, there was a police officer at each window, and they asked us to get out of the car and then started peppering us with questions about "Why we were in this part of town."

I was taken back by the questions and as I opened the door and got out, I protested to the officer. As fast as the words came out of my mouth, I was thrown up against the side of my car with the door slamming behind me. I was just about to give the man a piece of my mind when he pulled a huge black flashlight out of his belt and shoved it under my chin, so I was looking him right in his eyes. He then moved his body right into me to pin me against the side of the car.

"Hey boy, what were you going to say? You guys are in the wrong part of town." He gave me a sly smile, but as I looked deeper into his eyes, I could see the hate shining brightly through. I looked past the officer and saw a few of the guys we just played with, standing there frozen. In the background, I could hear William's voice trying to explain to the other cop why we were here and that we were invited by the other guys in the lot to play basketball. My mind was becoming numb and then I became nervous that if this guy ever asked me for my license and registration I was screwed. Then I thought to myself, I had not even brought my wallet. It was back in my room. Panic started to set in, and the more I tried to move my body to straighten up, the man kept his body weight on me.

I tried to think about how this was going to end when all of a sudden the other policeman yelled, "Roy, these guys are okay! I know this kid's father. He runs the CYO basketball in the city."

The guy that had me pinned backed up, put the flashlight away, dusted me off, and was back in his cruiser before I could say "Boo." His partner gave William a half-assed apology and then retreated to his car and drove away.

William and I got back into our car and drove past a few of the guys, and they waved, knowing full well what had happened. We drove back to the shelter with no music and no conversation the rest of the way. I was not sure if Will was in shock or just embarrassed for inviting me in the first place.

The whole way back to the shelter I couldn't stop thinking about how we were treated. We were just minding our business and were trying to get some exercise and have some fun. Was this the kind of treatment Blacks had to endure on a regular basis, or was this just one policeman with a bad attitude? I pondered the thought.

I LAY ON MY bed reading *The Catcher in the Rye* and was getting very sleepy. The day had been ruined and my mind was jumbled. As I drifted off to my happy place I started to dream. It was so clear, more than other dreams I had from time to time.

I was sitting at the desk in my bedroom and was looking down at my Civil War college history book. I started to question why I was in my room at home, and then I remembered it was the weekend and my college roommate had a few of his friends coming up from Connecticut to visit him and enjoy a weekend in Boston. He asked me if I could stay in a friend's room or go home for the weekend, since I lived so close to the city. He was a good guy and we got along well, so I cut him a break and went home after my classes on a Friday. My parents were thrilled to have me. I told them I had a big history exam on Monday morning and would need to study at some point. I helped my mother and father do some chores around the house that they just could not get to, which needed some manual labor. I was a good helper while I was at home since that is the way they trained me from the time I was a little boy. This help had diminished since I had gone to college.

As I sat at the desk in my room, I looked at my history book on the battle of Gettysburg and how it was a battle in the Civil War that had turned the tide for the Union army. I was reading about a commander of the Union Army named Joshua Chamberlain, who had commanded the 20th Volunteer Regiment from the great state of Maine. He was a civilian and signed up to fight in the great war and had a knack *for being brave, commanding troops, and using very smart military strategy to fight and win battles.*

He had won the battle of Little Big Top, which turned the tide for the Union side, and they routed the Confederate troops. They sent them retreating to Maryland and Virginia. The losses on both sides were devastating. Some battlefields in the area had dead and wounded bodies strewn side by side from one side of the field to the other. His commanders were very pleased with his men and his leadership, and he was promoted to a higher rank after the battle.

I was reading page after page of this great battle, taking notes and highlighting passages that I thought were important to remember. My professor was the Dean of History at Northeastern and he was an expert in Civil War studies. I knew I could not double talk him if the test was more essay than multiple choice or short answer. I kept concentrating and trying to comprehend as much information as possible about that major battle when all of a sudden, I heard a noise. It was the sound of my father firing up the Briggs and Stratton lawn mower. I knew I needed to stop studying and come to the rescue. I would finish my Saturday chores and then come back to my studying later in the afternoon. I wanted to get all my work done so I could go out with my town friends on Saturday night. I had not been home in a while, and I had a lot of catching up to do with them.

I resumed studying in my dream later in the afternoon and realized there would be questions on the exam about an all-Black regiment from Ohio. I forgot all about this part of the test. My heart jumped a little with a sense of dread. I put my Gettysburg textbook away in my backpack and pulled out the other book. It had a picture of a Black recruit in the Civil War, running with his regiment across a battlefield. His face looked brave and determined.

I flipped open the cover and turned the page until I saw my yellow highlighted lines and began to take in all the information. It seemed that the Black citizens of Ohio wanted to help out with the war effort, but the Officers and the regular army did not want Blacks involved unless it was in the roll of a laborer to help on bases, or behind battle lines. After Lincoln sighed the Emancipation Proclamation in 1863, Union troops were taking incredible loses on the battlefield and could not fill the void fast enough. The order was given to recruit Black soldiers to fill the regiments and they were more than glad to sign up.

There were many reasons why the men wanted to join the ranks, from the steady money for their families, stature in the community, and wanting to give back, after President Lincoln freed their brothers from slavery. The new recruits were sent to Fort Monroe to train, and then sent to their new assignment in the 27th United States Colored Troop. It was a group that consisted of escaped slaves, freed domestic workers, and a conglomeration of many people from several different manual occupations. The text went on to say that 179,000 Black troops participated in the war, and 38,000 died.

I was getting tired in the midafternoon from droning though information and trying to figure out what facts were important for the test and what were not. My eyes started to droop as the afternoon sun beamed in with its warmth and I drifted off to sleep.

THE SUNBEAM HIT ME in the eye and shocked me back to life. I couldn't believe I was still alive. The last thing I remembered was on a battlefield in Petersburg Virginia and was fighting for my life against the Confederate troops in one of the final battles of the Civil War to preserve the Union. The battle was long, tough, and bloody. The last thing I remembered was hand to hand combat with a tall, scruffy Confederate soldier, and he was getting the best of me. His bayonet came down and stabbed me in the leg, and then his riffle but hit me, and the lights went out.

I kept opening and closing my eyes since the sunlight was hitting me right in my retina. As I tried to lift my arm it was constrained for some reason. As I rolled my body back and forth, I realized that I was covered with dead bodies from both sides. My mind was shocked into reality and the brutality all came back to me. I struggled further to *make my way to the sunlight. I kept pushing with all my strength and felt myself getting to the surface. As I reached the top, I wished I could go down and bury my body forever. The battlefield as far as you could see in any direction was littered with dead bodies. My mind was still adjusting to the calamity I had been a part of. Everyone was dead and the wounded had been carted away to behind each enemy line. There was a quiet stillness to the battlefield. How long had I been knocked out? It must have been days. The stench of the dead reminded me it must have been days.*

I stood up as a dead soldier fell off me and his eyes were still open. It was one of my comrades from my troop. He was a young man like me, fighting for a cause, and was cut down in the prime of his life. His skin was turning white which I assumed meant he had been dead for a time. I reached down and closed his eyes and said a prayer. After several minutes, I began stepping over bodies until I got to the edge of the battlefield, always being aware of my surroundings and watching out for any enemy soldiers lurking in the area. I reached down and grabbed a rifle from a deceased Union soldier and grabbed the ammunition to fire it. As I walked, I stumbled over and over due to the mountain of humanity laying in my path.

Once I got to the edge of the field, I collapsed from exhaustion and felt a pain in my lower leg. I pulled up my pants and saw a deep bayonet wound that looked like it was getting infected. My heart dropped as I was thinking about how I would treat myself and make it back to my regiment. I ripped a piece of cloth off a dead soldier and poured some water from my canteen on the red flesh and cleaned it as best I could.

Afterwards, I looked out across the battlefield again and focused on all the humanity fighting for the cause. My friends and the Union army were fighting for our freedom as people and were willing to die for the cause. I thought about that for a minute and realized the sacrifice to leave your family, and friends and train to go into battle, and the chances of being wounded or killed were very high. I felt an overwhelming feeling of guilt about all the people who died for the cause in which they were not directly related. I started to cry and then wail to the point that I looked around to see if there were any Confederate soldiers still in the area. After about a half hour, I knew I needed to go west towards Lynchburg, to try and hook up with Union soldiers and get back to my comrades.

The area was mysteriously quiet, and my footstep noise was magnified. I made my way to the nearest railroad tracks and went west. The morning air was starting to heat up and the humidity was settling in. I could hear the birds chirp and come to life and other animals walking through the woods with me.

I stayed over to the edge of the tracks on the down slope to avoid detection, in case enemy troops or civilians came from the other direction. I was not as worried about a troop train since most of the tracks had been blown up or dismantled by Union soldiers to take away the Confederate's ability to move troops, supplies, and other needed contraband to continue to fight the war. I kept thinking about what my commanding officer told me if I was ever captured. The Confederates would brand me as a traitor to the South even if I was a free man, a free slave, or an escaped slave. General Grant tried to have Blacks fighting for the Union be treated as any other soldier, and Jefferson Davis agreed, but battlefield law, and the law of Jim Crow South overruled all law. That very fact kept bouncing around in my mind and made me even more paranoid and troubled.

Every few miles I would go into the underbrush and rest and drink from my canteen. I kept looking for any markers or signs that would give me a guide to where I wanted to be. I also prayed that maybe I would see some Union soldiers marching South to clean out the last bastion of Southern resistance. The Confederate troops had been decimated, their supply lines cut, and their morale diminished. They were fighting for their very lives and a way of life, until their commanders ordered them to stand down. Chaos and mob rule was the order of the day.

As the mid-afternoon sun beamed down on me, my leg started to ache, and I stayed off to the side and sat resting my body and using some of my grandmother's old natural remedies to treat my stab wound. I washed the red oozing cut in a nearby stream and refilled my canteen with fresh water.

It seemed like I had been walking forever. I looked through some sapling trees growing near the tracks and spotted a farmhouse and barn in the foreground. It was red with several outbuildings, and looked to be unoccupied. I held my rifle straight ahead and made my way through the brush, closing in on the barn. Everything was so quiet you could hear a pin drop. As I opened the barn door to see if any animals were alive, I stepped into the shade and out of the mid-afternoon sun. My eyesight was masked for just a split second and then a blow from nowhere came crushing down on the back of my head. The lights went out.

It seemed like days. My mind was groggy, and my eyesight was coming into clear view. The back of my neck was killing me. As I adjusted my vision, I could see two older people. A man and a woman were kneeling, looking over me. They were saying things to me, but it was garbled, due to my concussed state. I tried to sit up, but then the woman put her hand on my chest and said lay down and rest. You have been through a terrible time. The man looked over at her and I noticed he had my rifle and was using it as a crutch to bend down next to me. They obviously hit me in the head.

As my body and mind were coming back into focus, the old woman reached behind her and picked up a bowl and spoon. The man then propped me up against a horse stall and began to feed me some gruel that she kept saying would make me better. I felt my leg wound and pulled up my pants and to my amazement, the wound on my leg had been cleaned and dressed with new bandages made of torn sheets.

I lay in the barn for hours talking to my saviors and I noticed that the old man was still walking around holding my rifle. I asked for it back and he said it was better that he kept it since soldiers from both sides were committing atrocities due to anger, lack of food, and low morale. He indicated he would give it back to me when I went on my way. I relented, because they were treating me with compassion and seemed to be fair minded, even though they were Southerners.

At night they bedded me down in a horse stall, since it would be a better hiding place if renegade Southern troops came rushing in to search for food, livestock, and anything else they could steal of value. I felt safe and did not want to inconvenience them in any way since the southern civilians had been through hell and back and were in the middle of all the mayhem. As I lay down in the hay, I relaxed and drifted off to sleep. I dreamed about my comrades in arms and all we had been through for two years. I looked forward to being a free man and going back to Ohio to work and live in a free nation. It was a sweet dream and one that made me feel confident about the future even if the cost had been so high.

As I lingered in my dream state, I was shocked back to life hearing loud voices and a scream. I opened my eyes and saw straw and then I rolled over brushing it off. I could hear the older couple pleading with what sounded like two men with a deep Southern drawl.

My mind and ears struggled to hear what the conversation was about, and it sounded like the men thought they were hiding food or animals. I lay down and covered my body with hay. I could hear the old woman scream and the old man plead that they had no food or livestock. They said that the Union army came through weeks ago and cleaned them out. The conversation went back and forth and then the barn doors opened and the sunlight beamed in.

Through the straw I could see two confederate soldiers with tattered uniforms, looking unshaven, and in need of food. The old couple looked like they had been roughed up a little and were terrified. The men were in no mood for excuses. They pushed the couple into the barn and began to search around for any animals that could be skinned, cooked and eaten, or fresh eggs. As they searched the woman kept saying they had nothing and no valuables to give them.

The men looked frustrated and kept going from stall to stall to make sure they had not missed a morsel of fresh food. I held my breath as they got closer knowing I did not have a weapon and was defenseless. One man kicked the straw and was only a few feet from me when he tripped over my leg and fell into the side of the stall. As he arose my leg was exposed. He put his riffle and bayonet down into the hay and I yelped from a slight stab wound to my abdomen.

He yelled to his friend who brought the old couple over to peer into the stall and stare at his catch of the day.

"Lookie here what I have found. One of our dark Union friends trying to get away North." He laughed, and as he said it the other man slapped the old man across the face and push the woman closer to the stall, berating them both.

The man with the gun poked me to get up which I did. I brushed off the hay and stared at both of them. I looked at the couple with a feeling of shame, having put them in a perilous position. I told the soldiers they did not know I was there, and told them they were both loyal to the South and the Confederate cause and Jefferson Davis. I did not know their loyalties, but at this point they were just trying to survive the war and it was getting harder everyday as things spiraled out of control.

The other Confederate left the couple and came into the stall and together they pulled me up to my feet and began berating me as a Black man fighting for the Union cause. They then asked me where I was from, and I said I was a free Black from Ohio. This caused them to laugh and then one of them said this was not going to help save me.

My heart dropped after the words came out of the man's mouth. They shooed the old couple back to the house. They were so scared they immediately left and then I was alone with these two desperate men.

One man tied my hands behind my back, and the other kept looking around the barn. The other man found a big piece of rope in another stall and began making a noose, and giving out a nervous laugh as he was making it. The other man was behind me poking me in the back with his bayonet to let me know they meant business.

A thousand thoughts were going through my mind. Was this where it was all going to end? I was so proud of my service to the cause of liberty and freedom for the Black race and I thought about the sacrifices that had been made and the death and destruction the country had endured to win the Black man's freedom. This war would secure the ideals that *were stated in the Declaration of Independence: Life, Liberty, and Pursuit of Happiness.*

The two men marched me out of the barn. The mid-day sun was heating up the air and making it sticky. I was sweating, and my leg was killing me. I limped along as I could feel the bayonet pinching my skin, prodding me along. As I was walking, I looked straight ahead and saw a big maple tree with a big branch protruding out. One of the men went over to a big stump with a hatchet stuck in it, and rolled it over under the branch. It had obviously been used to behead poultry to clean and then cook for food.

The other man with the rope came over, and threw the noose over the branch and pulled it back and then came over to his friend and put his hand under my arm, and the two of them began dragging me towards the stump. My heart started to race, and I panicked and started to fight them. I kicked and fought for my life. I was thrown down to the ground and the two were looking down at me, and snarling.

One man yelled at me, while the other began poking the bayonet into my stomach. They said "You can die here or swing from the tree. Which will it be?" Then broke out in laughter and dragged me up from the ground.

They put the noose around my neck and made me step up on the stump. One went to the base of the tree, tied off the rope, and took all the tension out of it. I started to pray in my mind, and thought back to my church in Ohio, and remembered the pastor saying God is always watching and always with you. I tried to bring my mind to another place that was peaceful, and absent of all the pain and suffering on earth. My mind floated for a minute, and then the stump was kicked out from under me. The rope began to tighten around my neck, and I tried to make my neck muscles tight to stop my airflow from being blocked. I started kicking my feet, even though I knew it was a futile exercise.

The more I fought, the more the two men engaged in nervous laughter. They were very proud of themselves that they had expelled another Black man from this earth. Just as my body started to relax and I was giving in to my plight, I heard a gunshot ring out, and the rope above me snapped, and I fell several feet to the ground with a thud. My head was turned toward the two men, and the look on their faces was one of sheer surprise.

Then I heard the crack of two more rifle shots, and I saw both the men's faces explode with blood, and be propelled back before they splattered to the ground. What had just happened? I struggled to turn my head in the other direction, as my hands were still tied behind my back. The glare of the sun hit me in the face, and I blinked my eyes a couple of time to adjust for the bright light.

As I did, I saw the older couple remerge from their house and a troop of Union soldiers headed toward me. There had to be twenty to thirty men galloping in my direction. One man had General stripes on his sleeve. I looked up to him and to my amazement, I was looking at General Joshua Chamberlain, the hero of Little Round Top at Gettysburg. He was bigger than life as he dismounted his horse and pulled a knife from his sheath. He picked me up with the help of another officer, and cut the rope from my hands. I adjusted my hands, as they were numb, and looked into his eyes.

"Hey son, it looks like we got here just in time," he said and then let out a chuckle. "These Southern boys don't think our Union guys can shoot straight. My Millinocket guys can shoot a red squirrel off a fencepost at one hundred paces." He laughed some more. He then walked me around the perimeter of the farm, questioning me on my troop, and where I last fought, and how I ended up here. He told me his troops were charged with rooting out the last bastions of Confederate resistance, and disarming the troops, and sending these good old boys home to their families. The South had lost the war, and it was time to make the peace.

As he was talking, I was taken in by this man's compassion and care for his fellow man. No one would know the 24th Regiment from Maine was an all-volunteer group that had fought long and hard over the past few years and contributed to the Union victory. He told me he appreciated the efforts of the 54th regiment from Ohio, and made me feel good about our group's victories, and our contributions to the war *effort. This man treated me like an equal, and I knew with more people like him, the future of my people would be bright.*

As I sat on my horse, I stared through the window of the Appomattox Courthouse for the signing of the end of the Civil War. So many people had died or were wounded, and it would be years before the South would be able to rebuild and adjust to an economy that did not depend on slavery. After my rescue from the farm, General Chamberlain invited me to the official surrender ceremony. I asked him why he would bestow an honor like this to a Black man? He went on to tell me his aunt, from Bangor Maine, was an abolitionist and very devoted to the plight of the colored race in America. She had made it possible for hundreds of enslaved people to migrate north and be saved from a life of misery in the South. Due to that reason, he had been raised to treat all men equally, and without recourse.

The year was 1865 and it was April 9th. I watch the generals and officers make their way in for the peace signing, and noticed General Lee's uniform was so new, and so clean, in contrast to General Ulysses Grant's uniform, which was dirty and tattered. He had just returned from the battle of Five Forks, and had not had time to get back to camp to freshen up for the occasion. This said a lot about the man, and the way all Union soldiers revered him as a military leader.

As I looked through the window, you could see the two leaders sitting across the table from each other, with other officers passing back and forth the documents that would end the Civil War. I had chills going up and down my body with history being made before my eyes, and the anticipation of what was to come in the future.

Chapter 13

I WAS COMING DOWN a steep incline and kept tapping the brakes of my car to keep a constant speed. The Allegheny Mountains were beautiful, and the views of rural Pennsylvania were striking. The ride from St. Louis had been longer than I had anticipated, and I was getting tired of driving and not having a decent meal all day. I had been gorging on gas station store items such as Slim Jims, potato chips, and Coke. My stomach was rumbling, and I knew exactly why.

As I was coming down my last big hill on I-70, I could see the city of Pittsburgh in the distance. It looked beautiful from afar, with the Allegheny and Monongahela rivers merging with the Ohio, with the city stuck right in the middle. The skyscrapers were shooting up to the clouds, reminding me why they called this the Steel City. Pennsylvania was home to coal mining, which was used in the steel mills in the outskirts of the city. This town and these mills were responsible for most of the steel to build war machinery in World War II and provided a high percentage of the steel used in the United States to build cars, buildings, and many other things used in American life.

It was a proud city that had prospered during the industrial revolution but was now coming down off its high perch due to the great recession, and many of the industrial jobs going overseas chasing cheap labor. Many mills were closing, unions were fighting to keep the progress it took decades to achieve, and small business was feeling the pinch because the citizens were either unemployed or had less money in their pockets.

As I banked off the ramp and down into the city, I could see the stores boarded up, the neighborhood was blighted, and people had a look of despair on their faces. I saw the homeless, and drug addicted walking the sidewalks begging for money, and average citizens dodging the people to get to their jobs or do their errands. A few beggars had on faded Pittsburgh Steeler Football hats and jerseys. Even with the recession, the city was so proud of their football team and were looking forward to a winning season.

As I drove, I quickly looked down at my map of the city laying on my passenger seat and scanned it for Broad Street, which was where the next Salvation Army homeless shelter and discount clothing store was located. I would be spending my next week here, trying to make a difference in the lives of the downtrodden, and learn as much as I could about the other side of life in America. The deeper I got into the city the more despair I saw, and the homes and businesses were in such disrepair.

I spotted the building down the street. I dodged a few homeless people and a shopping cart, then pulled into the chain-linked fence parking lot and shut off my engine. I opened my hatchback, threw in my tapes, and pulled out my overnight bag. Then I shut the lid and locked it. As I made my way around to the front door, several people came up to me for money, with many different excuses. All of them sounded desperate, and made sense. I kept saying hi to them, and not breaking my stride as I headed for the front door.

I skipped up the stairs and made my way into the building. Above the front door was a cross, and directly to the right was a peace sign that was spray painted in orange paint. It was late in the afternoon, and as I turned the corner into the main hallway I walked right into a huge Black man. I looked up into his eyes, and a big smile came to his face. I swear I could count every shiny white tooth in his head.

"Sorry!" I said quickly.

"Well son," he said with a jovial baritone voice, "where are you going in such a hurry?"

"I am looking for Mr. Gregory Jackson, the house manager. My name is Jimmy McPherson, and I'm a volunteer from Boston."

"I'm Greg. I wasn't expecting you until tomorrow."

He put his arm around me and led me to his office on the first floor. As I sat down in a chair in front of his desk, he opened a bottom drawer of his desk and pulled out an employment application. He handed me a pen and I started to fill out the paperwork and Greg talked about the history of the shelter, and all the good things they were doing for the community. I kept reading the employment questions and raising my head up and down to let him know I was interested in what he had to say. He did not touch on his own personal history, which I thought was odd, but I let it go since it was none of my business. All I needed to know was he was knowledgeable of the place, had a big heart for the downtrodden, and seemed to be a nice person.

All of a sudden, I heard a loud rap on the door, and Greg said, "Come in."

The door whipped open, and a young girl flew through the door talking a mile a minute about something that had happened over in the secondhand clothing shop. She was talking so fast that I could not tell if it was a problem with an employee or a customer. I could not keep my eyes off her. She was so beautiful, with light brown skin that was silky smooth, a small Afro, average build with a multicolored top, and dungaree bell bottom pants and white sandals.

Greg raised his hand to her, which was an indication for her to stop talking and start listening.

"Sarah, I want to introduce Mr. James McPherson to you. He will be helping us out this week, and I want you to mentor him," he instructed the young girl.

She looked at me, and then back at Greg, and I stood, dropped my pen, and we both went to pick it up at the same time, and hit heads. We both stood up fast, and she was apologizing up and down for her stupidity. I told her it was all my fault, and as we looked into each other's eyes a beautiful smile came to her face. It was tugging at my heart, and I had never had a feeling like this in my life. Her voice was so soft, and her mood changed immediately.

"Well Mr. McPherson, nice to meet you," she said with a whispery voice like Marilyn Monroe. "Once you finish and get settled in your room, Amos will guide you down to the clothing center, and I will walk you through your duties."

She looked into my eyes for recognition of what she had said, and I agreed with a nod and a smile, and she was off as fast as she arrived.

I talked to Greg for another half an hour, and he walked me through the history and clientele of the place. I filled him in on my background and then went to my room to get unpacked. I was dying to remove my makeup and take a shower since my skin was getting more irritated as the weeks and months dragged on. I knew I didn't have time, so I sucked it up and went to the men's room to wash up, brush my teeth and change into a new set of clothes, so I could impress my new friend.

I was introduced to all the workers in the clothing center by Sarah, and was immediately accepted by them, and into my new role. Most of the people there were young, some volunteers, and very idealistic about the world and what they could contribute to it. There were no preconceived thoughts about the homeless, drug addicted, or alcoholics. They treated everyone the same, with dignity, and respect. As I talked to most of the employees over time, a lot of them were from tough backgrounds. They had to scrape and claw for everything they got out of life, but they were taking it all in stride and made the most of their job, and educational opportunities.

My job was to take the clothes that were donated to the shelter, wash them in big commercial washer and dryers, then check the size, fold them, and put them in piles on a series of big, long wooden tables. Then another person came and scooped them up and put them up front either in bins or on racks. There were several people up front waiting on customers and trying to keep the line moving.

Some people could pay the small fee for their purchases, and some could not. The help did their best to take care of all the people and did not differentiate due to lack of money. All customers were treated the same.

Sarah took me under her wing, and we grew closer as the week went on. She was so nice and had a great outlook on life. She was a paid employee and had just completed her second year of community college. She was transferring her credits to the University of Pittsburgh and was waiting to be accepted into a liberal arts program with a major in psychology, and a minor in sociology. She also talked about her parents and sister, who was much younger than she. The father worked in the Edgar Thomson steelworks in the town of Braddock, right outside Pittsburgh, and she also lived in the same working-class town. Her mother was a housewife and was thinking about getting a part time job to get back in the workforce because the steel union said the jobs at the steel mill were going away.

We were inseparable the whole week, and on Thursday after work she asked me if I wanted to go on a late afternoon picnic to a favorite place of hers. I was a little taken aback, but agreed right away. After work, I freshened up and then met her out by her car in the lot. She waved me over when she saw me, and I jumped into a 1963 Ford Falcon. It had a lot of miles on it, but it was in pristine shape. She was so proud of her ride. As I jumped in the passenger side, I looked in the back seat and saw a picnic basket. I thought to myself, was this planned? It gave me a comforting feeling as we drove out of the city and up into the suburbs and the Allegheny mountains.

The conversation with Sarah was so easy and natural. I felt like I had known this girl my whole life. I thought back to my college days and you would have to stand on your head to get a girl to notice you. This was a nice change of pace for me, since I never had a steady girlfriend to confide in. We had been driving for about twenty minutes as we meandered higher up the surrounding hills when we pulled into a park with a dirt parking lot and came to a stop. In the foreground you could see many picnic benches, steel barbecue grills, and trash barrels around the property, and a beautiful view of the city and valley below.

As the car came to a stop, Sarah climbed out, retrieved the picnic basket from the backseat, and locked the car with her key. There were not many people here at this time, and we had the pick of any table. She picked out a nice table near the edge of the park, which had a beautiful view of the surrounding area.

"So, Mr. College Boy, tell me more about you and your life," she spouted. She gave a heartfelt laugh, and started unpacking the basket. She had two chicken salad sandwiches, two bags of potato chips, two Cokes, plastic wear, and a few napkins. She also had packed two beers which she claimed she stole out of her father's fridge at home, since she was still underage. She seemed very pleased with that major theft.

I was not surprised back by her question, but I knew I could only tell her part of my story, since she would probably throw me off the cliff if I said I was white and on a field trip to write a thesis paper to graduate from college. I tried to be forthright with her without showing her my whole hand. It was hard and I felt guilty, but I knew it was for the best. I gazed across the table into her eyes as we ate our meal, and after we were finished, she came over to my side of the table and cracked open one of the beers and snuggled up to me. My heart skipped a beat, and then I became paranoid that my makeup was amiss, and I would blow my cover. I tried to tell her some funny stories of my life and college years, but she had other things on her mind.

I took a long swig of my beer and looked back at her beautiful face, and into her eyes, and her lips came to mine. We kissed, and had our arms around each other, and we stayed like that for some time. In between kisses, and snuggling, we sipped our beers, and I felt like I never wanted this moment to end. She was so beautiful, and full of life and had such a positive personality. It was like God made an angel and brought her down to earth to help the disadvantaged people in life. She had no negativity, and wasn't jaded in any way.

We stayed at the park until dusk, and then she drove me back to the shelter. We hardly talked on the way home, and just let our romantic interlude set in, and take heart. As we pulled up, some of the homeless guys were on the front steps, and this made her feel uncomfortable to kiss me before I got out of the car. We both held hands and looked into each other's eyes. Then she asked me to attend her church with her on Sunday morning. Her little sister was doing a solo in the choir, and she wanted me to meet her parents and her little sister. She said she had a voice of an angel and wanted me to experience it.

I said yes without really thinking it out and regretted my decision as soon as the words came out of my mouth. I had planned on leaving for the next city on Friday after work, and then went over the itinerary in my mind. I was supposed to be in Baltimore on Monday morning, and that would mean after the Sunday morning service, I would have to make up an excuse to Sarah to get on the road as soon as possible. I got out of the car and made my way through the crowd, giving a few peace signs and high fives. I had a lot to think about in the next few days to piece this together.

I STOOD OUTSIDE THE First Baptist Church of Pittsburgh, not far from where the shelter was. I drove my car to the church since I was in a bad part of town and did not want to walk the distance. I had worn my Sunday best, which consisted of Chinos, a madras short-sleeve shirt, and loafers. I made sure I had makeup in all the appropriate places, since I knew I would be looked over pretty closely by Sarah's family.

I made my way over to the front walk leading up to the church and saw several families making their way into the church. The pastor, a big man with a big welcoming smile was greeting people, shaking hands, and hugging little children. I thought back to my church in Massachusetts, and this brought back fond memories. I had drifted from the church while in college, but I knew when I settled down in life I would go back. The world had become a scarier place since I was little, and I felt the church was a good place to pray that people would just get along, and come together.

As I looked up from surveying the crowd, I saw Sarah and her sister walking towards me, with her parents not far behind. The younger sister was cute like Sarah, with braids and ribbon in her hair, a light blue summer dress, with bobby socks and white sandals. Also, a big smile like her sister pasted across her face. As they approached, I greeted both, and stuck out my hand to the young girl. As I reached forward, Sarah put her hand on my back, and leaned in for a peck on my cheek. I was a little surprised by her affection in a church line, and I could tell looking back at the father that he was not pleased either.

The parents caught up to where we were standing, and Sarah introduced me to her family.

"Momma, this is Jimmy. He works at the shelter with me in the clothing area." Dad was waiting for his own introduction. "Daddy, Jimmy is very interested in the steel mill, and how everything works. Maybe you can show him sometime," she told him with an enthusiastic manner.

My heart dropped when I heard the words come out of her mouth, since I knew I would not be sticking around the area after the service ended. I shook hands with all the parties, and Sarah's sister Nicole was grabbing my hand so hard I didn't think she would ever let go. Before you knew it, the pastor gave the high sign that the service was about to start, and my new friend grabbed my hand, looked into my eyes, smiled, and we walked into the church together and sat down.

Once we were in the pew, I realized the seat was padded with a nice cushion, which our Catholic church never had. The Catholic priests wanted to keep you uncomfortable so you would pay attention. I grabbed a prayer book from the rack in front of me with nervous anticipation and started flipping the pages like I knew what I was doing. Sarah's little sister and mother kept looking down the row at me and smiling. The father looked ahead stoically. The Baptist church service would start with music, then a welcome, then an invocation, a hymn, pastor's comments, God's words, Benediction, and postlude music. My heart sank as I read the format, thinking I was going to be there all day.

I was wrong of course, and the service was exactly an hour. The choir was great and sang a lot of Southern Baptist songs from long ago. The pastor gave the congregation some words of hope, and in the middle of things Sarah's sister Nicole made her way to the choir for her star performance. She looked nervous as she paraded up to the front of the crowd. Sarah and her mother held hands with a look of anticipation in their eyes. The choir started the song called "I Need Thee," and Nicole sang along, and in the middle, the young girl was singing the third and fourth verse all by herself, with the choir swaying.

She finished up her two verses with a bang, and her sweet voice bellowed into every corner of the church. She was so proud of herself as she stepped back into line, and as I looked down the row, this family couldn't have been prouder and even dear old dad had a smile breaking through his stern face.

Pastor Clough finished up the service after the benediction and then ended the proceedings. After the choir sang the final song, we waited for Nicole at the back of the church as she made her way towards us, being congratulated by her peers. Sarah grabbed my hand again as we all made our way down the front steps, and I noticed some of Sarah's friends were staring at us, probably wondering who the new guy in town was. I swallowed hard, walking slowly back to the parking lot as we patted Nicole on the back, showering her with praise.

As we entered the lot, I was almost ready to say my goodbyes and leave when Sarah's mother invited me out to breakfast at a local diner down the street from the church. It took my mind a few seconds to realize what she just said, and I did not have time to come up with a good excuse. I looked over at Sarah, her sister, and then into her father's eyes. He was looking through me as if this part of the celebration was already discussed and agreed on. He was not happy about it, and I sure wasn't excited about it, due to my schedule and not wanting to break Sarah's heart any more than I already was going to. I chickened out from drawing the line and said yes, and then Sarah and Nicole begged their parents if they could ride with me to the diner.

We followed the parents down the street, out of the ghetto, and past the homeless and less fortunate to a fifties style diner right on the edge of the river. It had that silver look to it and had probably been there for many years. Nicole was jumping all over the backseat, and I prayed that the little sister would not open my eight-track cassette box which was on the floor next to her. This would expose me as the honky that I was. Also, my bag was packed, and right over the back seat in the hatch back area, and if the sister looked back there, I would have a lot of explaining to do.

I grabbed a seat from another table inside and pulled it up to the edge of the booth that Sarah's family had settled into. The waitress, dressed in a fifties outfit, put five menus on the table, brought five glasses of water, and then made her way behind the counter to deliver some orders to her other customers.

I buried my face in the menu, even though I knew I was having bacon, eggs, home fries, and toast. I kept going over in my mind how much money I would need to pay for the whole meal and Sarah's family. I was on a budget and the expenses from my little field trip were starting to add up.

Once we ordered our meals and the waitress disappeared there was an awkward silence, and then the mother asked "James, Sarah said you have graduated from college last May. What are you planning on doing with your life?"

All eyes turned to me, and I felt like I shrank in the chair like one of those cartoon characters on the Saturday morning shows. I thought for a minute what I was going to say. I was a history major with a minor in political science with no social work background or experience. I'm sure they also thought I would be staying in the area, since I'm sure that's what Sarah told them. The seconds ticked by while I drew up a response in my head.

"I'm not sure what I want to do with my life. Around my school in Boston is a very depressed neighborhood, and my college helps out the community. I thought it would be nice to go to another city and see if I could help the disadvantaged and compare it to my experience back home." I exhaled after my statement and wondered if they were buying it.

Sarah jumped in and told her mother everything I told her this week about me and my family. This only made me feel worse than I already felt. This was a meal to introduce me as her boyfriend, and not just some casual acquaintance she met along the way. My anxiety was rising, and I gorged myself on the food and tried to let Sarah do all the talking. I chirped in once in a while, when it was really needed.

The parents were a nice, hardworking middle-class couple, and lived a decent life. Sarah would be the first child in their family to go to college, and they worshipped the ground she walked on. The little sister looked up to her in every way. The steel works job was good paying, and I worried inside what the father's prospects would be if the mill had more layoffs. Pittsburgh had a one-dimensional economy, and little by little it was fading away, as the world changed to a global economy. None of us realized what wreckage lay ahead as the country was transitioning to a service economy.

As the meal finished up and the waitress put the check on the table, I reached for it at the same time Sarah's father reached for it. He gave me a look that could kill. He was a proud, humble man who had always provided for his family, and this day would be no different. I immediately let go of the check and thanked him profusely for the meal and his generosity. He looked at me and gave me a halfhearted, "You're welcome." He then stood up and went to the counter to settle the bill.

Sarah's mother asked me what my plans were for the rest of the day, and I lied, and said Greg had some chores for me around the shelter to get ready for another busy week. She and Sarah seemed satisfied with my response, and we all walked out to the parking lot together. I gave my well wishes to the family, thanked the father again for the meal, and then Sarah held my hand for a few seconds, looked into my eyes, smiled, and gave me a peck on the cheek. Then said she would see me at the shelter tomorrow afternoon.

I agreed to the same, and gave her a halfhearted goodbye then turned and headed back to my car. As I was walking a wave of guilt settled over me. I reached up and brushed a tear from my eye, knowing I was letting go of the best thing that had ever come into my life so far. I drove down the street, making sure the family was not going the same way, got up on I-70 headed southeast to Baltimore, and turned up a Jethro Tull tape as loud as it would go to drown out the sound of me crying like a little baby.

My sleep pattern was topsy turvy and it seemed like I was going from one side of the bed to the other. I couldn't get Sarah out of my head. I felt like I had made a huge mistake leaving town without saying goodbye and wished it had gone different. I had not even thought about the personal feelings I would encounter along the way, with my cross-country field trip and thesis paper. I tried to keep that part separate in my mind, but my heart had not gotten the message. Did I just leave behind someone who could have been a life partner and changed my life forever? Then I realized she was Black and I was white. I speculated how society would look at us, and how Sarah would have been accepted into my family, and also hers. Even Sarah's feeling for me might have changed when she found out I was a white kid from Boston, and I was doing all this on a lark to write a paper and get my diploma from college. She might be offended and write me off because I had misrepresented myself to her.

I continued to roll around the bed. I opened my eyes, and the room was dark, and for a while I forget what motel I was in, and what town I was in. My mind was groggy, and I adjusted my eyes to look at the clock on the nightstand. It read 4:00 in big red numbers. I knew I did not need to get up until seven to shower, put on a new layer of makeup, eat, and get to my new destination. I closed my eyes and drifted off into another dream state.

For some reason I was dreaming I was in a church, sitting next to Sarah's little sister her pew. Then my dream became clearer, and I realized I was in the rectory hall in the basement of a different church. There was a little girl named Rebecca Williams, and she had just finished practicing in the junior girls' choir of her church. She was holding a copy of today's church service program. It read 16th Street Baptist Church, Birmingham, Alabama. The date was September 15th, 1963.

I stressed and strained in my sleep. Why was I here? I felt like I was in an episode of the Time Tunnel show which I watched as a kid. The little girl kept folding up the program, and then opening it up. Her friends Addie Mae Collins, Cynthia Wesley, Carole Robertson, and Carol Denise McNair were walking towards her with pending excitement. Their Sunday school teacher let them practice the three songs they would be singing at the 11:00 o'clock service, and this would be the first time the junior choir would be alone up on the alter without the adults running the show.

Rebecca looked down at the three songs on the program. They were listed as "Oh Freedom," "Lift Every Voice and Sing," and "Go Tell It on the Mountain." The girls had practiced these songs for so long they could recite them in their sleep. The girls swept me away into the ladies' room to freshen up, since it was a humid day in town, even though we were almost into fall on the calendar. The girls were combing their hair, splashing cold water on their faces, and laughing with nervous excitement.

I was hoping the church service would bring the community together, since the past month had been violent in Birmingham, with school desegregation and the civil rights movement being at the forefront. Our church was a meeting place for the civil rights leaders to plan marches and design literature to keep the populace informed on the movement. I was proud of our civic leaders and hoped God could guide us to a better place in the community.

I opened the door of the ladies' room to look at the clock in the hallway, and it read 10:15 AM. My parents said they wanted me to meet them on the front steps of the church so I could accompany them to their pew and sit with them until the church service started at eleven. Then my group would walk up to the front and line up for the opening hymn. I said my goodbyes to my girlfriends and tore out of there to meet my family.

I went up the stairs to the main floor and walked to the front of the church. As soon as I opened the huge wooden front door, the morning sun hit me in the eyes, temporarily blinding me as I stepped out and stumbled. The pastor grabbed me from falling and gave me a jovial pep talk on taking your time. He knew me well and was so happy I would be singing the church songs today. I was nervous to keep up a conversation with him, but as more people came up the steps, he turned to greet them, and I faded away to the other side. I peered out to see my parents. As I strained my neck to check the parking lot, I saw my momma and daddy walking up the gravel path towards me. My heart went pitter patter, as I realized the big debut was almost here.

The congregation was marching in, and as my parents got to the top stair, I leaned forward to give my mother a hug, and my father patted me on the head, and asked if I was ready for my big day. I nodded yes, and we turned, greeted the pastor, and made our way to our usual seats in the church. The three of us said a prayer to God, and I handed my church program to momma, and then she grabbed the song book from the seat next to her and opened it to the first song we would be singing.

I kept looking over to the side door which led downstairs, wondering when my four friends would be up to meet their parents. We would all form the children's choir up front. I looked behind me at the churchgoers streaming in and saw the clock read 10:22. I heard a loud rumble, and then the right side of the church stairwell exploded with so much power I could see the outside world through the wall, which had been destroyed. We all turned our heads quickly to avoid the fragments of splintered wood and flying debris. There was a cloud of smoke and dust which enveloped the church. People were running and screaming to get out the front doors.

Before I knew it, my Daddy picked me up in his arms and raced to the front of the church. The pastor was coming the other way into the church to see what the damage was and help anyone in the church that was wounded or hurt. My mother was right behind us, running down the stairs into the parking lot.

As we were making our way to our car, I looked back to the back, right side of the church and it was blown to pieces. My heart sank when the realization set in that that was exactly where the ladies' room was, where I had just left my friends. I started crying and telling my father we had to go back, but he forcefully put me in the car, and said we needed to leave the area in case there was a secondary explosion.

As we made our way home, I looked down at my beautiful blue dress and it was soiled with splinters, soot, and blood. I looked at the back of my parents sitting there, saying nothing to each other. We were all in shock, and I reached across the backseat and grabbed my favorite doll, held it close to my heart, and started to wail uncontrollably. We were God-fearing people and had not bothered anybody, but some people in our community had hate in their hearts, and not even God could shake it loose.

Chapter 14

I LOOKED OUT OVER Baltimore harbor from my Howard Johnson's second floor window. It was a beautiful August summer day and the humidity still lay in the air. I opened my window and shut off my air conditioning. I could smell the fish and crab wafting in the air. I saw schooners, sailboats, tugboats, and a variety of other vessels. Across the bay, you could see many large cargo ships and oil tankers on the horizon. Straight ahead and to my left were many run-down warehouses and several small businesses on Pratt Street that were open, but looked dreary.

It was Tuesday morning and I had arrived Monday night and checked in with no problem. I had gotten a good night's sleep, had a great meal in the dining room, applied my makeup to change my complexion, and was ready to step out to my next stop on the tour. This week I would be at the Salvation Army House on Light Street, up on the other side of Federal Hill. I purposely picked this hotel because the house superintendent said they had no room for volunteers, and all their space was reserved for the disadvantaged and homeless. This hotel room would be my home for the next two days. My level of anxiety had left me, knowing I would be in a tranquil space after work and could recharge my batteries every day. This would help me bring more energy to the job and hopefully give me time to document my day, and my trip so far.

As I walked out the door, I received many second glances since I had changed my looks to be a Black man. I felt confident that if security stopped me, I had a room key, and a receipt to my room paid in advance for the week in cash. The sunlight hit me in the eyes, so I pulled my sunglasses out of my top pocket and put them on. I took a right off Pratt Street, and was on Light Street, which went straight up the hill, and bordered Federal Hill. The homeless shelter was on the other side of the park. I saw many people on their way to work, tourists venturing around the harbor, and other people who were either homeless, drug addicted, or lost in some way. The balance of the people looked to be involved in the boating or fishing industry. The harbor looked over-industrialized and depressing. I felt with a little investment it could be a nicer place, but city budgets were stretched to the max.

I kept a steady pace down the street, and noticed the businesspeople and tourists gave me a second look. They had a look of fear in their eyes, and some walked to the other side of the street. I didn't know if I was being paranoid or if this was really happening. The homeless and the down and out did not give me a second look. I checked my looks up and down and felt I looked very preppy and non-threatening. As I walked further up the hill, I saw some old granite stairs which led up to the park at the top of Federal Hill. I decided to take a short cut to the shelter through the park.

As I crested the top step, I was surprised what a view I had of the harbor and the city of Baltimore. I could see for miles in all directions. I looked to the left and saw my hotel about a mile away with its green tinged sign. I turned my head to the right, and I could look out into the harbor and see Fells Point, and then the water wrapped around to the right. There was Fort McHenry, where a major battle had been fought in the War of 1812. Then the water headed out to Annapolis and on to the Atlantic Ocean. It was a spectacular view, and I stood there and gazed for a few minutes.

All of a sudden I heard, "Hey man, can you spare a dime?"

I turned suddenly and a middle-age Black man was standing in front of me with tattered clothes, smoking a cigarette, and pushing a shopping cart with all his worldly possessions in it. His voice was soft, but crusty, as he gave me his excuse for the day, why he needed money. I had a brief conversation with him and reached into my pocket and pulled out a quarter. I put it in his hat which was stretched out in front of me. He gave me a knowing look of thanks and went about his business.

I peered around the park and noticed it was run down and the grass had not been mowed in weeks. Every few steps you could see a monument to the city or a Revolutionary or Civil War plaque or statue. The granite was stained by pollution, and the brass signs with the identity of the landmark was discolored and in need of polish. It gave me a feeling that this was a pretty important city and had a lot of significance in American history. One thing I noticed right away was there were no tourists in such a famous place. I thought for a moment and then it came to me, the park was run down and the homeless had taken over all the turf.

I looked to the other side of the park, and I noticed all the homeless and addicted were making their way down the street away from where I was standing. It seemed strange, so I followed their lead. As I was walking through the neighborhood it looked like most of these homes were bigger than most, but run down. I thought to myself I bet this is where the steamship captains and richer people lived, since it had a great view, and seamen could look at their ships tied up down on the docks below. As I made my way down the street, I took in all the sights and sounds and kept a good distance back from the homeless, since I only had so many quarters in my pocket.

Before I knew it, I had my answer with this parade of people. Light Street must have wrapped around Federal Hill, and I was looking right at The Salvation Army Shelter which was an old Victorian home that had been remodeled into a place for the homeless to sleep, get a good meal, and maybe some addiction counselling. This would be my place of work for the next week, and I couldn't wait to get started.

I blew in the front door past some of the residents, saying hi and being friendly. I was holding the door for an older man who looked like he needed help, but he waved me off. I turned fast and walked right into this big guy. I bounced off his chest, and I stepped back and looked up at this big fellow.

He gave out a big jolly laugh. "Where are you going in such a hurry, son?" he said with a continuation of his jovial laugh.

"Hi Sir," I answered with uncertainty. "I'm looking for a Mr. Taby Allen, the house manager."

"Well, you have come to the right place. I'm Taby, the house manager, and I assume you are Mr. McPherson?" He stuck out his hand.

I grabbed his hand and shook it until so much time had gone by that we stopped. He put his arm around me, and he said, "Come with me, and I will introduce you to the staff, and show you to your job for the week."

His arm around my shoulder was crushing, and as we walked down the hallway to the cafeteria, everyone passing me was saying hi to Taby and treating him with the utmost respect. He had a calm manner and was a people person.

Once I got settled and introduced to the staff, Taby assigned me to the kitchen, mainly washing dishes and putting them back on shelves. The room in the house was smaller than most shelters I had been in. This was a tight-knit group and got along well. There were ten volunteers on the day shift and evening shift, and five on the night shift. The sleeping capacity was smaller than most and the cellar of the home was filled with cots that could sleep twenty men at a time. There were also ten beds in the top floor of the home organized in the same manner. These beds were held for walk in business after hours. Taby told me he never wanted to turn anyone away because if they did, he knew the person would be sleeping on a park bench down the street, which troubled him greatly.

He told me after the second day working in the shelter that his father had been drug addicted and on the streets after many years of his mother trying to get him help, and keep the family together. He saw the pain on her face, and always worried about his father wandering the streets of Baltimore.

During the mid-week, Taby approached me after lunch and said he messed up the work schedule and had too many people for the afternoon and dinner shift. He asked me if I wanted to take the rest of the day off and do some sightseeing around the city on my own and I jumped at the chance. I was on a tight schedule from city to city, and this would give me time to take in all the tourist spots, and then work on my notes and catch up with what I had learned on my journey. So far it had been very depressing, seeing how many people were affected by poverty and drug abuse, and its casualty list and toll on society. I was taken aback by how it was also hidden from the main population; if you never looked beneath the surface, you would never notice.

I went back to my hotel room and freshened up and then asked the main desk person directions on foot to get to Memorial Stadium. This was the home of the Baltimore Colts and the Orioles teams. I had always been interested in both teams as a child and collected baseball and football cards on all of them. I remember having Johnny Unitis and Brooks Robinsons cards. I was told the stadium was in a residential area of Baltimore, so I asked the front desk where Thirty-third Street was. The nice man at the counter had a big change in personality since I had checked in as a white person. He made me stand there for a few minutes, and then he asked what I wanted in a put off way. All I could make out was he told me to go down Light Street and take a right on Orleans Street. I thanked him for his time and walked out the front door on to the street. I could feel the man's eyes burning a hole in my back.

As I started my journey, I noticed the sidewalks were sparse except for a few tourists, and some businessmen rushing back to the office. The sun was shining, but the city in general looked drab and in need of some sprucing up. The pollution was bad, due to the fact this had been an industrial city in the past, and most of the buildings and warehouses were in need of updating or at least sandblasting to remove the stains on the brick.

I walked what seemed like a few miles and as I made my way down the street the city was far behind. The homes were a variety of multifamily dwellings and row homes. Most were in disrepair, and a lot of people were hanging out on their front steps due to the heat, and the kids were playing stick ball or kickball. Several fire hydrants were unscrewed with water spraying into the streets, and the little ones were having a ball running through the stream. The smiles on their faces were priceless, and they did not have a care in the world. Then as you looked at the parents observing all the fun, their faces told a different story of poverty, adversity, and despair. They talked in low voices, and when you looked into their eyes you could see the sadness, and I'm sure they were praying to God to get them through one more day.

After I turned on Orleans Street and looked way down the hill, I did not see anything that looked remotely like a sports stadium. I started to get nervous, since I was very far away from the downtown area of Baltimore, and I was not in the best part of town. As I moved further down the street, I saw a school on my left. The sign said Dunbar High School. The school was closed for the summer with no activity going on except some kids playing basketball on the courts on the left side of the school. The children's ages looked to be young teenagers and it was the shirts against the skins. They were playing hard and having fun.

As I walked by, I noticed a mother pushing a baby carriage and a young boy standing next to her having a very serious discussion. I cut across the street and as I approached, I could hear the mother say "Reggie, you are not going to play pick up with those boys. They are too old for you."

The boy mumbled something which I could not fathom, and then the mother reached across and slapped the boy on the hands, knocking the basketball out of his hands for a second. He quickly regained the ball and then noticed me coming and was quiet.

The mother turned quickly as she saw me approaching her. By the look on her face, she was paranoid I was going to rob her. She put her arm around the young boy and pulled him close and I smiled to diffuse the situation.

"Hi Ma'am," I said in a disarming way. "Could you tell me how to get to Memorial Stadium?"

She looked back at me with a skeptical city look, and then said "Honey child, you are way out of your way. The stadium is two miles down this street, and then take a right on Thirty-third Street for another half mile. It will be on your left, and you can't miss it." She looked back at me for recognition that I understood, and the little girl in the carriage woke up from her nap and started to fuss. The young boy looked right up at me and didn't smile. I looked at his face and was sad to see the despair. To have someone so young who looked already defeated in life was heartbreaking. I would never forget that look.

I thanked the young mother for her time and started making my way down the street, dodging the trash cans and dogs on the way to my destination.

After about a half hour I made it to the Stadium. It was not what I expected. It looked much smaller than it did on TV, and they were right that the residential neighborhood hid this gem from the rest of the world. There were several tourists meandering around, waiting for a tour, even though the baseball team was on a road trip to New York. I tried to chat to some of the white tourists, but they were stand-offish and then I remembered I was dressed as a Black man. The body language was very obvious, even though I was dressed like a tourist myself.

I walked around the stadium a few times and engaged the people from the neighborhood, and they filled me in on great stories and historical events with the two sports teams from past history. The locals were engaging and so proud of their teams, and I learned so much more than was printed in sports magazines. After some time, I asked a local how to get back to Pratt Street, and they pointed down the way. I understood enough to feel comfortable to continue my journey.

My mood was good, and I looked at my watch and it said four o'clock. I walked about a mile, taking it all in, when I saw a sign for Fells Point. I entered a nice little hippie hamlet with shops, small businesses, and young people and tourists meandering here and there. I could also see and smell marijuana wafting through the air.

I started to get hungry, since I had not had any food since breakfast at the shelter. I ate while I worked to not take away from my mission to help and feed the poor. In the distance I saw a long wooden building that had several signs for eating establishments. I opened the door and stepped into a building with multiple restaurants with many different themes and kinds of lunch items. This was before the advent of the food court. The noise was loud as people went here and there, trying to figure out what they wanted, and what food had the best value.

I looked up and down for a while and then saw a burger and fried food joint up ahead. It had eight stools at a counter, and one was empty. I jumped on the spare seat, and grabbed a menu on the counter, and started flipping through it. No one next to me gave me a second look, but this big cook dressed in a white outfit and a chef's hat gave me a look of distrust. As I surveyed the customers and patrons walking around the building, I noticed none who were Black. I thought back to many years ago when white lunch counters did not serve Blacks, but I knew this was not the case now. I had every right to be here.

My nerves were getting the best of me and then the man stepped forward and said, "What do you want?" in a stern voice. His eyes were piercing and looked right through me.

I spouted out, "I would like a cheeseburger, medium French fries, and a Dr. Pepper."

The man did not give me any recognition, just set a napkin, fork, and a bottle of ketchup in front of me, turned and went back to his duties. I assumed he got my order, and would cook it, and serve me soon. I sat there looking at a free paper that someone had left on the counter. After what seemed like twenty minutes, I was giving up hope that I would ever be served. My stomach was growling, and I was just about ready to walk away when the big man put a plate in front of me with my food, opened the soda pop bottle and stuck that in front of me. Then slapped down the check and said he needed the money now.

I knew he did not do this with any other customer, but I put my hand in my pocket and pulled out a few bills. I paid the man and said, "Keep the change." As fast as I transacted the business at hand the man turned on his heel and went back to what he was doing. I ate my lunch in silence and tried to stay positive and look for the best in people and mankind.

After I was done with my meal, I came out of the food building and noticed all the hippies sitting in the park talking, laughing, throwing Frisbees, and smoking pot. The smell of marijuana and cigarettes was wafting in the air. It seemed like such a fun atmosphere, and reminded me of a warm spring day on campus, after a long cold winter in Boston. It was called spring renewal and we knew the warm season was coming and there would be so much fun with good weather, baseball, sports playoffs, and the beach.

I stared at the kids for a while, and then looked over to the dock where small ferry boats were taking the tourists back to the inner harbor or out to Fort McHenry Park to see where one of the final battles of the War of 1812 was fought. I kept standing there, looking at everyone come and go and thought to myself, I should go on that tour. I wanted to learn more, but then I looked at my watch and realized my time was almost up. It was six o'clock and I would need to get back to my hotel and get ready for another day of work.

I grabbed a tourist map and charted a path back around the inner harbor to Pratt Street and Howard Johnson's. As I made my way down the street in that direction, I saw many nice shops including art studios with abstract drawings, music shops, drug accessory shops, and many others that had various themes. I saw a big poster of Jimmy Hendrix and Janis Joplin in the window of a music store, and it drew me inside.

As I entered, many young people were surveying all the great albums the owner had inside. I looked around and saw an older man behind the counter, cashing out a young couple. He eyeballed me, and I did not think anything of it. I started to check out the store and kept looking up and down at the albums and the great posters on the wall.

I started to look at Led Zepplin, The Rolling Stones, The Beatles, The Kinks, The Who, and many others. Most of the patrons in the store were white and then I got paranoid that I was looking at white people's music. I immediately swung over and started to look through Black bands like The Jackson Five, Marvin Gaye, Sly and the Family Stone, and Stevie Wonder.

Suddenly, I felt someone in my personal space. I looked up quickly and the man at the register was right there looking at me, and then said, "Can I help you with anything, son?" in a put off sort of way.

I quickly said, "No thank you, I am only browsing," with as much confidence as I could muster. He walked away as soon as I finished my response. I thought it odd but continued my journey around the store. All of a sudden, I looked at my watch and it said seven o'clock. I had lost track of time and needed to get back to my temporary home. I made my way for the door at a fast pace. As I walked out the door, I felt a hand on my shoulder. I turned fast to face the person.

It was the store manager again, and he had a look of suspicion on his face and in his body language. He stared at me for a few seconds, which seemed like hours and then said, "Do you have anything of mine on you?"

What was he talking about? I stood there and then said, "What do you mean?"

He reached his hand down and pulled my shirt out of my pants to see if I had any contraband stuffed down my pants. He noticed my skin was white, but my face was black, and immediately backed away and retreated inside.

I was rattled, and mad, but knew I would need to be on my way. I reached into my pocket and pulled out the tourist map and studied it intently. After a few minutes I decided to cut through Little Italy because this would be the most direct route back to my hotel. I sped up my pace marching down the sidewalk. As I got further and further away from Fells Point, the tourists diminished, and the street became empty. There were many warehouses, and some were boarded up and abandoned. As I came around the corner, I started to notice a nicer working class residential neighborhood with a few Italian restaurants. Most of them did not have many customers since it was a weeknight, and the dinner hour was close to over. The atmosphere gave me a warm fuzzy feeling of the North End of Boston and all its history and heritage.

As I made my way down the long street, I could see three teenagers sitting on a step outside a rundown row home. They were smoking cigarettes, drinking soda, flipping coins, and swearing up a storm. I switched from one side of the street to the other side to avoid any trouble. I did not look their way as I went by, but could see their faces out of my peripheral vision. They had a look of hate in their eyes.

All of a sudden, a coke bottle went zinging by my face and smashed on the cement front steps of someone's home. The glass splintered and flew on to my clothes and all over the sidewalk. Then I heard a barrage of racial epithets and the one of the kids say, "Stay the fuck out of our neighborhood!"

I was shocked but not surprised. I had been educated in being a little more street smart from going to college in the inner city and realizing I was not in Disneyland anymore. I picked up my pace and shook my pants to get the glass off. I looked back to make sure the kids were not following me.

After about twenty minutes of fast-paced walking, I was back on Pratt Street, and I could see the orange roof of my hotel, and the twenty-eight flavors of ice cream. It was a sight for sore eyes, and I celebrated with a strawberry ice cream cone. I sat out on a wall across the street next to the harbor. The businesspeople and tourists were gone, but it was not dark yet, so the beggar's and flim-flam men had not descended on the area yet.

I stared at the boats on the docks in their slips as they bobbed up and down and I noticed an older Black man coming up from beneath a big schooner cabin. He looked tired and was sweating after a long day in the sun. He held a can of beer in his hand and sat down on the edge of the boat. Then he picked up a toolbox and rested it beside him. I thought him to be out of place, since he did not look like a man of means, when all of a sudden, another man came up with a drink in his hand, took out his wallet, paid the man, and they sat for a few minutes and talked. The man was dressed to the nines and walked around pointing things out around the boat. The other man was nodding his head in agreement. He was obviously a hired hand to keep this expensive wooden boat in great shape. They talked to each other in a very relaxed way and after what seemed like a half hour the workman picked up his toolbox, walked up the dock to the street and jumped in a vintage rundown car.

I sat there for a while watching the sun set and thought about all I had seen. Some of it good, and a lot of it bad. Poverty, homelessness, race relations were not what I thought they were in America. I felt I was educated in the ways of the world from college, and studied many different cultures and history, but once I reflected for a while, I realized I did not know anything.

I DRIFTED IN AND *out of sleep that night. I was feeling out of sorts, and I did not know why. I could feel my body floating in the air. I was way up in the air and looking down on Baltimore harbor. My body*

was coming down in a place called Fells Point. It looked like a small fishing village.

There was a man sitting in the back of a large schooner. His name was Frederick Hall. He was a free slave whose mother worked as a maid for Captain Moses Grandy of Annapolis. She had escaped a plantation in the South and made her way north with her young son with the help of some local abolitionists. The captain was sympathetic to the cause and took them in and raised the boy like a son.

At a young age, he taught him about the sea. He took him on a large boat that transported passengers from Baltimore to Philadelphia, New York, and Boston. The boy learned the art of the trade from repairing ships, to working on rigging, to making sails, cooking meals, and serving passengers. When he got to be an older teenager, the captain got him a job on a shrimp boat in Chesapeake Bay, and the boy saved his money to eventually buy his own ship, and work for himself.

In 1803, one fifth of sailors were African Americans in the maritime industry and many were slaves in the past who were given their freedom and paid a fair wage. The ship owners felt they were more reliable than the Roustabouts, because they were sober, stable, and married.

The date was September seventeenth, 1814, and the Battle of Fort McHenry had just ended. The fighting lasted for seventeen hours, and the British ships had taken over the harbor and the battle was bloody and long. The cannon balls were flying in all directions, and a few had gone into the city and blew up a few houses and started fires.

After the smoke had cleared, Fort McHenry was still there, the American flag was still flying, and the United States of America had won the battle and vanquished the British out of the harbor. My boat had been commandeered to take the wounded and dead soldiers ashore to either a hospital or the graveyard. I was done with my duties for the day. I had taken ten trips today and many more the last three days. The Fort was now secure, and the War of 1812 would be winding down.

I filled up my bucket with salt water, took my sponge, and continued to clean the blood off the bottom of the boat. I scrubbed over and over to *sanitize the wood and bring it back to the original shine. The sun would bleach the wood, and new varnish would seal it again.*

As I dumped the bloody bucket over the side, I saw the water lapping on the posts of the pier, and crabs trying to walk up the poles and falling off back into the water. I heard something behind me and turned. One of my friends had dropped off a copy of the Baltimore Patriot on the back of the boat, and he gave me a wave as he left.

I decided to take a break from my duties and catch up on the news of the week. I went down to my cabin to get out of the hot sun and started paging through the paper. As I flipped through, there was a story of a person by the name of Francis Scott Key and a poem he had written. As I read further into the article it said this man had gone to the British in the harbor to negotiate the release of one of his friends accused of working for the Americans in the war. It seems he was running into a dead end when the battle started, and he had a ringside seat for the whole exchange.

He wrote this poem after the battle and called it Defense of Fort Henry. It was in the paper.

I read through the poem. The last verse read, "O'er the land of the free and the home of the brave." I thought back to my childhood working on the plantation and the way we were treated, and felt bad that this second war against Britain had not done anything to free my people. In fact, the British were offering American slaves freedom if they would fight for England in the British Colonies. It was not fair that this great nation had not granted all Americans freedom.

I sat there for a while pondering the thought. Maybe someday that dream would come true.

Chapter 15

I saw the Philadelphia skyline as I was driving down the Pennsylvania Turnpike at a good rate of speed on a humid summer day. I would spend the next week in the city of brotherly love, and this would be my final stop before I made my way home to Massachusetts.

I was getting a little homesick since I had been gone for over two months on my little road trip, but I had all that anticipation on my mind of going home, seeing my parents, writing my thesis paper, officially graduating from college, and hitting the job market full force. I would then start my life as an adult.

My eyes kept gazing at all the highway signs as I did not want to miss my exit down into the city. As I scanned the horizon, I saw the baseball and football stadiums for both Philadelphia sports teams. Then I saw the exit sign for the city. I moved over to the right, turned down the volume of my eight-track player so I could concentrate on directions. As I came down the ramp, my dashboard light lit up red on my panel. The engine started to sputter, and my heart was jumping out of my chest. I could not stop here, or I would be rear ended by a car or a truck. That would be a horrific situation if it happened.

I took my foot off the gas, and let gravity bring me down the ramp, and I prayed there was no red light at the bottom. The engine kept sputtering, and then backfired a few times. It sounded like my muffler fell off, but I knew it had not. I was on Broad Street, and as I drove by the big stadium, I saw the Philadelphia Spectrum sports facility where the Seventy Sixers basketball team, and the Flyers hockey team played. I immediately pulled into the parking lot and shut my car off, before it blew up. What had happened to my car? The engine had been running fine all summer.

I got out of the car and walked toward the ticket office and prayed it was open, and had a payphone to call a tow truck. As I walked into the ticket office, I noticed there were a few people in line, and I thought that odd, since the season for hockey would not get started until October. There was a nice gentleman standing there helping people get in the right line, and he directed me to a payphone on the opposite wall. I went over and pumped a dime into the phone and dialed the eight hundred number on the back of my AAA card. This had been a godsend in the past, since I usually drove clunkers for cars, and they were always breaking down. Now I had a fairly new car, and it still broke down.

I dialed the phone number and waited on hold, listening to some nice passive music, until a woman answered and ask me what she could do to help. I let her know my problem, and that I needed a tow, and said I wanted to go to a Chevy dealership in the city since my car was fairly new. I did not trust any local garages to look it over. She agreed, and said a truck would be there within the hour.

I hung up the phone and turned around and the ticket line was growing. Everyone had their Flyers jerseys and hats on, and seemed pretty excited about the prospects. Why was it so busy this early on a Sunday morning? As I thought about it, I looked up and hanging from the ceiling was a big white banner, promoting a pre-season charity hockey game between the Broad Street Bullies and the Big Bad Bruins. All proceeds would go to the Greater Philadelphia Food Bank.

I got so excited, and when I saw the date, it said Wednesday night. This was one of the biggest rivalries in hockey and both teams were at the top of their game. I knew it would be a high scoring event, and there would be plenty of fights featuring Wayne Cashman and Dave Schultz. They were guaranteed to mix it up at least one time a game.

I decided to jump in line and buy a ticket, and as I stood there, I asked a fan behind me how these two teams were playing before the season started. He advised me that the National Hockey League gave the teams special permission to start early because this was a good cause, and it would give the league good publicity to kick off the regular season. As I waited, I thought back to how many great hockey games I saw on TV and that the Bruins were a team on the way down, and the Flyers were a team on their way up.

After I purchased my ticket, I went out into the mid-morning sun and stood behind my car. After a few minutes a tow truck driver pulled up. I explained the situation, and he hooked the car up to the truck. I pulled out my overnight bag and eight-track tape box, and jumped into the truck with the man. I told him where I was staying and he dropped me off a few miles down Broad Street at the local Holiday Inn, and then he continued on. I had an empty feeling inside me as I saw the tow truck pull away with my car behind. I hoped the repair would be a minor one, since my money supply was dwindling.

I checked in, took a shower, and then a nap. After I woke up, I sat by the pool, read a book, and drank a few Cokes. It was a nice day, so the pool was crowded with people from out of town, and parents dropping their kids off at the local colleges in the area. I took in all the nice-looking girls, doing their best to show off their figures.

That night I had an early dinner in the dining room, went back to my room, applied my makeup for the week, made sure my wig was combed and groomed, and turned into bed and flipped on the TV. The Sunday night programming was poor, and I passed out, and then woke up after eleven o'clock to the local news which consisted of city fires, hold ups, murders, and disfunction. The whole time I was watching, I did not see any white people. It was all Black people, and families. I kept thinking to myself, how do the people live a normal life under these circumstances? It all seemed so unfair, and why couldn't this cycle of poverty be overcome?

In the morning, a ray of sunlight peered through the drapes like a laser and hit me in the eye. I immediately woke up and rolled the other way to look at the alarm clock. It read seven fifteen. My alarm had been set for seven thirty. I hit the top of the clock to shut off the alarm before it rang, and looked at the TV in front of me. It was still on, and a rerun of the nightly news was replaying on the tube. The commentator said it had been a hot, violent weekend in the city, and the police and fire departments were stretched to the breaking point. They were interviewing police and fire officials and they all had frustration and exhaustion in their voices.

I snapped off the set and made my way to the bathroom to wash up, check my look, put on my hair, got dressed, and repack my bags. I would be staying at The Roosevelt Darby Center at 802 North Broad Street, which was a men's shelter on this side of the city.

I went down to the dining room to gorge on the breakfast buffet, and then call for a taxi, since I did not know how far the shelter was from my present location. It was another beautiful, hot summer day in the city, and I tried to stay optimistic about my week's activity helping the disadvantaged.

The taxi driver pulled up in front of 802 North Broad Street, and it was no more than one mile from the Holiday Inn. I looked at the meter and realized there was a minimum amount when he pulled the flag down for this occasion. I paid the man, and got out with my bags and tapes, and made my way to the front door. The building was three stories high, made of tan brick, with the kind of windows that had wire running through them for durability and would repel rocks or objects. It was in disrepair, but so were most of the structures I had seen in the neighborhood. There were several metal shopping carts lined up, with a variety of logos and names on them from different nearby shopping centers. I thought for a moment, "What is this?" and then I realized this was where most homeless people kept their life's treasures, as they made their way around town to try and survive another day.

As I climbed the steps, several men were standing there talking to each other, and each person was trying to out-talk the other with an exciting adventure they had been exposed to the day before or during the summer. The cigarettes and coffee were flowing, when a smaller Black man came through the door, whining and complaining, with a larger man tugging on his ear, and going up one side of him and down the other. The sea of people parted, and as the two men reached the bottom step, the larger man said, "Don't come back tonight. You are banished for a week, and you better improve your temperament if you want to be a guest here again!"

The smaller man sputtered for a few seconds, turned, and made his way over to the side of the building to retrieve his cart.

Then the larger man turned to me and said, "You aren't going to give me trouble, are you?"

I looked up at him with the sun in my eyes, and he looked like Man Mountain Dean. He had to be six five, with a crazy big afro, and was wearing a bright Jimmy Hendrix outfit with all sorts of colors. His shoes were brown sandals, and his accent was that of New York, Jersey, or Philadelphia. I snapped to attention when he addressed me.

"My name is Jimmy McPherson. We talked on the phone last week. I am here to volunteer at your shelter," I finished, with as much of a commanding voice as I could muster. I looked at him nervously, waiting for a response, when he turned away from me and then stuck his arm out with his hand commanding me to follow him back into the building. I raced through the crowd of men with my stuff, not wanting to be left behind.

THE WEEK HAD BEEN going well. I was getting settled into my new home for a week. Chad Brooks, the house manager, had introduced me to my new work friends, and I had sized Chad up as a serious guy who grew up on the field of hard knocks, but cared about his fellow man deeply. He never showed a compassionate side to his workers or overnight guests, but as I saw him work and interact with people, I knew he had a warm place in his heart.

The residents looked the same as at the other places I had been. They were all ages, their faces showed despair, and they looked like they had given up on life. Their clothes and shoes were tattered, and in need of repair, but they appreciated a safe, dry, place to hang their head for eight hours, and get out of either the warmth or the cold, depending on what season it was.

I gave it my best shot and tried to interact with all the residents, and be as positive as I could be. I listened to their concerns as if they were the only person in the world. Over the past summer I had learned a lot, but also, I learned a lot about people and life itself, and how precious it was. Everyone of God's children had something to offer to the world, and once given a chance most people would be able to find it.

I had just finished up getting the sleeping quarters ready for another night, and I asked Chad if I could leave to attend the hockey game at the Spectrum. He knew I was a good worker, and never had to be supervised, so he gave me permission.

After the afternoon shift, I ran up to my room to freshen up, brush my teeth, check my look as a Black man, and headed out on foot down Broad Street. I was going to stop at Gino's Philly Cheesesteak, which was famous in the Philadelphia area, and see what all the fuss was about. I figured it was on my way to the Spectrum, and I might as well see a little of the city while I was here. I would walk double time to have my dinner and still make it to the arena before the game started.

As I made my way down Broad Street my bladder began to feel full. I had been drinking more water than usual since it was hot and humid, and I did not want to get dehydrated while doing my job at the shelter. It seemed the more I walked and pounded the pavement, the more I had to go. My pace was starting to break into that of a speed walker, and I thought back to what one of the volunteers said to me back in Chicago. "When your Black, never run when you can walk. It will draw way too much attention." It took me awhile to understand his message, but eventually it came to me.

As I looked ahead, I saw the sign for Gino's and my body and bladder relaxed for a minute. I stepped up to the takeout window, and before I ordered I asked if they had a men's room. The scantily dressed girl at the window was probably seventeen years old, had long, teased blonde hair, the face of a shark, and was snapping her bubble gum over and over. She pointed down the street, and said Doyle's Pub, and then waited for my order. I indicated I would be right back and turned and walked away.

I walked back the way I came, but on the other side of the street. The rush hour traffic was starting to form, and the smell of exhaust fumes was in the air. It hung low due to the humidity. As I made my way down the block, I noticed a lot of boarded up windows in stores, and others had big gates that closed over the front windows and doors. It was only five o'clock, but the owners of the stores had closed, and gone home.

Just as I was getting worked up that the young girl had given me bad directions, I rounded the corner, and a sign hung out that said Doyle's Pub, with a Ballantine beer bottle on the sign. I turned quickly and stepped from the light into the dark. As I entered, I stopped for a moment to readjust my eyes, and see where I was. I blinked a couple of times and all I could see were men sitting at tables smoking cigarettes and drinking. The room was filled with Formica tables and chairs, and the booths were made of highly varnished mahogany and green padded seats. There was a loud murmur of background noise.

I looked up to the bar. It was filled with working class people having a few drinks after a long hot day. I assumed most would leave after a few, and go home to their families. I saw a big, bald, bartender, taking glasses out of a small sink and drying them. He was eyeballing me like a hawk.

I walked to the end of the bar, where the waitresses would order drinks, and tried to wave him over. He purposely looked the other way and struck up a conversation with a customer. I kept trying to get his attention and started bouncing back and forth with the pain in my bladder getting worse. I started waving frantically and then a patron looked at me and then back at the bartender, and said, "Hey man, this guy wants to talk to you," in a loud obnoxious way.

The bartender turned on a dime and marched toward me and stood two feet away on the other side. I looked up at him and he was larger than a mountain and looked like he had been a professional wrestler in his earlier years.

He blurted out, "Can I help you with something, son?" Then glared.

"Yes sir. I was looking for the men's room."

He looked back and responded, "We don't have a men's room." Then looked me right in the eye.

I kept thinking, "What is this guy's problem?" Then I looked down at my hands holding on to the bar, and they were Black. I looked around the place and everyone in the pub was white. I studied the faces of the men at the bar, and some were snickering, and looked the other way.

I looked back at the bartender, and said "Thanks anyway." I turned and headed to the door as fast as I could. The sunlight hit me in the face, and I stumbled down the steps and almost fell into a parked car. I regained my footing and raced back toward Gino's. I looked ahead and saw two policemen sitting at a picnic table, eating their Philly Cheesesteak, and I was all ready to ask them for help when I spotted what looked like a bath house on the other side of the street in a park with several basketball courts near it.

I banked across the street, walked past the chain link fence, and entered the red painted building. Inside it had little light, it smelled bad, and there was mildew all over the urinals, toilets, and sinks. It looked like it was hardly used or cleaned. As I looked further you could see abandoned liquor bottles, cigarette buts, and needles. It had the smell of stale urine in the air.

I needed to go so bad I decided to hold my breath and get this over with. I stepped up to the urinal and started to relieve myself. It felt so good, and the longer I went, my body started to come back to normal. I was so caught up in my own thoughts, I did not hear that the basketball thumping outside had stopped.

After I was done, I washed my hands, and decided to not dry them, but let them air dry. This place was disgusting, and I kept thinking about the germs and me eating a big greasy Cheesesteak sub. I turned away from the sink toward the entrance when I was staring at four guys looking back at me, and one started bouncing a basketball. Two were dressed in normal shorts and tee shirts with logos on them, and the other two were dressed in dungarees, tee shirts, and bright shiny high sneakers. They all had short Afros, and one guy was sneering at me.

The smallest of the bunch started to circle me and look me up and down. My heartrate was going up, and I replayed over in my mind how I could be so stupid to get myself in this situation. I started to size up my options when the leader stepped forward.

"Hey man, what gang you with? Where are your colors?" He stood and waited for an answer. His grasp of the English language was not good. This was Philly slang with a city accent.

I responded nervously, "What did you say?" I waited for an answer.

I heard a click, and a snap. Then I saw a switch blade come up from his side, and he stuck the tip of it to my throat and backed me up to the green cinder block wall. I hit my head as I met the wall, and then he said. "Are you some kind of a wise ass, man!? I asked you a question."

I looked over his shoulder and the other three guys were jumping around nervously, loving every minute of it. They were laughing and talking and did not look like they were in a hurry.

Just then, I heart footsteps echoing at the entrance, and then I saw the three men's facial expression change from one of laughter to one of fright. My friend who had the blade at my throat looked to his left, pulled the knife away, and brought it down by his side. As this happened, I looked to my right and saw two blue uniformed cops step into the room. It was Philly's finest, and I was never more happy to see them. One man was small, and one was huge, and both had their normal hand cuffs, guns, Billy clubs, and they were wearing black leather gloves which I thought was strange. They both kept smacking the batons into their other hand, in a rhythmic fashion.

The bigger cop walked over to the other three men and stood right in front. The shorter cop walked over, and stared down the guy right near me, and then looked back at me. As fast as a flash that Billy club came down on the guy's wrist, and I heard a yelp, and the switchblade went skidding across the cement floor. I backed up away from the action, and then the cop put his other hand on the baton, jammed it under the guy's throat and backed him into the wall where I had just been standing.

"Hey man, what the fuck? You can't do that to me!" he demanded.

The cop looked back at his friend and smiled, and then let his grip on the baton go for a second, and then brought it down on the guy's elbow, and then his knee. He fell to the floor, retching in pain. Then the cop kicked him in the stomach and the guy let out a gasp. The kids in the corner started bouncing around on their feet, not knowing what to do. They were obviously scared that the bigger cop was going to dismantle them one at a time.

The smaller cop turned away from his prey and walked purposely toward me. He put his baton in the pouch on his ammo belt and raised his hands like he was going to hit me. My body stiffened to await my fate when the man started dusting me off, looked right into my eyes, and said, "Boy, you're in the wrong place. Why don't you move on down the street and get to where you're going." He then gave me a smirk.

I turned on a dime, thanking the two cops as I raced out of the building and back on to the street.

I crossed over and was walking past Gino's and then saw the picnic table the two cops had been sitting at when I walked past before. Their food was still there, and half eaten. There still was steam coming off the cheesesteak. A lit cigarette was still burning at the side of the table as it had been put down knowing they would be right back.

I realized that those cops could have sat there and let me get my ass kicked, but they took the time out of their dinner to save me, knowing I was Black, but not from the neighborhood. I had lost my appetite, but still wanted to make it to the game. I looked at my watch and knew I would need to hurry.

I DID NOT KNOW if I was awake or asleep. I seemed to be spinning through the air like I was going through a time tunnel. I was hovering over a small rickety cabin with a barn, out houses, and several fields surrounding the structures. It was dark and the only thing that burned was a candle on a kitchen table inside the house.

The date was September 10th, 1912, somewhere in Forsyth County, Georgia. The man of the house was trying to explain to his young daughter, and wife, that they needed to get their belongings together and go into the woods as soon as possible to save themselves.

The past few weeks had been up and down. One of their neighbors had found a young girl by the name of Mae Crow beaten and left to die down by the Chattahoochee River. The sheriff had arrested three men, one being a young Black man by the name of Robert Edwards. Somehow, they beat a confession out of him, and he was in jail awaiting trial.

The Crow family were well known and respected by all the residents in the area. After they got wind there had been an arrest and a confession, the citizens worked themselves into a frenzy, and approached the jail. Hundreds of people congregated outside, and were yelling and screaming for the law to send this man out to meet justice the Southern way. The sheriff came out with his twenty-two riffle and talked to the crowd and did his best to get them to disperse. The deputies were inside guarding Mr. Edwards in his cell and were more scared of the crowd that their prisoner.

After several minutes the crowd rushed the jail, right past the sheriff and deputies. They knew most of the citizens standing in the street, and did not know how to stop this spectacle, short of shooting one of their neighbors.

When push came to shove, they stepped aside and the prisoner was dragged from his cell by the agitated townspeople, beaten with crowbars and sticks, and brought outside. He was either knocked out or dead when he reached the street. Several men threw a long rope around a telephone pole and hoisted his limp body up high. The men took turns with their pistols and shot guns using the man's body as a target, spinning his lifeless body around and around as the crowd of bystanders roared.

The next day he was cut down and spread across the courthouse lawn for viewing.

A few weeks later, the beautiful Mae Crow died from her injuries. On the day of her funeral, groups of white men talked quietly with their hats in their hands, their eyes filled with anger.

As nighttime fell over the area, many men set out on horseback toward the Black folks and their cabins, which were clustered in the woods and meadows along the river. They posted notices on trees, used guns, torches, and dynamite to scare the hell out of their Black neighbors. The message was clear, get out of Forsyth County pronto or end up like Mr. Edwards.

The father, mother, and child emerged from the cabin, hearing the horses coming, the ungodly screaming and the torches making their way through the forest and getting close to their farm. They had to leave all their worldly possessions and the life they had built there and run for their lives. They cried as they scampered down by the river and got into a canoe they used for fishing. The father launched the boat, and they paddled across the river and out of Forsyth County forever.

After it was over there would be nothing left of the farmhouses, fields, churches, or anything the Black families had held dear. They would have to start over again being sharecroppers and saving all over again to be independent.

I heard a congested cough, and a man clearing his throat. I started waking up, coming out of my daydream state. As I opened my eyes, I noticed I was on a bench sitting outside Independence Hall in Philadelphia on Chestnut Street. The park bench was located on the plaza just outside the front door. I had the middle of the day off from the shelter, since my job was to get everyone up and out in the morning and strip the beds to have the laundry service wash the sheets. Then we would remake the beds in the late afternoon and await the arrival of the residents for the next night. Then I would be on for a four-hour shift in the middle of the night to babysit our guests.

As I came to, I remembered I was waiting for the school group tours to get finished, which were always booked in the morning. I had not known that prior to coming down for the tour. I heard another cough and looked to my right. At the end of the bench an older Black man was seated there in his overcoat and tattered shoes. He looked back at me with a dazed expression as he took a swig out of a wine bottle encased in a paper bag. He then grumbled some comment, but it was very garbled.

Just at that moment, I saw the front doors of the hall burst open and excited school age children came running out from their tour and head for the school buses that were lined up down the street. Some stopped along their way and got some food and drink from the many street vendor carts which lined the area. I could not tell if they were city kids or suburban kids. But anyway, they got a good old education today on American history.

I jumped up from my seat and headed against the traffic, since it was after twelve o'clock and it was time for the general public to be able to come into the hall. I walked past the Liberty Bell, which had been rung on July 8th to celebrate the first reading of the Declaration of Independence. It was enshrined at the front door with unbreakable glass and a beautiful brass plaque. I walked through the front doors and immediately felt the cool air conditioning and breezed past the ticket counter since I had already bought my ticket earlier. The kids kept coming at me going for the front doors, but eventually I made it through the sea of humanity.

As I looked to the right and left there were pictures and displays of our forefathers who were in the Continental Congress and were essential in drafting the Declaration. I looked up into the domed ceilings and there were artists drawings of Revolutionary War scenes. My mind flashed back to my American history classes in college, and how exciting it was, and all I had learned. I was here where it all started. It gave me goosebumps just thinking about it.

As I continued to walk, I saw up ahead a few people congregating around a display with a scroll and inlaid gold around the edges. As I made my way through the crowd to the front, it said August 2, 1776. I paused for a moment trying to recall that date. I thought the Declaration had been finished on July 4th. I pondered the thought and said to myself I would look that up as soon as I got back home.

I looked at the scroll and writing and was amazed by the penmanship these men had. I saw John Hancock's signature and how it was said he made it larger to make sure the King of England would not miss it.

I started to read the Declaration. It said "We hold these truths to be self-evident, that all men are created equal. That they are endowed by their creator with certain unalienable rights, that among these are life, liberty, and the pursuit of happiness."

I stopped reading and stepped back and reflected on the document. This was the basis for our democracy but, thinking back on all I had seen and heard this summer, it had not trickled down to so many Americans of color. I knew the basics of life that hard work and education were the roadmap to the American dream, but how could so many people be left behind? How could I have missed so much living in my suburban bubble? I pondered the thought as I continued to tour the museum, reflecting on all these things bouncing around my mind, and soul.

Chapter 16

I WAS SITTING ON a Greyhound bus making its way down Route 95 in northern New Jersey. My tour of the northern United States had come to an end. It was Friday of Labor Day weekend and my fact-finding mission was over, and I needed to get back to my real life, and future.

I had made a reservation at the Holiday Inn in Philadelphia on Thursday for overnight, and made it there after my rounds at the shelter to take one last shower, scrub my skin with soap and a special chemical solution to take all my makeup off, and cleanse my skin to get it to respond to the fresh air, and diminish my acne and pimples.

Chad Brooks at the Roosevelt Darby Center would find a letter on my pillow that I had a family situation that I needed to address and had left in the middle of the night. I knew he would be disappointed, but he would get over it.

My Chevy Vega was still at the dealership. I had talked to them mid-week and they said I had a blown engine, but the good news was there was a class action suit ruling against General Motors for their aluminum block engines. They were defective to hot and cold temperatures. The General Manager of the maintenance department told me that they would fix it for free, but they would need a few weeks to start the process due to the amount of business they had.

I had a conversation with my father conveying that my car was in the shop, and I would be taking the bus home, and needed to be picked up in Park Square in Boston at the Greyhound Terminal. He was not pleased but said he would be there at the allotted time.

I noticed the bus slowing as we were taking the exit off the highway. The sign said Newark, New Jersey. After this, the only stops left were New York City, Hartford, and then Boston. We banked down the ramp, and what I saw was astounding. The city was horrible, with boarded up storefronts, burned out buildings, some in the midst of being demolished, litter and filth, and so many adults meandering around looking like they had no destination in mind.

I remembered back in my sociology readings in college about the race riots in 1967, the people killed, and the destruction to personal property. I remember it was a long hot summer that year, the industrial base and jobs had diminished, white flight of citizens to the suburbs was in full swing, and the political leaders of the city had not made adjustments to compensate for the loss of jobs.

Many Black citizens were thrown out of their housing to make room for urban renewal, which consisted of new commercial buildings, but no new housing to take its place was planned. The population became homeless, and frustrated.

Then one hot summer night a Black taxi driver had been arrested and beaten by the police on the way to the station. The rumor spread through the neighborhoods that this had taken place and the local Black citizens marched on the police precinct and began pelting the building with rocks and bottles. All hell broke loose, and fires were started. The police were activated with riot gear and Billy clubs, and the rest is history.

As the bus made its way into the Greyhound terminal, I counted back on my fingers how long ago that was. After a few seconds I said to myself, seven years, and nothing of substance had been done to improve the city or the people's lives who lived here. It looked like Dresden, Germany, in World War Two. The city had been bombed by the Allied forces to knock out the industrial might of the country to wage war. The buildings were levelled, the citizens dead or buried alive in air raid shelters, and many more people displaced.

How could a city in the United States look like this? Boston was a beautiful city with many skyscrapers, beautiful parks, well-kept housing, and people walking the streets with optimism in their eyes. What I was looking at was a war zone, with people who had given up, and with no future to look forward to.

I was going to get off the bus and hit the men's room before the final leg of my journey, but decided to use the restroom at the back of the bus instead. I sat there thinking about my journey this summer as the passengers departed the bus. I had seen so much and learned even more. Some of it was inspiring, like all the great volunteers who cared so much and devoted their time and energy. But this was outweighed by the level of poverty in the country, and the tide was so hard to stem due to the sheer volume of people who needed help. I got lost in my thoughts as I watched the people come and go. I had a dark feeling about it all and tried to block it out with better thoughts and dreams.

Chapter 17

I was standing outside the Greyhound Bus terminal in Park Square on a balmy Friday afternoon. The rush hour had started, and all the businesspeople were scurrying here and there, trying to get out of the city and on the way to their Labor Day weekend destinations, and the official end of the summer. I stood on the sidewalk with my bag, dodging work people, tourists, drunks, and assorted misfits. My head started to hurt sucking in rush hour traffic, and carbon monoxide being blown out of bus exhaust pipes.

I scanned the crowds of cars racing through every light to see if one of the cars was my father coming to pick me up. I kept scanning the rows of cars but no luck so far. I was dead tired from my long day, and the anticipation of facing my mother and father, and summarizing what I had done this summer. I had many scenarios cooked up in my head, but after coming up with several good stories I decided to tell them the cities I had been in, but leave out the part about not graduating from college and needing to write a special thesis paper to get my diploma.

A brown Ford Torino shot across several lanes of traffic, making many cars honk, and then I saw my father pull up to the curb. He had both hands on the wheel and made no effort to get out or give me a friendly wave or hug. I grabbed my bag, opened the back door, and threw it on the seat and closed the door. I then opened the front passenger door, hopped in, and said "Hi" to my father.

He did not look at me or say anything. He just pulled out into traffic and meandered down the street, merging.

"Where is Willie?" he questioned with a suspicious tone.

I panicked after I heard the question. I forgot that I had told them that Willie was going with me on my cross-country trip. A million thoughts raced through my mind to come up with something plausible. Then out of nowhere I spouted, "His father and mother picked him up a few minutes before you got there." I waited after the remarks came out of my mouth for my father to tell me I was a big fat liar. I couldn't be sure if my mother had called his mother in Lexington to check up on how our trip was going. I had called home many times over the summer, but they never asked me about Willie.

I looked over and studied my father's face. He looked okay but was staring straight ahead, keeping his eyes on the stop and go traffic. I started to get uncomfortable just sitting there with no conversation, so I reached over and pushed the AM radio to a rock and roll station up the dial. As fast as I did it my father reached across and pushed the button for the talk radio and news station he had been listening too. I looked back at him for a split second.

He said, "When you get your car back from wherever it is, you can play your own music."

The rest of the way home we did not talk, and I wished I was a junior at Northeastern, and could check into the campus dormitory and not go home. The anticipation of seeing my parents, having a good meal, and looking to the future had been blown.

Winchester, Massachusetts

I sat at the dinner table as my mother served my father and myself a meal that was fit for a king. It felt like a holiday meal without the fanfare. The house looked the same, the yard looked the same, and the mood in the house was the same as when I left. I stuck my fork into my chopped sirloin steak and balanced some mashed potatoes and peas on my fork before I put it in my mouth. It tasted so good, and I had already thanked my mother for such a great meal. No amount of appreciation got a rise out of my father.

My mother kept peppering me with questions of my summer and the cities I had been too, and the places I had seen. She was obviously overcompensating for my father's lack of interest and conversation. I answered all her questions, I told her what cities I had been to, and what I had seen. She looked perplexed as to my choice of geography. She asked why I never made it to California, and I said I ran out of time which seemed odd to her.

"Now Jimmy, when you get unpacked, give me all your clothes to wash, and everything in your room is fresh and clean, so keep it that way, dear," she answered in her usual soft-spoken voice.

Before my father could hop all over me about doing any chores, I decided to cut him off at the pass.

"Well, I gotta stay in my room for the weekend to get some things done and get organized. On Tuesday, I'll be able to help you guys do any chores you have around the house," I stated with a firm, confident voice.

My father immediately stopped eating and put his fork down on his plate so hard it made a snap on the edge of the plate.

"What do you have to do that is so important that you can't help around the house after being gone all summer?" he demanded. Then he looked over right into my eyes. I flashed back to when I was a kid and had done something wrong, and he caught me in a lie.

"Well, Dad I have several job leads that I managed to come up with on the phone over the summer, and I need to design a good resume, and some cover letters to go with it. I also might have an appointment in Boston on Tuesday to discuss a life insurance opportunity." I sat back in my chair and my father's stiff manner started to relax and he sat back.

As he went for another forkful of food he said, "That sounds like progress."

I did not even mention a makeup job on Broadway or in Hollywood, since that was pie in the sky and I needed a paycheck fast.

I looked over at my mother and she smiled back at both of us, and the conversation started to flow in the normal manner that I was accustomed too. My blood pressure dropped a couple of points, and then the mood got brighter, and the food got tastier. I looked over on the stove and I saw a lemon meringue pie on the stove. My mother usually only served this at special holiday meals. I was in seventh heaven after that.

I SAT AT THE old desk in my room with my trusty Smith Corona typewriter in front of me. It was Saturday morning and I had slept like a baby the night before. It always felt better and more secure being home in your own house. I told my mother that I would take all my meals in my room for the next three days and she was amenable to that, since she wanted success for me, and to keep my father in good spirits.

I sat there looking out the window overlooking the backyard, and my heart dropped seeing the length of the grass. I knew my father had let it grow knowing I would be home to do some honest landscaping during the long weekend. I did not look forward to tackling this job, but if that was my only punishment for bailing out on the summer, so be it.

As I looked around my room, I noticed pictures of Boston sports stars, teams, surfing and skiing posters, and many other relics of a childhood, well lived. I started to have flashbacks of a young life that went by so fast, and now I was an adult and would be going out into the world to make my mark. My parents had given me a good start and worked so hard to present me with every opportunity to be successful. I was determined not to let them down and make them proud of me.

I kept scanning the walls of my room, and noticed the kids' wallpaper under all my posters and relics hanging. It had fairytale characters on it from my childhood, and was in no way appropriate for a teenager or a kid in his twenties. I kept looking at it and playing my life over in my mind, and the realization came to me that I needed to get a job, move out, and live my life as an adult. It gave me a sinking feeling.

I looked down at the typewriter, put a new sheet of paper in the machine, and cranked it into position. I gave my notes one last review, and started to think of a name for my thesis. At first, I thought I would name it "Roadtrip 1974." Then I started kicking around some more adult titles in my mind. Then it came to me. I would title the paper "Lily White Like Me," thinking that this encompassed my being so clueless about how people lived outside my protected bubble in America.

I put the title at the top of the page and began to type feverishly. The typewriter had been my trusty companion during college, and the ink tape was as dark as it had been my freshman year. The carriage went back and forth as I put my fieldtrip and story down on paper. It was more of a sociology experiment than a history paper, but I knew it was a story that had to be told.

As I finished each page, I proofread it, and used my Wite-Out to fix any imperfections before I took it out of the machine. With each new page and summary of my notes, I gained more confidence. I was amazed with all the places I had been, the people I had met, and the volunteers who gave up their time to take care of people in need. As heartbreaking as the things I witnessed were, it made me feel better that people cared about their fellow man and woman, and would pitch in if needed to catch them before they fell.

The story was easy to put down on paper, and the words fell out of my head and constructed what I thought would be a compelling story with observations. My mother came up to the room every few hours to see if I was okay, or needed anything. I know she missed me so much this past summer, and was happy I was home from college, and safe from my field trip.

It was a new chapter for me, and I wanted to make the most of it. I put my head down and continued to strike the keys with renewed confidence.

Chapter 18

I sat there in Dean Smith's office, staring at a mosaic picture on the back wall behind his desk. It was a multicolored Aztec Indian in front of a huge tan pyramid. The more I looked at it, the more I got lost in the three-dimensional illusion. The more I looked around the office, the more I saw on the walls which for some reason I overlooked the past few years. I had been in this office several times to discuss courses and my overall performance, but I was probably so scared I couldn't concentrate on anything around me.

It was Tuesday, the day after Labor Day, and the school campus was coming back to life. I was dressed up in my Sunday best since I had to tell my parents a white lie, saying I had a job interview in Boston. I suppose I was kind of telling the truth, since I would be looking for a job once the Dean accepted my thesis, and I officially graduated from college. Then I could put that on my resume and get going with the rest of my life.

I had been sitting in a chair, facing the Dean, for about an hour and a half. He was methodically taking each page of my thesis out of the typewriter paper box in which I had stored it, due to its vast size. It contained all my thoughts, observations, and conclusions from my summer's work. As he peered across each page, he seemed thoroughly engrossed in its content, but gave no hint that he either liked it or thought it was an amateur piece of field trip summary.

He moved his head and eyes up and down each page, closely studying the content, while moving his spectacle glasses down on his nose, and then a few minutes later back up on the bridge. I tried to study his face for any indication of acceptance, but he had a good poker face.

I looked at the clock behind his desk, and it read eleven thirty. The time had flown since I had sat down, and I promised my underclass friends that I would meet them at the Cask and Flagon Pub for one last lunch and goodbyes before I ventured out into the world. I started to fidget more in my chair, and I knew the Dean was not even close to being done. I did not want to bother him, since any mood change could affect my final mark, and future. I bounced around the situation in my head and tried to come up with a solution.

Finally, I cleared my throat, and Dean Smith looked up and stared into my eyes.

"I'm sorry to interrupt, Dean, but I have a job interview downtown in an hour and need to leave to get prepared. Is it okay if I head out, or would you like me to stay?" I finished with a questionable tone in my voice.

"By all means, Mr. McPherson. You do what you need to do, and I will continue to read this nice piece of work. So far, I am impressed with the content and effort you have put into this paper. Call me later this afternoon and I will give you my final impressions." The Dean put his glasses back on the bridge of his nose, gave me the slightest of smiles, and then said, "Good luck."

I got up, waved back to him, breezed through the outer office and gave a wave to the office assistant, and was on my way. I felt like a million dollars, as I practically skipped down the hallway, down the stairs, and out the doorway of the Daniels Building, and across the quadrangle to Huntington Avenue. I was floating on air as I made my way along and gave a couple of students the peace sign.

Crossing the grass portion of the Quad, I looked back to study the EL Center, and the library building that I had spent so much time in over the past few years. I had a melancholy feeling for only a brief minute, remembering all the trials, tribulations, and good times I had along the way. It was a great five year adventure, and I had learned so much, and met so many nice people.

I got to the edge of the street, and as I looked up, I saw a Black Vietnam veteran standing there with hat in hand asking for donations. He looked tired and worn out from living on the street. He was about thirty-five years old, with short black hair that had a hint of gray. His uniform was worn, with all his badges and medals ripped off, and his black army boots were scuffed up with holes in them. I wondered why his rank, badges, and medals were gone from the uniform, and I thought maybe he was ashamed of his service in the military. I pondered the thought for a few seconds as I looked into his eyes.

I reached into my pocket for some change. I had none. Then I took out my wallet, and looked inside, and had no one-dollar bills. All I had was one five-dollar bill, which was for lunch with my friends. I stood there for a second trying to decide what to do. As I looked at his face it finally hit me. Had I learned nothing this summer about the poor in society who had been left behind? It affected people of color so often, and if it was ever to change didn't it start with me and everybody else?

I pulled the bill out of my wallet in watchful view of the Veteran and put it in his hat. There were a few nickels, dimes, and quarters already in the hat. Once I placed the bill in the hat, he immediately took it out and put it in his pocket. It was as if I had given him a million dollars. He gave me a slight smile, and said "Thank you," under his breath. I then side stepped him to cross the street.

I started across Huntington Avenue to the other side, when I heard my name being yelled from the Northeastern side of the street. I assumed it was my classmates, so I looked back to wave to them. The morning sunlight hit me in the eyes, and blinded me for a brief moment. In that moment, all stood still.

Out of nowhere, I was pushed with a sudden violence, which propelled my body in the air, and I hit the hot black pavement and rolled into the gutter. My head glanced off the curb, and I was slightly stunned. I heard the roar of a car engine, the squealing of brakes, and the roar of acceleration. Then I heard what I thought was a thud of a body not more than twenty feet from where I lay. I opened my eyes as the dust from the street blew particles into my face. When things came into focus, I saw that Vietnam vet lying in the middle of the street, his body broken and twisted.

I crawled over to his body and saw blood emanating from his nose, ears, and the back of his head. He had a compound fracture of several bones, and was laying there unresponsive. I put my hand behind the man's head and lifted it up. His eyes were open, and I studied his irises to see if there was any life left in him.

After only seconds, I heard a police car pass us on the left screaming down Huntington Ave. I assumed it was after the speeding car that caused this accident. Then another Boston Police car pulled up with an EMT ambulance only a few feet away from where we were. The siren went off but the lights remained on, and a crowd started to form. An emergency medical person and a big Irish cop started to pull me away from the body, and I lowered the man's head ever so gently, resting it on the hot pavement. My friends started dragging me back to the curb and sat me down. I looked down at my hands and saw the blood and started to cry hysterically. I kept looking at that poor man and knew he had just saved my life from a speeding car. He put his life on the line for me. A true selfless army veteran and person.

I sat there thinking about his life and what led him to this moment as they scooped up his body and put him into the emergency vehicle and drove away. My friends kept patting me on the shoulder saying it would be all right when I knew it would never be.

Chapter 19

1983

I rolled around in my bed in a dream state. My body was tired, but my mind was going ninety miles an hour. I woke up to the sound of my baby daughter coughing with a loud bark in her voice. My wife, Mary, was holding her, sitting up in bed, and rocking back and forth and trying to get her back to sleep.

I yawned and rolled over to meet my wife's eyes. She had a look of fright in her eyes. My body was tired as I got home late last night. I had attended a Northeastern basketball game with a friend and alumni who was a season ticket holder. We had courtside seats at Matthews Arena, and I was fixated by the new recruit they brought in. He was a tall, lanky freshman, going up and down the court with ease.

In the second quarter, a ball went out of bounds. The young kid came over to right where we were sitting to pass the ball inbounds. The referee handed the player the ball, he turned to focus in on a teammate to pass the ball inbounds. Then, at that moment, his face came into focus. I almost fainted. I was looking at that little boy who was standing with his mother outside Dunbar High School in Baltimore. I was shocked to see that little boy was Reggie Lewis. He had grown up into a man, and I was so happy he had gotten out of the ghetto and had an opportunity to have a great life.

As my daughter's coughing got louder, my wife nudged me a little and I sat up in bed. She handed little Sarah into my arms, who then snuggled her little head on my shoulder, and let out a cough that sounded like more of a congested bark.

My wife was a pediatric nurse and ran down the list of treatments she had given our daughter that night including medication, Vicks Vapo Rub, hot and cold mist treatments, and nothing had worked. We talked things over for a few minutes when she suggested we stand outside in the cool winter air on our patio. She indicated this could clear her airway and let her breathe more freely.

I slipped out of bed with my little girl on my shoulder, and we went out to the living room, slipped on her coat, and made our way out to the back of the house. The night air was so crisp and clean, but hit us like a wall of cold. We danced around the patio, holding our daughter, bouncing from one foot to the other to stay loose and warm, and prayed this would solve our dilemma.

I looked into my wife's eyes to get a read on how things were going, and my daughter was waking up from being outside. I tried to cradle her to keep her small body warm, but as she woke up and squirmed, the coughing started with a more rapid pace. I could see my wife getting frustrated and the nerves were setting in when she said, "Jimmy, I think we need to take Sarah to the hospital to have her evaluated."

She looked back at me with longing eyes and a desperate look on her face. I thought about how we would pull this off, since my five-year-old son was asleep in the other bedroom, and I did not have the heart to wake him up and throw him into a cold car. I also did not want to send my wife and daughter out in the middle of the night to the hospital. Who knows who was on the road or what the driving conditions were like. I made a quick calculation in my mind and then I said I would call our next-door neighbors, the Robinsons, to see if the wife could come over and babysit for a few hours while we went to the Emergency Room.

The Robinsons were a nice Black family from Seattle. They moved in next door about six months ago, and we only saw them when we were out raking leaves, shoveling our driveway, or checking our mail. They were about our age and had children about the same ages. As of yet, we had not had any formal get togethers, since we both had busy lives. From what I had gotten from our short conversations, the husband was a computer engineer who worked at Microsoft, and the wife was a nurse. I remember about two months ago, my wife came back from the mailbox with their phone number, and a promise if we ever needed them to call.

My wife was in full agreement with the arrangement, so I picked the phone off the wall and made the call. It rang several times, and I started to wonder how close they were to the phone at night. Then I started to calculate all the bad things people get calls for in the middle of the night, and I felt guilty to be bothering them at this late hour.

All of a sudden, I heard a woman's voice on the other end of the line. I blurted out my name and explained the situation, and asked for her help. She didn't have to think twice. After only a few seconds, she agreed to come over, and I hung up the phone. My wife started running around to get prepared for our guest, and going over in her head what she would need to explain before we both went out the door, and on our way.

After only a few minutes, I was putting on my boots on the front hall stairs and saw a woman's face peering through the glass of the front door. I waved to her, and almost tripped over my laces as I lunged to open the door. I pulled the door open right as my wife and daughter came up behind me. The neighbor came walking through the door, and I said, "Thank you for coming," in a rushed manner.

She introduced herself as Gail, and we chatted for just a few minutes and then we showed her my son's room, the phone on the wall, and the couch and television. We then raced out the door, and on our way.

After a few hours and a lot of anguish, we returned from the hospital to our house. Our daughter had an X-ray, more potent nebulizer treatments, and everyone was feeling better.

As we turned the top of the stairs in our foyer, I saw Gail's head pop up from the couch and she indicated to my wife and I that everything was okay, and that our son had not woken up. She then asked how Sarah was, and we gave her a resounding positive "better," all at once. We then laughed at ourselves.

My wife turned to Gail and thanked her for coming over on such short notice, and then asked her if she would like to stay for a cup of tea.

I looked back at our neighbor, who after a moment of thought said yes, probably not really wanting to stay, but not wanting to turn down our hospitality. The women both turned into the kitchen area, and I continued on to my daughter's bedroom to get Sarah settled in bed and check on my son.

After fifteen minutes, I walked back out to the kitchen and the women were sitting at each end of the table with a cup of tea in front of them, totally engrossed in their conversation. I went to the refrigerator and got a glass of juice and sat back down between them. I smiled briefly at Gail and just sat there and listened. I realized they were both nurses and worked at our local hospital, but on different floors. They were throwing out names of doctors and nurses to see if they each knew any of them, and were telling war stories from their time working. The conversation was free and easy, and if I closed my eyes, I could imagine the same conversation with one of my wife's good friends that she had known for a lifetime.

This family next door was no different from us. They had the same hopes and dreams that we did for their lives and families. I thought back to my cross-country trip many years ago, and then thought about race relations in our country and how people were really all alike, even if they came from different places, and from different backgrounds. I sat there with a content feeling, listening to the conversation, the laughter, and it gave me a warm feeling inside.

Maybe if we all looked at the world through our rose-colored glasses things would improve for all people of all races.

SUGGESTED READINGS

RACE AGAINST TIME BY Jerry Mitchell Simon and Schuster 2/2000 New York

Inside The Minstrel Mask by Anne Marie Bean, James Hatch, Brooks McNamara Wesleyan University Press

Thesis Paper by E. Joey Brackner Jr. 1981

Journal of African Dias Pora Archeology and Heritage by Lydia Wilson Marshall Depauw University

A short history of Reconstruction by Eric Foner Brook News, Inc. 1988

To Be Loved by Berry Gordy 1994 Rosetta Books LLC

Scott Joplin, The Man Who Made Ragtime, by James Haskins, Double Day Co. 1978 Garden City N. Y.

Diary Of A Midwestern Getto by Doreen Ambrose Van Lee ISBN: 1-4241-4676-3 Memoir of a Childhood at Cabrini Green

The Slave Trade by Hugh Thomas, Simon and Schuster 1997

They Were Her Property by Stephanie E. Jones Rogers, Yale University Press 2019

For Their Own Cause by Kelly D. Mezurek, Kent Press 2016

Birmingham Sunday by Larry Dane Brimner, Astra Publishing House 2010

Black Jacks, by Jeffrey Bolster, Harvard University Press, 9/1998

Blood At The Root by Patrick Phillips, W. W. Norton Company 2016

Made in United States
North Haven, CT
10 July 2022